THE MUMMY

* Forthcoming

THE MUMMY

RICCARDO STEPHENS

with a new introduction by
MARK VALENTINE

VALANCOURT BOOKS

The Mummy by Riccardo Stephens
First published by Eveleigh Nash in 1912
Reprinted by Hutchinson in 1923
First Valancourt Books edition 2016

Introduction copyright © 2016 by Mark Valentine
This edition copyright © 2016 by Valancourt Books

Published by Valancourt Books, Richmond, Virginia
http://www.valancourtbooks.com

ISBN 978-1-943910-28-1 (trade hardcover)
ISBN 978-1-943910-29-8 (trade paperback)
Also available as an electronic book.

Set in Dante MT

INTRODUCTION

Dr. Riccardo Stephens was the author of a handful of books in the late Victorian and Edwardian period that deserve to stand with the macabre work of Robert Louis Stevenson and Arthur Machen. They have the same dark verve, sinister atmosphere, and strange, imaginative plots. It is a mystery why he is not better known in the field of the fantastic in literature. Although some of his books were issued by the relatively minor publisher Bliss, Sands & Co., others came out from established houses such as John Murray or Blackwood & Sons, and his last and most remarkable was first published by Eveleigh Nash, who successfully promoted similar writings in the supernatural fiction field by Algernon Blackwood and William Hope Hodgson.

Very little biographical information about Riccardo Stephens appears to have survived. He seems to be the Riccardo Britton Stephens born on 28 February 1860 in St. Austell, Cornwall and baptised on 29 July 1860 at the Wesleyan Methodist Chapel, Croydon, Surrey. Our best source about him is a note in *Lyra Celtica, An Anthology of Representative Celtic Poetry* (1896), edited by Elizabeth Sharp, and with an introduction and notes by William Sharp, to which Stephens contributed three poems, "Witch Margaret"; "A Ballad"; and "Hell's Piper": these seem to be among his earliest writings in book form. This tells us:

> Dr. Stephens is a Cornishman settled in Edinburgh, where he practises as a physician. He has not, as yet, published any of his poems in book form; but, none the less, has won (if necessarily, as yet, a limited) reputation by his exceedingly vigorous and individual poems. He has written several "Castle Ballads" (of which the very striking "Hell's Piper" given here is one) – poems suggested by legendary episodes connected with Edinburgh Castle ... for Dr. Stephens is one of the many workers, thinkers and dreamers who congregate in the settlement founded by Professor

> Patrick Geddes ... New Edinburgh, as University Hall is sometimes called, an apt name in more ways than one. Dr. Stephens is a poet of marked originality, and his work has all the Celtic fire and fervour, with much of that sombre gloom which is held to be characteristically Cornish. "Hell's Piper" has lines in it of Dantesque vigour, as those which depict, among "the shackled earthquakes," the "reeking halls of Hell," and the torture-wrought denizens of that Inferno. "The Phantom Piper" will never be forgotten by any one who has once read and been thrilled by this highly-imaginative poem.

Patrick Geddes was a leading figure in Edinburgh in the last two decades of the 19th century, and it seems that Stephens was a keen and loyal member of the circle of artists, writers, teachers and others around him. Influenced by the Celtic Revival led by Yeats and others in Ireland, Geddes wanted to see what was termed a Scots Renascence, and to create a new educational and cultural quarter in Edinburgh. A man of prodigious energy and vision, he set up courses in the arts and sciences and gathered disciples at his foundation University Hall (distinct from the University itself), "a community of students from different academic disciplines living together and co-operating with one another".

Riccardo Stephens, together with his friend, the future Antarctic explorer William Speirs Bruce, lived in University Hall around the period 1888-1891. Stephens was also involved with the Old Edinburgh School of Art founded by Patrick Geddes in 1892, and with Geddes' quarterly journal *The Evergreen* (1895-6).

He evidently first practised medicine in Edinburgh, but by 1908 *The British Medical Journal* referred to him as a doctor in Sutherland, in the far north of Scotland, on the Atlantic and North Sea coasts. It quoted an incident from his novel *The Eddy* (1908) as an example of the lack of security of tenure for doctors working for Poor Law Committees in the country, who could be dismissed at the whim of parish authorities. We also know that Stephens was commissioned as a Captain in the Royal Army Medical Corps during the First World War, and his appointment was gazetted on 20 April 1915: but after that he disappears from view until his death was recorded in December 1923 in Salisbury, Wiltshire. Probably more will become known about him as interest in his powerful fiction rises, but at present the mysteries around him seem strangely to complement his work. However, clearly, like Arthur Conan Doyle, another Scottish doctor, he mingled his medical duties with writing. He was the author of seven volumes of fiction as well as poems, stories for periodicals, and at least one play.

Dr. Stephens seems also to have been the author of two pamphlets published by the Sunday School Union: *Your Health and How to Keep It – For Boys and Others* (1897) and *When a Boy Smokes* (1898, reprinted from *Young England*). At first glance these seem to fit oddly with his literary work. But there are indications that Stephens came from a staunch Methodist background in Cornwall, so possibly he continued to have connections with the church and produced these out of a sense of duty to his earlier faith.

However, his lasting writing was in the dark fantastic. The note in *Lyra Celtica* praises Stephens' "sombre gloom" and this was indeed evident in his poems. "Witch Margaret", for example, tells of the immolation of a witch burnt at the stake in Edinburgh: ". . . her cloak of flame and smoke / The winter air shall fill; / For they must burn Witch Margaret / Upon the Castle Hill": and it also dwells upon the tortures she suffered beforehand: "Upon her body, all in black, / Fell down her red-gold hair; / All bruised and bleeding from the rack / Her writhen arms hung bare; / Red blood dripped all along her track, / Red blood seemed in the air."

Stephens' first novel certainly reinforced his reputation as an adept in the art of the macabre. *The Cruciform Mark – The Strange Story of Richard Tregenna, Bachelor of Medicine (Univ. Edin.)* (1896) is written under the unmistakeable influence of Robert Louis Stevenson, particularly his *Strange Case of Dr Jekyll and Mr Hyde* (1886), which has rightly been described as taking place in a London very like Edinburgh. The setting and characters of Stephens' book clearly draw on the author's own background as a medical student in Edinburgh and in particular the Geddes circles.

The narrator investigates reports of apparent suicides or

mysterious deaths amongst young male students and staff at the university. It gradually becomes apparent that there is a link between them, which leads to a young woman who has mesmeric powers. In Machen's *The Great God Pan* (1894), Helen Vaughan, the daughter of Pan, under the name of Mrs. Beaumont, drives gentlemen to their doom through the unspeakable terrors she reveals: Miss Verney, in Stephens' novel is a similar *femme fatale* whose very stare, "cold, beautiful yet hideous" conjures up "undreamt of horrors". The theme is not unlike Michael Arlen's later dark thriller *Hell! said the Duchess* (1934, also available from Valancourt).

His next book, *Mr. Peters* (1897), opens with the lynching of an innocent foreigner in an American wild west settlement. But it soon shifts to an Edinburgh boarding house some years later, where Mr. Peters, "tall, swarthy, dark-eyed" and with "a sphinx-like calm" arrives and flurries the housekeeper with his exotic ways and graces. We soon know that Mr. Peters has a mission: he is the son of the victim and has been raised with revenge in mind. The story of his stalking of his quarry, whose traces he has followed to Scotland, is oddly intermingled with scenes of romantic interest and light humour. The tale is assured and full of lively characters but lacks the sinister power of his earlier novel.

However, Stephens' subsequent work, *The Prince and the Undertaker, and What They Undertook* (Sands & Co., 1898), marked another change in style and theme. It is an extravagant episodic romance which probably owes something to Stevenson's *The Suicide Club* (1878, collected in his *New Arabian Nights*, 1882). Like that story, it has a prince in exile, although Stephens' character is in poverty, unlike the opulent Prince Florizel of Bohemia. The tone is equally jaunty, however, and both princes become involved with a series of colourful characters in the stranger quarters of London. They also both encounter a young man intent on taking his own life and save them from their dark journey by pursuing curious and fantastical adventures. In Stephens' book this takes the form of a series of conversations with piquant individuals each with a tale to tell: the Undertaker, the Barber, the General, the Musician, the Physician, the Artist and finally the Young Man (the Prince himself).

However, Stephens' book also has a particular origin in what I have called the Jacobite Sunset, the revival of interest in restoring the House of Stuart to the throne of England that gathered impetus in the last years of the nineteenth century. It was thought that the anticipated ending of the ageing Queen Victoria's reign, together with doubts about the suitability of her son, Edward, might prove auspicious for an attempt to regain the throne for the Old Cause. Amongst the adherents to this romantic idea were many literary figures of the Eighteen Nineties, including the pale poet Lionel Johnson, Baron Corvo, and the ritual magician Macgregor Mathers, a founder of the Hermetic Order of the Golden Dawn. The movement also had devotees amongst Scottish nationalist circles, including some in the Geddes communities, where Stephens probably encountered it. But this conspiracy is diverted in his book into another plot involving subterfuge and disguise, with the Prince proving to be a loyal friend and subject.

Two volumes of romantic commercial fiction were also issued around this time: *Mrs. De la Rue Smythe* (Bliss, Sands, & Co., 1898) is a series of brief humorous sketches depicting dialogues between the narrator, Dr. Tregenna (a Cornish name) and the eponymous lady, a cosmopolitan hostess with decided opinions. There is a sort of mild sub-Wildean ambience to the volume and the pieces were probably written in response to the success of E. F. Benson's *Dodo: A Detail of the Day* (1893) and Anthony Hope's *The Dolly Dialogues* (1894), which had offered similar light society banter.

The Wooing of Grey Eyes (John Murray, 1901), a novella collected with seven short stories or sketches, is a stormy romantic melodrama. The narrator, Jim Dalrymple, a breezy 27 year old, is told he has inherited Hawksheugh, a house on a cliff edge in remote country (probably based on Sutherland). He finds the place desolate and bleak, with the wind whistling through the keyholes and windows, and the sea moaning below. The estate itself is bare and grey, and there is a surly, saturnine gamekeeper. Everything seems set up for another study in the macabre, but although there is certainly a Gothic mood, the story is about his love for a young woman he meets while out walking, who holds a secret that will affect his happiness. A twist ending leads to a tumultuous finale.

The book is of interest for confirming a decided trait in Stephens' work towards concealed information, the revelation that all is not what it seems. This is partly of course an artful literary device, but may also suggest something in his own character or biography that is still yet to become apparent. One image that recurs in his books is that of a woman's pale and haunting face. Stephens is an inventive writer with an exuberant imagination and this repeated motif is therefore not due to a limited palette: it is hard to avoid the suspicion that the eerie, hovering vision had some personal significance for him.

The Mummy (1912) was his last published book, and is here presented from the later Hutchinson edition of 1923. That was almost certainly produced to capitalise on the discovery of the tomb of Tutankhamun in 1922 by the Earl of Carnarvon's expedition led by Howard Carter, in order to gain from the fervent popular interest in Egyptology that this inspired.

There had already been many other literary explorations of the Mummy theme. The archaeologist E. A. Wallis-Budge had published his study *The Mummy: Chapters on Egyptian Funereal Archaeology* in 1893. *The Mummy*, a comedy by George Day and Allan Reed, in which a pharaoh is brought to life again using a "galvanising battery" invented by an eccentric professor, was staged in London and on Broadway in 1896. Theo Douglas' fantasy *Iras: A Mystery*, in which an Egyptologist is haunted by the spirit of a mummy he has excavated, was published in the same year as the play.

There was a perennial interest in Egyptian themes among readers, especially in plots connected with magic and the occult. Guy Boothby scored a great success with his *Pharos, The Egyptian* (1899), about a modern magician who is a reincarnation or survival in some form of an ancient mummified sorcerer. The rebirth of ancient Egyptians in modern times is also the theme of *The Mummy and Miss Nitocris: A Phantasy of the Fourth Dimension* (1906) by George Griffiths, the author of scientific romances. In Bram Stoker's *The Jewel of Seven Stars* (1903), the spirits of an Egyptian witch-queen and her cat (both of whom were mummified) assail an Egyptologist as part of the sorceress's attempt to be revived in the 20th century.

Mummies were not only deployed in supernatural fiction but also in stories involving ingenious crimes. In Arthur Machen's *The Three Impostors* (1895), a character (based on a former employer, the proprietor of *Walford's Antiquarian* journal, with whom he did not get on) is despatched by being mummified. And R. Austin Freeman's *The Eye of Osiris* (1911), featuring his detective Dr. Thorndyke, was one of the most successful crime novels to make use of the sinister allure of the Egyptian relic and its potential for disposing of oblivious victims.

One of the strengths of Riccardo Stephens' novel is that he presents a set of engaging and picturesque characters from bohemian circles who have their own interest quite apart from the sinister influence of the mummy: he also has the confidence to remove some of them from the scene. He is skilful in building up the baleful atmosphere surrounding the mummy with considerable power and pace, and also attempts an audacious piece of misdirection in the plot. This may not quite convince us, but together with the strong characters and the taut tension it suggests a bold, adventurous author determined to go his own way. *The Mummy* was certainly a fitting conclusion to the literary career of a master storyteller and mysteriously lost figure who should now at last gain the keen readership he is due.

Mark Valentine
August 2015

MARK VALENTINE is the author of several collections of short fiction and has published biographies of Arthur Machen and Sarban. He is the editor of *Wormwood*, a journal of the literature of the fantastic, supernatural, and decadent, and has previously written the introductions to editions of Walter de la Mare, Robert Louis Stevenson, L. P. Hartley, and others, and has introduced John Davidson's novel *Earl Lavender* (1895), Claude Houghton's *This Was Ivor Trent* (1935), Oliver Onions's *The Hand of Kornelius Voyt* (1939), and other novels, for Valancourt Books.

THE MUMMY

CHAPTER I

I AM CALLED IN

I was sitting at breakfast one February morning, about nine o'clock, two years ago, with Mudge, my servant, ex-sergeant of Marines, at my back telling some yarn about what he said he had done at Ladysmith.

Though I live in the West End, it is only in a little flat over a grocer's shop, in a small side-street off Piccadilly, where my patients are principally the servants (and principally the men-servants—butlers, coachmen and such-like) from the big houses and clubs.

A couple of news-boys began yelling something through the morning fog, about exclusive information and special edition of the *Daily Tale*. I knew nothing would satisfy Mudge till he got a copy. So I sent him out.

Presently the outer door was pushed open, and a man's voice asked loudly whether the doctor was in.

"Second door right-hand side of lobby," I shouted, and the man was in before I could swallow another mouthful.

He was a well-set-up young fellow, and well dressed. But I noticed he had no gloves on, and he was looking considerably upset.

"Sorry to come in on you like this," he said, "but there has been a sudden death in Albany—a man I know—and I want you to come round at once."

"Poor fellow," I said, leaving the paper-knife to mark my place in the magazine. "Are you sure he's dead?"

"I'm afraid there's no doubt about it."

"Poor fellow," I said again. "If he's dead, I may as well finish my breakfast," and I took another mouthful.

"You damned cold-blooded cormorant," said the young fellow very angrily. "Will you come or won't you?"

"Not unless you want me," I assured him, "but I'm ready if you are," and I turned into the lobby for a hat, munching the last of my breakfast. Of course I didn't mind his remarks, for though my comment was quite logical and reasonable, his sentiment was natural enough. I took a fancy to the young fellow at once. I made for the door, patting my hip-pocket, to make sure that my hypodermic case was there. It is an old servant, and reminds me of a good many queer things if I sit down to overhaul it. But the queerest had not happened when I felt it in my hip-pocket that raw February morning.

A taxi-cab was at the street door, and there was hardly time to ask any questions as we went. Maxwell, as he told me his name was, said that he and another man had gone round to breakfast at the Albany, and had found their host lying on the ground.

"Poor Scrymgeour's man Seymour," he said, "knew you and gave me your address."

It seemed futile to ask questions when I was about to see for myself, and Maxwell did not appear to be a talkative man. We sat quiet, and in a few minutes went up a stair of the Albany and knocked at A 14.

If you know the Albany you may remember that at the foot of this stair there is a very badly-lighted corner. Just as we turned that we almost ran against a woman who had either just come down, or had come along the corridor beyond.

These Albany suites consist mostly of dining-room, bedroom, bathroom, and kitchen, and a pigeon-hole for a servant. The three first are *en suite*, and also each opens into the hall or lobby. Seymour took us straight to the bedroom from the outer door. Entering, one faced a high carved mantelpiece over the fire; and above the mantelpiece was the half-length portrait of a man in the dress of Charles the Second's time.

On the ground lay wooden steps, of the sort one uses to reach high book-shelves. One side was twisted and broken. On the hearth a big, heavy man lay, his head turned a little over his shoulder, his face half-hidden. It was easy to see before handling him, that his neck must be broken, and when I touched him I found he was not only dead, but cold. He was in evening-dress, and his face, the face of a man about thirty, was strikingly like that over the mantelpiece. The resemblance was increased by a small pointed beard, and by the dead man's hair being just a little longer than most men wear their hair in town nowadays.

A young fellow, whom I judged to be Maxwell's companion to this projected breakfast, joined us through another door than that by which we had entered, and bowed rather ceremoniously to me, without saying anything.

"Your friend is, of course, dead," I said, rising from my knees, "and he has been dead several hours."

"And will you be so good as to tell us the cause of death?" asked the young fellow who had just joined us. His voice was pleasant, though high-pitched, his manner was polite almost to affectation.

"A broken neck," I said, "vulgarly speaking. More accurately, there is a separation of the cervical vertebrae, and probably complete rupture of the spinal cord."

"But would you kindly oblige us with your opinion as to the cause of the broken neck? I hope I am not asking too much."

I looked at the young man, at the body, the steps, and the portrait.

"I cannot take the place of the coroner's jury, you know," I said. "The general appearance of things suggests that your friend was using the steps—perhaps examining that portrait—and that the steps broke, and the consequent fall did the mischief."

"Quite so. That is what we thought. I am greatly obliged to you for your opinion," said the young man.

"But my opinion," I went on, looking at them both with some curiosity, "isn't of the slightest value, except as to the injury. The police must be told at once, and things had better be left exactly as they are until the police come. There will be an inquest."

"Is that absolutely necessary?" the man called Maxwell asked.

"Absolutely, I should think. But the police will tell you," and I turned to leave the room.

Now as I turned I was thinking about the poor fellow on the floor, whose face was, I dare say, a good deal more grave and dignified then than it had been while he was alive; and I was wondering whether I could do anything to make matters easier for his friends, who both seemed a good deal concerned, though they made no fuss.

While thinking, I made absent-mindedly for the nearest door. I heard the two friends say simultaneously, "Not that door!" but they were too late.

I had pushed it open, and my attention was immediately caught by a queerly-shaped something, half-hidden under a settee.

"Thanks," I said, "but if I write a note for the police—I know the inspector—it may save you trouble. I can write it here, I suppose?" and I walked in, and sat down at the table directly facing the thing that puzzled me. Then I wrote a note, very deliberately, and the composition took me some time, and between the sentences I stared hard at the peculiar object under the settee. Upon my word, the more I looked at it, the more it seemed as though a coffin had been provided before I was called in.

"What's that?" I asked at last, pointing to that thing with the pen.

"That?" It was Maxwell who answered. "That's a mummy case, with a mummy inside. Poor Scrymgeour was interested in such things."

It was my first introduction to the Mummy. I wish it had been my last.

CHAPTER II

CAUGHT IN PASSING

The death of this young Scrymgeour excited a good deal of interest, because he was related to several well-known people, and was himself rather a character. I had to perform a post-mortem examination with another medical man, to make a report thereon, and to appear at the inquest.

The only evidence besides my own was given by the three men whom I had met in the Albany.

Seymour, Scrymgeour's man, stated that he slept in the house, but on the evening before the death he had gone to see

The Merry Widow, had returned late, found the lights out, in the dining-room at any rate, and had "retired," to use his own word, without seeing his master. The next morning, when his master's guests arrived, he went into the bedroom and found the electric light on. He then saw the body lying on the hearthrug, cried out, and the two gentlemen joined him. Later Captain Maxwell went for the doctor, whose name and address he, Seymour, had supplied. He was not a heavy sleeper, but had heard no noise. He would certainly expect to hear a fall, if it happened after he was in his bedroom. The light might be switched on in the bedroom without his being able to notice it from the lobby. He thought the accident had occurred before he returned from the theatre.

The evidence of Maxwell and his friend Perceval was hardly more than corroborative of Seymour's. Both said they had arranged on the previous evening to breakfast with Scrymgeour. Scrymgeour had seemed quite well and in good spirits. He left the club before they did, about eleven.

I was examined as to my visit and my post-mortem observations. I annoyed an inquisitive juryman, a druggist, by speaking of the dead man as a heavy man, without having weighed the body. Also no one had measured the precise height of the steps, and I declined to give a dogmatic opinion as to the height from which the fall of a man, say thirteen stone, would cause a broken neck. I said a hangman might be able to say, if the information was absolutely necessary.

Then Perceval rose, and asked whether he might be allowed to make a statement, which he thought might be useful in clearing up the matter, and the coroner agreed.

"My dead friend," he said, "belonged to an honourable family, and had an amiable weakness. He delighted in genealogy and family histories. He possessed several old family portraits; but his favourite was one of Sir Charles Scrymgeour Scrymgeour, a soldier living in the time of the first and second King Charles.

"This hangs in his bedroom over the mantelpiece, and he was fond of showing it to his acquaintances, and of hearing them comment upon the family likeness. I have known him mount the steps already spoken of, and dust the frame of the portrait himself, calling attention to various characteristics in his ancestor's face. I have thought it possible that he was examining the picture when the steps broke and caused his fall."

The jury, after a certain amount of delay, due, everybody was sure, to the druggist, returned a verdict of death by misadventure, in accordance with the medical evidence.

Curiously enough, the medical man himself was not altogether satisfied. I left the place feeling that the verdict was a common-sense verdict, and sure that the druggist was a bumptious ass. Still, I had noticed one or two things which did not precisely square with the general evidence, although they did not contradict it.

For example, Maxwell and Perceval stated that they went by invitation to breakfast with Scrymgeour, and Seymour also referred to it. But there was no breakfast laid in the room, certainly the dining-room, where I went by mistake. Now, were they all three lying, or was Seymour late with breakfast, or were Maxwell and Perceval before time in their appearance?

Perceval's manner while giving evidence, and particularly while being questioned by the druggist (who obviously thought all men liars and rather wanted us to know it), was conspicuously unconcerned and matter-of-fact. But he passed me on his way back to his seat—and I was surprised to see by the light of a straggling ray of the cold February sun, that his immobile face was covered with little beads of sweat.

The inquiry was closed, and I made my way back to Piccadilly.

A block in the traffic at Piccadilly Circus kept me hanging for a moment on the edge of the pavement, and when I lost patience and made a dash for it I was stopped in mid-stream, between the two currents.

A voice I knew spoke close to my ear. It said, "Well, thank God we kept her name——" and then it stopped suddenly. Half-turning, I found that I stared directly into a motor-brougham, from which Maxwell and Perceval stared back at me. It was Maxwell who had spoken, and Perceval had him clutched by the arm. At that moment the traffic moved on; I had to make a dash for the pavement, and left them without a word or a nod. But we had recognised one another, and I was more puzzled than ever.

CHAPTER III

For a fortnight after the inquest my life in my flat over the grocer's shop was as monotonous as usual.

I had seen nothing during that fortnight of my fellow-witnesses, Maxwell and Perceval; but I heard something of them from my patient Seymour, the dead man's servant. He came to me complaining of sleeplessness and palpitation. Not yet having found another place, and his late master's things being still in the Albany, Seymour slept there. More correctly, to use the old expression, he "lay" there, for he slept little. When he did, he was apt to dream, so he told me, of being forced to enter his master's bedroom, knowing what he would find on the floor.

I prescribed for him upon very unorthodox lines, and spoke of his master's friends. Maxwell, I had learnt from the Army List, was a Sapper and had the D.S.O. Seymour told me he was a "talented officer" and a "great traveller." Seymour himself, by the way, is thin, melancholy, clean-shaven, lantern-jawed, dignified in speech and movement, with a tremendous liking for elegant language.

He was obviously sorry for me because I didn't know Perceval's lineage. "Cousin, sir, to the Earl of Moy and Merricourt, *and* heir. A gentleman, sir, if I may say so, with a great deal more in him than meets the heye. A very delusive gentleman."

I was talking to Seymour and Mudge one evening when my bell rang, and Mudge answered it.

"Bearer waiting reply, sir," said he, and stood to attention, while I read the note he gave me. There was a crest on the paper, an eagle displayed, motto *Ad Solem*, and an address, "Dene Court, Sussex, S.O." "Doctor Armiston is urgently requested to meet Doctor Thorne in consultation at Dene Court to-night. The car will wait for him, and will be at his disposal for returning in the morning."

It was then about half-past eleven.

I knew nothing of Dene Court, or who lived there, and I am not accustomed to such messages. However, I told Mudge to put a change of clothes into a bag for me, and as Seymour helped him I was ready in a few minutes, and down in the street, where an electric-brougham stood with a chauffeur in livery.

"Back before lunch to-morrow, I suppose," said I. "Good night, both of you," and as the car started I nodded to Seymour, who was standing on the kerb.

It might have been the electric light, but his face looked perfectly ghastly.

CHAPTER IV

THE MUMMY TRAVELS

The night was so dark that I could see little of the road as we went, once we had passed beyond the lamps of the suburbs.

I began to get dismal.

First I speculated idly upon the reason which had induced people to send for me in particular as a consultant—I having no delusions (I think) about my small reputation. I am indolent, and seldom write to the medical journals, being ready to assume that what comes under my observation has been already noticed and probably recorded by others. But I wondered whether any one of my few contributions had led to this journey. Then I remembered that I must be passing in the darkness through many places which had been familiar to me as a boy. I grinned at the memory of the great things which at that time I had expected to do in life. I must have been a fool at fifteen. But having a strong suspicion that I continue to be a fool at fifty, I couldn't congratulate myself. There's no fool like an old fool.

The hour's journey was lengthened almost to three by fog, and was sufficiently dreary. I was far enough from the cheery frame of mind proper to the consultant, when we stopped before the great gates opening on to a carriage-drive. A rough calculation suggested that we passed through an avenue of about a mile, before we stopped again in front of a large pile of buildings which stretched into the darkness on either hand.

I was received by the stoutest butler I have ever seen. A huge man, shaking like a jelly with grief. A ridiculous sight, had it not been for the conditions of my visit; but from his appearance I formed the worst possible prognosis of the case I had come to see.

I said nothing to him about that, of course, nor he to me. He directed a footman to take charge of my bag, and led me himself across a large hall, where a wood-fire blazed, to a room where the table was laid for a meal. Here he pressed me to take food, and asked me to excuse him, as there were things to attend to. A groom, he said, had driven to fetch the doctor who was to meet me, but they could not be back for half-an-hour. He left me, and I munched a biscuit and sipped a glass of very fine port, sitting in an easy-chair by the fire.

The house was perfectly still, and no one else, rather to my indignation, came near me. I remained quite alone until my *confrère's* arrival.

Dr. Thorne was a smallish, dry, hard-bitten man of forty or so, with a tanned face and slightly bowed legs. His eyes were a flinty blue, his general appearance was distinctly horsey, though I learnt afterwards that he was a great deal more than a mere horsey man.

He said politely that he was delighted to make my acquaintance, and absent-mindedly helping himself to port, he sniffed it, shaking his head at the fire, standing with one elbow on the mantelpiece.

"A sad case!" he said, showing real trouble. "A sad case, isn't it? A charming fellow, I assure you, and I have known him from the time he went into knickerbockers."

"I've heard nothing whatever of the case," I said; "I've seen no one but servants since I came. Is there anything you think I should be told before we chat with your patient?"

The blue-eyed man, who was staring moodily into the fire, moved so abruptly that he knocked his wine-glass off the mantelpiece and it smashed on the fender.

"Patient!" he said. "God bless my soul, sir! he's dead. Was dead for some hours before we sent for you."

"Why did you send, then?"

"Well, the case is a curious one. Very sad, very sad! And the hounds to meet here in two days' time. One of the best days of the season generally. Not certain if they'll be out again at all. Respect for the dead, you know, and all that sort of thing. A most charming young fellow. Rode straight, and family of course greatly respected. Hope they won't miss a day's hunting for *me*, though, all the same, when my hour comes."

"Why did you send for me?" I asked again, rapping on the table, and the other man started.

"Yes, yes," he muttered. "There I go, rioting as usual till I'm whipped off. Disgrace to my profession. A mere hunting man."

He sat silent for a minute or so while I waited, and then he began to speak quietly of the case.

"The boy," he said, "is a D'Aurelle. You know the family, of course. His father is one of the richest commoners in England, and has refused a peerage, as more than one of his forefathers did. The boy was the only son—about twenty-two, and in every way a manly fellow. Lady Hélène d'Aurelle, his mother, was ill last autumn, and has wintered abroad with her husband. Hugh, the young fellow, has spent a good deal of time in town this winter —they say there was some special attraction—but he hunted here regularly. He came down about a week ago, and, when I met him, told me that he would be here for about a fortnight. Two days ago he was riding hard to hounds, with a couple of friends. He had three visitors, I think, if not four, down with him. Yesterday afternoon the butler found him lying dead in a sort of *salle d'armes*, where apparently he had been using Indian clubs. He had not been at lunch, but it was an understood thing that he and his guests acted independently of each other till dinner-time. They supposed he was lunching at a neighbour's house some few miles away."

"What do you suppose to be the cause of death?" I asked. "There is some uncertainty?"

"None whatever!" the blue-eyed man answered briskly. "There's not a shadow of doubt about it. He overtaxed his heart two years ago. He was in the Oxford boat. The run of two days ago was unusually stiff. Are you a hunting man?"

"No."

"Ah, well, you've missed one of the great pleasures of life; given a good scenting day, a good mount, and a country you know like a book. The first whimper of a trustworthy hound in covert—I know all their voices——" He broke off abruptly. "Poor fellow! He'll never hear them again. Well, well! As I said, it was a hard day, and he rode hard, and we killed some fifteen miles from home. He spoke of stiffness next morning, and, undoubtedly, to try and work it off with heavy clubs was a fatal mistake."

"And why am I called in?"

"In the absence of his people, and to avoid any source of error or of gossip, an independent opinion seemed advisable. It gives me the pleasure of making your acquaintance," and he bowed pleasantly to me across the fire.

I muttered something banal about the pleasure being mutual, and after a word or two more we went upstairs. I was inclined to repeat my question of why I was called in—with special emphasis on the personal pronoun. But I was tired of ringing the changes on that query, and the point seemed of no particular importance, except to myself.

Passing along one of the upper corridors we found the big butler evidently on guard at a bedroom door. He drew himself up to attention as we neared him, and stayed where he stood, making no move to enter the room with us. There were candles in a candelabrum, and they flickered in the draught. This made his huge shadow go through strange changes; and indeed I think his fat body still shook with grief, though he made no sound, even when Thorne said a friendly word in passing. Thorne told me that the man had served in the Guards, had saved the elder D'Aurelle's life in the Egyptian war, and had been the dead man's first teacher in boxing, fencing and many other things.

The boy (he looked no more than a thoroughly manly boy) had been strikingly handsome. His clean-shaven face had a set look, as though he were making an effort with clenched teeth —and something of a frown. There seemed no reason for doubting Thorne's decision about the cause of death. I examined the body; and returning to the corridor asked the butler a few questions about the finding of it, and also chatted a little longer with Thorne, who was ready to give all possible information—being anxious, he acknowledged, to avoid a post-mortem in the parents' absence, if he honestly could.

I finally said that I was quite prepared to sign a joint certificate, giving heart-failure, due to over-exertion, as the cause of death, and this was agreed upon.

It was then between five and six, and chilly, as it always seems to one who has been up all night. A bedroom was ready for me, and I am sure that the servants, of a somewhat old-fashioned type, would have offered me every attention. But I took an unreasoning dislike to the place, and felt, also, that I must be a burden on the distressed house.

I also declined Thorne's pressing offer of a bed at his place, and asked Mott, the butler, privately, whether he thought that I could arrange with the chauffeur to take me back into town at once. It ended in my getting a breakfast while sundry preparations were being made; for Mott seemed to brighten up quite visibly at my suggestion. Indeed, until he conducted me himself to the car, I was rather puzzled at his hurried way of speeding things.

Passing down the steps from the big hall door to the carriage-drive in the grey morning light I talked to him, trying to remove some vague uncertainty that he seemed to feel, about the cause of the boy's death. He didn't express it openly. Indeed, he wouldn't acknowledge it, and I decided that he merely felt special responsibility because his master and mistress were away.

The flight of steps was high, and in going down I looked on the top of the car.

My bag was there, and also a long, pretty broad, sinister-looking object, partly muffled in rugs.

"I brought nothing but a bag," I said, staring down on it.

The man Mott looked down too, stammered, and then the guardsman in him seemed suddenly to get the upper hand of the butler.

"'Twas an order I got from him," he said. "The d——d thing was to go to town this morning, anyway. Twice this week he said, 'Remember, Mott, as I might forget, or be away, that the Thing's to go back on the twenty-fifth.' It's me that's glad to be quit of it. Though if you ask me I say it's too late."

"What is it?" I asked, but really I already knew.

"A blasted Mummy," said Mott.

CHAPTER V

COWARD CONSCIENCE

From Dene Court, which I left fantastically obscured by wreaths of morning mist, through which I saw the hatchment over the porch, and the flag drooping damp and dull at half-mast), to Piccadilly I thought of nothing except the silent passenger upon the roof, racking my brains to imagine if there was any possible connection between the two sudden deaths, one in the Albany and one in Sussex. I never had a more unpleasant journey.

When we reached my rooms I decided these points as far as possible for myself, without consulting the astonished chauffeur. Probably Mudge, who was standing on the kerb, waiting to take my bag, has been too long with me to show or to feel astonishment at anything. I climbed to the level of the car-roof and examined its burden. Yes—to all appearance this was the mummy-case which I had seen a fortnight before. I had noticed a large dark stain on it, about the size of a dinner-plate—and here was the stain.

I could not very well stay to examine the thing carefully. Its shape was too suggestive to the passer-by, and my own position was conspicuous. I only settled one more point before getting down. I looked for an address, and found it:

PROFESSOR MAUNDEVILLE,
21, Courtenay Street, W.

Over my coffee and a cigar at night I tackled the affair again. Here is a summary of my thoughts:

Within a fortnight I had been called upon to certify two sudden deaths. Both had occurred apparently without witnesses. Those concerned were both young men, bachelors, well-to-do, of good social position. In the first case the death seemed accidental, and the cause of the accident seemed obvious. In the second case it had been foreshadowed as possible under certain conditions, namely over-exertion and fatigue. These conditions had apparently been present.

Both cases, so far, might occur in any man's practice, but certainly not with the coincidence that was left to be accounted for.

In each instance there was a mummy in the house (more accurately a mummy-case, for I knew nothing about the contents). Moreover, it was apparently the same mummy-case.

Further, whereas in the first instance I had been fetched apparently because I was near by, and already known to one of those present, in the second I had several hours' journey to make, and went where I was an absolute stranger.

I decided to know as quickly as possible whether the two dead men had been acquainted, or had had mutual acquaintances. I rang the bell.

"Where's Seymour?" I asked Mudge.

"Gone to a music-hall, sir, to get rid of the 'orrors.'"

"What horrors, Mudge?" asked I.

"Dunno, sir. 'E seems scared of something, and says 'e won't sleep alone in the Albany at any price."

"Well, keep him here when he comes back," I said, "but don't disturb me. I don't want to see either of you to-night. More coffee!" and then I was left to myself.

Personally I cannot concentrate my mind without unlimited coffee and cigars; and sometimes I cannot concentrate it at all.

That night I got nothing for my vigil except an attack of biliousness, and a certainty that I must interview the men connected with my Albany experience—Perceval and Maxwell. Yes, I also reached the unpleasant conclusion that if I hadn't been a conceited humbug I shouldn't have left Dene Court directly I saw that mummy on the car, and should at least have returned and torn up that death certificate, refusing to sign any without further investigation. I had a miserable night.

It was the early morning when I fell asleep, and in consequence ate a late breakfast in a shocking temper.

I was in the middle of it when the front-door bell rang. "If it's anyone to see me," I said to Mudge, "I'm engaged and shall be all day. I won't see anyone but Seymour. If it's a patient, tell him there's a younger and better man at the bottom of the street." Nevertheless Mudge returned in two or three minutes, and said that two gentlemen had insisted that they must see me, and were waiting in the lobby.

"Must!" I said. "How much did they give you?" and Mudge was so worried that he mentioned half a sovereign before he knew what he was about. I told him to return the tip and show them the door.

"They're gentlemen, sir," said Mudge. "One's an officer."

"Tell your officer what your orders are; I'm engaged," shouted I.

Mudge saluted stiffly, went out, and returned.

"Gentlemen say they must see you, sir."

"Must"—again! I was much annoyed. Merely because a poor fool has studied medicine, may he never have peace? I thumped the table, and of course was angry with myself for doing so.

I beckoned Mudge to come nearer, and he came and waited until I felt that I could speak coolly and slowly. I spoke very softly and deliberately, so as not to say anything unreasonable. I whispered to Mudge that what I paid him for was to obey orders, and to keep people out just as much as to let them in. I pointed out to him that I was not the "slave of the ring." That, theoretically, this was a free country, and that if I chose to tell him to turn away fifty officers of the regulars he must do it. I was going on to say with some emphasis—Mudge needs things to be put clearly —that I would see these patients condemned before I allowed them to interrupt my deliberations, when I saw that I hadn't his undivided attention. His eyes wandered to the mirror over the mantelpiece a little behind my chair, and to my left, and he began to grin weakly and idiotically. I twisted in my chair, and found that the two patients were standing just inside the door, and that they were Maxwell and Perceval. I was an ass not to have guessed that it might be they; but I was altogether absorbed in my puzzle.

For a moment no one said anything, and I sat staring at them. Then the situation struck me as being rather comic, and I began to laugh, while my two visitors remained perfectly solemn.

So I merely told Mudge to give them chairs, and to obey orders if anyone else came. Then I sat back and waited for them to explain themselves.

CHAPTER VI

A DOUBLE CONSULTATION

As a matter of fact, Perceval began with a careful apology for their intrusion, which I listened to without any comment.

When his apology, very formal—stilted, in fact—was at an end, I said, "Well, in any case I wanted to see you both. What do you want?"

Perceval explained that they had come to consult me about their condition. "Of which," he said, "we have reason to think very seriously."

They both looked remarkably fit, though as solemn as owls, and I began to wonder if they were playing some trick.

"My fee for each is a guinea," I said, and each of them, without saying anything, produced two guineas, and put them on the table.

I asked them which wished to consult me first. "The other," I said, "can stay here till I send in for him."

But they both objected to this. They wished, they said, to consult me together.

I was inclined to say more, but decided that to give them their own way might explain things best.

"What have you to complain of?" I asked Maxwell, and poured out more coffee, while he considered. First he said that he wasn't complaining—hoped he had more sense; but his story finally was that he suffered from nerves and palpitation of the heart. He thought his appetite bad, and was always expecting something to happen. What sort of things? Oh, horrid things. Anything horrid.

"Such as mummies, and sudden deaths!" I suggested, on the spur of the moment; but whatever the state of his nerves might be, Maxwell let that remark pass without even showing that he heard it; and after feeling his pulse, which was going quietly at sixty-five, and seeing his tongue, which was as clean as any healthy baby's, I turned to Perceval. The latter complained in a high, level voice that he was restless and irritable, and always wanting to be alone.

"That's why you brought your friend with you, I suppose?" I suggested.

"When I'm alone I can't bear myself," he explained; "besides, Captain Maxwell doesn't count, doctor. We're old friends and understand one another; don't we, Max?" and Maxwell nodded, without troubling to say anything.

I overhauled Perceval in a general way, and then sitting back in my chair considered them both, while they watched me.

"Remember, we want your frank opinion," Maxwell said at last, "and whatever it may be we'll take it all right, and be grateful for it; won't we, Percy?" ... and this time it was Perceval who nodded without saying anything.

"Oh, if you want it, you shall have it," I said. "You've paid me for it, and you've *got* to have it. How you'll take it, and whether you'll be grateful for it, is another matter, which doesn't particularly concern me. My frank opinion is that there's nothing the matter with either of you. Either you're suffering from guilty consciences, which for the time I leave to yourselves, or else you're trying to impose on me, which seems a waste of time. I'm inclined to think both of you liars, and clumsy liars. I trust you find my opinion satisfactory."

To my surprise, they took this quietly, and merely sat looking at one another and seeming to consider. It is true that Perceval, who was much the fairer man, flushed a good deal; and Maxwell clenched his hand, which lay on the table before me.

For a minute or so I waited to hear what they would say, and they said nothing, till at last Maxwell turned to Perceval.

"Well, I suppose that will do?" he said.

"Altogether satisfactory, *I* think," Perceval answered; and they both rose, bowed politely, muttered a word or two of thanks, and went away.

I never was more puzzled in my life. I was so puzzled that I decided to make no effort to keep them, and to say nothing more, until I had time to think things over alone. I sat and stared at the four guineas, still lying on the table, till some sound made me shift my gaze, and I found Mudge watching with his usual expressionless stare. When I gave him leave to speak, he said that Seymour was waiting to know whether I wanted to see him, and I told him to send that melancholy individual in.

He came, looking very much upset, and I told him to sit down near me.

"I'm going to ask you several questions," I said, "but you will understand that I have no authority to make you answer them. You must please yourself. But if you answer fully and honestly you may save trouble. Will you do so?" and I watched him while he considered the matter, which he did for a while, biting his nails.

He was certainly unhappy, and looked as if he had not slept.

"Why haven't you shaved?" I asked sharply, and the man jumped in his chair, raising a startled hand to a blue chin with a hurried apology. I accused him of drink and excessive cigarette-smoking, but he denied my charges and sat still gloomily biting his nails.

"Well, will you answer my questions?" I asked again.

"I'd like to hear 'em first," said Seymour rather superfluously, but I understood what he meant.

"You heard where I was going two nights ago?"

"Yes, sir."

"You know the place?"

"Yes, sir."

"You were surprised?"

That man's renewed attack upon his nails set my teeth on edge before he replied. Then he said he didn't know.

"You looked it at any rate. Both surprised and frightened," I said. "Did you guess what was wrong?"

"I was afraid something was wrong," Seymour allowed.

"Do you know what was wrong?"

"I know now, sir. I didn't then, of course. But yesterday I made inquiries at Berkeley Square—at the town house, sir."

"Did your master know this young Mr. d'Aurelle?"

"Yes, sir."

"Did Captain Maxwell and Mr. Perceval know him?"

Seymour sat gnawing his nails with indecision for some seconds.

"They may have met," he said at last. "I don't say that they did or they didn't. It's not my business, anyway."

"And you think it isn't mine?" I suggested. "Would you be interested to hear that there was a mummy at Dene Place? Or did you hear that too at Berkeley Square?"

But at this point Seymour turned a paler yellow than ever, and rising unsteadily said I must excuse him, but he didn't feel well. He was staggering towards the door when I jumped up, got hold of him, and forced him down upon the sofa, otherwise he would have fallen. It cost me a good glass of excellent cherry-brandy (the first stimulant I laid hands on) before he reached his normal shade of yellow again.

I had for the time to stop my questions, and before night, when I had meant to continue them if possible, something happened which made me decide to leave him alone for the time.

CHAPTER VII

THE PLAIN SPEAKERS

I was out most of the morning, but came in for lunch, as I was not inclined just then for chatter with men at my club. In consequence, I saw my letters by the midday post soon after they came, and one amused me a little. The envelope, over which I idled for a few seconds, was of thick rough paper, was rather long and narrow, and carried an interlaced monogram S.P.S. stamped in black.

Inside was a small sheet of rough-edged note-paper, and on that was printed the following:

"You are invited to join the Plain Speakers. A member will call this afternoon, to answer any reasonable questions you may wish to ask."

What I took to be a punning crest or device was stamped in colours at the top of the paper. It was a skeleton, seated, and wearing robes, and a full-bottomed wig—presumably in fact a Plain Speaker.

Well, I didn't see the necessity for forming a club or society of plain speakers. One speaks plainly or otherwise according to one's taste, condition and habit, and possibly one's income. More than one old friend had already accused me of speaking too plainly. People who formed a society for that purpose were likely, I thought, to be weak-kneed individuals. It seemed to me, too, that the invitation had not been sent by any intimate friend; for the envelope was scrupulously addressed with a great many letters after my name, representing my membership of many learned and quite unimportant societies. I judged that my address had been copied from a medical directory. I crumpled the card up and tossed it into my wastepaper basket. Later I forgot all about the thing, and went out.

There is a fashionable flower-shop at the corner where my street meets Piccadilly. I was on the opposite side, but I crossed as usual just there, liking to get a sight of whatever flowers there might be. I saw the first daffodils of the season in the window, and while I was looking at them, and wondering whether I wouldn't tell the florist to send some across to my rooms, she took the whole lot out of the window, perhaps a dozen bunches, and showed them to a customer, a man. From the manner in which she presently set them aside, I inferred that he had bought the lot; and glaring at him discontentedly enough, for I had really meant to take some, I found that this man was Maxwell.

He dictated some address to the girl, and then turning to the window as though to see what else might be there, he noticed me, and at once came out into the street.

"I was on my way to call, doctor," he said.

"Why?" I asked, wishing to be sarcastic. "Do you feel worse?"

He made no answer to this, but invited me to go into the shop for a moment with him, unless I would prefer turning back to my rooms.

"I don't meet patients professionally in florists' shops," I said, "but I don't know that I care to turn back either—unless you mean to explain this morning's visit."

"If you'll be reasonable for a moment," he said, "and listen to me, I don't think you'll regret it. Come into the shop," and I followed him.

Once inside, and in a quiet corner away from the counter, he faced me and spoke, holding out a small card.

"You got, or will get, an invitation to join a society called the Plain Speakers."

I took the thing, the size of an ordinary visiting card, and saw that on it there was a little seated skeleton, in wig and robes. That and nothing else, except his name in pencil.

"I got it," I said.

"Will you join?"

"Do you think I need practice in plain speaking?" I asked him; and the man laughed good-temperedly enough. I had a good look at him before I answered his question.

He was a tall fellow, and very lean. He was naturally dark-complexioned, and made darker by exposure. One could see the line of demarcation caused probably by the collar of a military tunic. His black hair and moustache were close cut. His face in profile reminded me of some heads of Roman soldiers which I had seen on medallions; strong-jawed, hawk-nosed, spare. I shouldn't suspect him of much imagination, and an admirable nervous system probably kept him good-tempered. On considering him in this way, however, I was surprised to remember that he had allowed me to call him a liar—or, at any rate, to say that I suspected him of being one. I decided that he would, perhaps, stand a good deal, if it helped him to get what he wanted.

"Well?" he said presently.

"Why should I join?" I asked. "What do you want me for? What should I get from it, in profit or pleasure?"

"I don't think it will interest you much, but it's a Step," said he.

"In the dark," I pointed out. "Where does it lead?"

"I can't tell you much that's worth telling," he said, "until you join. The society may amuse you, or it may not. My friend Perceval and I want you to join." He stopped a moment, and looked at me steadily.

"You are interested in mummies, I fancy," he said. "I believe you might learn something new—and perhaps teach us."

"I hate mysteries. What on earth do you mean?" I grumbled.

"Mysteries are not in my line, and they're not to my liking," Maxwell said. "But a promise is a promise, even if it's a d——d silly one. Join the Plain Speakers. Then Perceval and I can say more. That's the only reason for asking you."

"What do I get by it?" I persisted; and the fellow looked me over with most impudent minuteness before answering.

"Can't tell," he said at last. "Depends on the sort of man you are."

"If you don't know what sort of man I am you had better find out before you go further," I said. "Come to me again, if you want to, when you do know. In the meantime, I shall be making more inquiries about *you*," and I turned to go about my business. I was tired of this circumlocution, and two people had already bumped against me in entering the shop.

But Maxwell laid a hand on my arm, and an uncommonly strong hand I felt it to be. It was impossible to get away without making more fuss than I cared to make while the young person behind the counter kept an eye on us.

"Listen a minute!" he said, "and then go if you must. You ask me what you'll get by doing what I want. You'll get a fee or two sooner or later, I'm afraid; but I understand you're not awfully keen about fees. Besides that you'll get worry and anxiety, and you may have to take risks. However, of course they're not in your line, and no one can blame you if you refuse them later."

"Confound you!" I said, "do you think a man's a coward if he doesn't wear a uniform? Get on with your enumerations of the inducements held out by your blessed society!"

"That's all, I think," he said, looking at me closely. "A man of your age won't be bothered like some of us, I suppose. Perhaps that'll even keep you from being interested."

"What the devil antediluvian age do you think I am?" I asked, "to be past bother and interests?" but he didn't say.

"I believe, though," he ended, "that you'd do as I ask, if you knew all about it. I think if you refuse now, and get to know about it later, you'll regret it as long as you live. That is, if you're the sort of man we take you to be. I can't tell you anything more unless you join."

I was nettled at his suggestion concerning my age and possible dread of risks. "I'll join, and be hanged to you," I said.

"Say what you please, so long as you join," he answered, smiling. "Come to the next meeting, for which you'll get a card —and after that we can talk plainly."

He gripped my hand very firmly, and went away without any more ado.

The next day I found another Plain Speaker envelope among my letters. Inside was a printed card, with the bewigged skeleton upon it:

"Your attendance is requested at the next meeting of the Plain Speakers, to be held at —— " Then followed the address of a great lady, and the time, 10 p.m.

CHAPTER VIII

POLITE SOCIETY!

On the date named for a meeting of the Plain Speakers, I had a note, signed Charles Aylmer Perceval, saying that the writer proposed to himself the pleasure of calling upon me at about 9.30 p.m., and of accompanying me to the meeting as sponsor, Maxwell, being detained until later by duty.

At the time mentioned he came and found me ready.

Ten minutes' stroll was enough to take us to our rendezvous, one of the big houses whose fine grounds and high walls would delude one into supposing London to be miles away, were it not for the unceasing low roar outside.

It is not necessary that I should give the name of our impressive hostess for the evening. She beamed graciously upon me from a height which seemed some inches greater than my own, when Perceval took me forward; and she said that she was afraid I should find the poor little Society rather frivolous, but that another learned man would no doubt help to improve it. Before I could disclaim any pretensions to special learning she turned away to greet someone else.

"Come and let me introduce you to the President for the year," Perceval said, with a finger on my sleeve.

"What the deuce does she mean by her remarks about learned men?" I asked. "Have you introduced me here under false pretences?"

"Not in the least, my dear sir," he assured me. "It's just the lady's way. A mere *façon de parler*. She knows nothing about you, except that you are called Doctor and are properly introduced by Maxwell and myself."

I stared at him with some surprise, for his rather sarcastic explanation seemed out of keeping with his usual careful politeness.

"Well?" he asked, smiling.

"You're showing yourself in rather a fresh light," I explained, "that's all."

"The light of Plain Speaking," he said. "It becomes a habit in time at these meetings, and may quite easily be carried to excess, I own."

We had crossed the room, and were now standing near a good-looking, grey-moustached man, who was pretty obviously a soldier, and whose face seemed somehow rather familiar to me.

"The President is engaged just now," Perceval said. "Maundeville, a charming and very learned man, by the by, is probably attacking him on some phase of modern warfare. Maundeville says that practically all soldiers are sentimentalists, and so waste life by their silly methods. He is rather amusing, but he won't let the President go yet. Let us sit here, and while we wait I'll tell you what little is necessary about the Plain Speakers."

He led me to a settee close at hand, and not far from the big wood-fire. The President, who was rather tall, and carried himself with an easy nonchalance, stood with his back to the fire, on a white bearskin, warming his coat tails and listening to Maundeville talking with tremendous vigour and fluency, and with somewhat emphatic but not awkward gestures.

Maundeville, who now faced us, was short and spare, but extremely muscular and vigorous, and his thin clean-shaven face was well-tanned. He seemed never at rest while talking, and when he laughed, as he did once or twice, he showed remarkably good strong teeth. His hair was grey but very thick, and curled slightly though close cut. His face was full of good nature, of *bonhomie*, and he made the President laugh twice at what I thought to be his arguments.

The drawing-room we sat in was one of a suite of three. Its colours were white and a dark shade of red. There were two large fires in it, but little furniture. A few chairs and settees were scattered about.

"The Plain Speakers," Perceval was saying as they gradually drifted in, "don't take themselves too seriously, and don't expect you to do so. The Society was started informally by a few people who decided that telling the plain truth was a luxury which they could too seldom indulge in. We meet once a fortnight during the season, at the house of any member who offers to receive us. A list of such houses is kept, and they are taken in rotation. Our rules are very few. The essential one is that at all meetings one must speak nothing but the absolute truth as one knows it. One need say nothing, one may refuse to speak, but we promise not to prevaricate in the slightest degree—of course, some of the women find that impossible. Nevertheless, we discover that the habit of truth grows upon one, and surprising admissions or statements are sometimes made. It is a point of honour with us not to use, outside, to anyone's disadvantage, any information thus gained—nor, of course, to repeat it."

He looked about him, hesitated a moment, and went on in a lower tone.

"Maundeville keeps the President interested," he said, "and no one whom I particularly want is here yet. I may as well explain further at once, or you will be bored.

"One thing has led to another, as usual, and some of the Plain Speakers have formed a little set, 'inner circle,' if you choose, with the professed idea of studying certain things. Maxwell and I want you to be with us there, but first we had to make you a Plain Speaker. I see our President is waiting for us," and he rose.

Maundeville had bowed and turned away, limping a little, and leaving the President laughing and looking in our direction. Perceval took me to him and introduced me formally. He gave my name, of course, but spoke of the other man merely as our

President, and addressed him as Sir. But while we chatted I recognised him as a man of very high rank, who had lately resigned an easy position, openly giving reasons worthy of a Plain Speaker for doing so.

After a few minutes he nodded to us, and turned to a lady who was passing.

"You're now a recognised member," Perceval said. "You need no further introduction to anyone here. Let us go back to our seat, and I'll give you some idea of what people are here already. You will know some of them by name at any rate."

The company seemed much more fashionable and distinguished than any I have been accustomed to meet, except at public functions.

I recognised one or two men as casual club acquaintances, and was interested to notice that generally, on recognising me, men would first look astonished, then laugh, and afterwards greet me more cordially than usual.

One man turned aside to say that he had more than once thought I ought to have been an original Plain Speaker. He was still talking when a lady tapped him on the shoulder with her fan.

"Go away, my dear man!" she said peremptorily. "Those two over there are discussing the Second Empire, and I told them no one knew anything about it but you and I. Go and put them right."

"Why didn't you do it yourself?" he asked.

"I can't be bothered, and I want to see this new Plain Speaker," she said—and he laughed and crossed the room. Perceval at the same time mentioned my name to the lady and offered her his place, which she took and peremptorily told me to sit beside her. I had already recognised her name as that of the authoress of certain much-discussed memoirs, and I waited with some curiosity.

"Well, I like learned men," she said, "for a change. And you look more learned than most of us. Drier, at any rate."

"I never was called 'learned' before in my life, that I know of," I said. "And the word has been used more than once since I came here. As for the other adjective I'm not responsible. At my age one begins to get dry."

"Well, that boy Maxwell told me you were learned," she said briskly. "Not that I suppose he is a judge. He said you were a born Plain Speaker, too. So am I. What on earth do you come here for? You can't know many of us silly folk."

"I came because I was invited," I said. "I didn't know whom I was to meet."

"Meaning that if you had known you wouldn't have come!" she chuckled. "But the talk is interesting sometimes; though the necessity of telling the truth—if you can—shuts some people's mouths altogether—thank goodness."

"I thought they were supposed to join for the privilege of speaking plainly?"

"Some of 'em joined to ask questions and some to hear others speak," she said, nodding. "Some find that they can't be truthful if they try."

"How do they find out?"

"Why, we tell 'em, of course! That's why it's amusing to meet here." She nodded towards the far end of the room, where our hostess was still receiving fresh comers.

"Lady Havers, you know . . ."

What she was going to say about our hostess I do not know, for she suddenly changed her subject with an exclamation of:

"There's Conder! He's a favourite of mine. Bring him over here!"

There was only room for two on the settee, and it was obvious that I had my *congé*.

"Since you're a Plain Speaker," I said, rising, "tell me why you took the trouble to talk to me."

"I was chilly," she said, "and the seat is comfortably near the fire. New members are always amusing for a few minutes. Now go and bring Conder here before anyone else takes this seat."

I did my errand, and moving away stood alone and watched the people—for the room was now filling up. Suddenly there was a lull in the chatter all through the room, almost a dead silence. People near me were all looking more or less openly in one direction, and naturally I wheeled to see what interested them. It was a newcomer—a tall fair girl, taller than any other woman in the room, and carrying her head high. She looked the more conspicuous because of the heavy masses of copper-red hair in which some emeralds flickered. Her dress was shimmering green, and a necklace and pendant of emeralds hung about her neck.

"There's a young lady," I said softly to Maxwell, whom I found by my side, "who looks more like the ideal heroine than anyone I've seen yet. Who's the girl?"

"What! You too?" Maxwell said, looking at me curiously, and I was annoyed.

"Now, what the devil do you mean by 'You too'?" I asked him. "I'm not surprised to hear that other folk agree with me. She's handsomer than any princess I've happened to look at."

"Poor O'Hagan, her father, would have politely asked you to say 'any other princess'!" Maxwell said. "He traced his descent from one of the Seven Kings of Ulster, and I've heard him tell her she could meet royalty on equal terms. That is Miss Nora O'Hagan, a second cousin of Perceval's."

While we watched, the girl left our hostess and went on into another room, bowing here and there as she passed. How tall she was! How well her red hair showed up against the white wall!

Well! The night went on, and I found, rather to my amazement, that I was enjoying myself. It was quite obvious that to be there was a sufficient introduction to anyone in the room, and that the Plain Speakers acted up to their principles. Of this I had several proofs.

After some time Professor Maundeville limped across to me (the limp was very slight, but I always associate it with him), and introduced himself at once as a medical.

"I never practised," he said, "but just studied the thing in London and Paris. I know a good many of the Vienna men too. Fascinating study, of course, but still quite empirical, you know. The Chinese plan is the best. Pay your man to keep you well. Wise folk, those Heathen Chinese!"

He kept nodding to men or bowing to women all the time he talked. He knew everybody, and spoke of them with the mild cynicism which all the older Plain Speakers seemed to feel.

"At one time we tried discussions on fixed subjects," he said. "Our hostess there is always ready to read a paper on anything; but her ideas of truth are—feminine. Yes, I'm a bachelor, like yourself. Oh, the thing has its uses. Men meet here who are not likely to do so anywhere else, and I've known useful work done among Plain Speakers. The women amuse themselves. But what on earth do you expect to do here?"

He beamed on me genially like the others, and I was about to explain my position as a Plain Speaker when Maxwell crossed the room and interrupted.

"Well, Maundeville, I suppose you're merely taking away our characters?" he said; "so I needn't apologise for interrupting. You might criticise that formula for me," and he gave him a slip of paper covered with symbols and figures.

Maundeville took it and at once became interested, and Maxwell turned away from him and spoke in an undertone to me.

"Go soon to the innermost room, by the fire," he said. "You understand?" and when I nodded he turned away, and at once began to comment upon the paper to Maundeville. I gathered that the figures related to a new explosive.

I left them a few minutes later and strolled away. I went slowly through the little knots of talkers in the middle room, wondering what some journalists would give to be there, and passed at length into the innermost room.

It was about the same size as the outer ones, and a small string-band was playing softly there; and staring down into the fire, with one green-shod foot on the fender, her elbow on the mantelpiece, her pretty chin on her hand, stood the red-haired girl.

I fancied she was listening to the fiddles, and since there was no one there waiting for me, I kept away from her. Indeed, I turned a shoulder to her, which brought me almost face to face with a young couple sitting opposite, a lady watching the orchestra, her partner watching her.

It would have been an interesting bit of psychology to compare what the muted fiddles breathed to each of us. Very different tunes, no doubt.

Now, I assure you that though, to avoid seeming to stare at the red-haired girl, I faced in the direction of the other two, I did not watch them. Nevertheless, they evidently thought I did so, for presently, after saying a word to the lady, and giving a little pat to an entreating hand laid upon his sleeve, as if to say, "Leave this to me!" the young fellow rose and strolled across to me.

"A good many Plain Speakers turned up to-night," he said, with a nod.

"I had no idea there were so many in all London," I acknowledged.

"Great institution! Useful practice!" he remarked gravely. "Helps no end. Bein' a Plain Speaker, I'm sure you won't mind my sayin' we, the lady over there and I, find your attentions most damnably inconvenient. No offence. See?"

He was a good-looking, resolute boy, and I sympathised with him.

"No offence whatever," I said. "But I was asked to wait here for someone."

"That's all right then," he said cheerfully; and then glancing over my shoulder, "So's Miss O'Hagan, I fancy." Then with a sudden inspiration, "Sure you aren't waiting for one another?"

"Gad, we may be, I suppose!" I agreed, and turned sideways to look. She was watching us.

"My apologies to your partner," I said formally to the boy. "I'll speak to Miss O'Hagan at any rate."

"That's all right," he said again, and we separated, he returning to his partner, who was watching us rather anxiously, while I moved towards the fire, where the red-haired girl waited.

I remembered that as I went I thought that at any rate, whether she wanted me or not, I should hear her voice. Heaps of women, as we all know, destroy a pleasing effect as soon as they open their mouths; and it might be so now, which would be annoying. As I drew near I saw that something worried her, though her face was quite still; for some filmy stuff about the edge of her corsage, or whatever you call it, was disturbed.

"I'm not sure," I said, "whether I was sent in here to meet Miss O'Hagan," and I stood waiting. Then I confess I got a disagreeable little shock. The girl returned my bow, with some formality and a very grave face. But directly her mouth moved all her face began to twitch most painfully, and it was some seconds before I could hear a word. What I heard was merely disjointed stammering, of which I could make nothing whatever, while her face was simply convulsed with her efforts. After this had gone on for perhaps twenty seconds, though at the time it seemed longer, I said "Stop!" and she became silent.

"Just listen a moment, Miss O'Hagan," I said, "and don't try to speak. Perhaps, being a stranger, I took you by surprise. My name is Armiston, Doctor Armiston. Captain Maxwell said that I was to come here, and I thought perhaps you were waiting for me. If you were not, please don't trouble to speak. Shake your head and I'll go back to the doorway." But she stood looking at me, neither saying anything nor making any sign.

"I may suppose, then," I said, "that Captain Maxwell sent me to you. Very well, I have nothing to do, I can wait as long as you like."

So I waited, standing near her by the fire, and looking more at it than at her. I could see the point of her small green shoe tapping the fender, and I could see a long slender hand, with three fine rings on it, gripping the mantelpiece hard. Presently she again tried to speak, but it was almost useless, though I avoided looking at her.

Finally I understood that she was trying to say she must write; and then I silenced her again, told her that Maxwell or Perceval could give her my address, since I had no card in my pocket, and then I left her as quickly as possible.

In the middle drawing-room Maxwell and Perceval converged quietly on me from different places.

"Was it Miss O'Hagan to whom I was to speak?" I asked Maxwell, and he nodded.

"Have you talked to her?"

"No. She seemed nervous," I explained, "and was stammering. An old trouble, I suppose?"

"Not at all," Maxwell said, exchanging glances with Perceval, and, of course, I was interested.

"Well," I said, "she found it difficult to talk, and I think she is going to let me have a letter some time. Now, unless there's any particular reason why I shouldn't leave, I'm going back to my rooms for a smoke."

"It was extremely good of you to come," Perceval said politely.

"Can we go back with you?" Maxwell asked. But I declined their company, bowed to my hostess, who had apparently forgotten me already, and went away.

When I got back to my room I sat by the fire for some time. The fact is, I had constantly before me a beautiful though contorted face, crowned with copper-red hair, and I was wondering how on earth that could help me in the matter of a mummy.

CHAPTER IX

I AM INVITED TO GO FURTHER

I had a sort of unformulated idea, until lately, that the man of fifty, provided he were fairly sane and not actually poverty-stricken, had many advantages.

Blood, speaking unscientifically, is supposed to cool considerably earlier than at fifty. The wisdom of experience is assumed to have accumulated.

It must be a matter of temperament and habit. At any rate, I have discovered that this comfortable mood of *laissez aller*, and refusal to marvel or admire, is not yet for me.

I left the Plain Speakers only to go home and think about them—and more particularly of the girl O'Hagan. Maxwell and Perceval had given me the idea that I was to be a Plain Speaker in order that I might learn more about a mummy; but it looked as though I had been taken in order to meet Miss O'Hagan.

What had she to do with mummies? What did she want to say to me? Why didn't she say it? Why did she stammer?

I took a good deal more interest in this case of stammering than seemed reasonable, in spite of my fifty years.

I was late at breakfast again, and was still sitting at the table at ten o'clock, turning over my letters and trying to choke off Mudge, who was telling me, who knew already, why he had joined the Marines. (It was, by the way, a girl. It always is. The way they get mixed up in things is absurd, and does more than anything else to make life a ridiculous and uncertain affair.)

Then the bell rang and Mudge went out, and came back to say

that Maxwell and Perceval wanted me to fix any time convenient for an appointment with them that day.

"Put them into the consulting-room," I said, and joined them a few minutes later, wondering whether these young fellows pestered all their acquaintances as they did me.

The two men seated themselves, Maxwell with a friendly nod to me, Perceval with a ceremonious inquiry after my health and an apology for the early intrusion.

"But we wanted to be sure of catching you," he said, "and knowing your practice kept you a busy man——"

Now I hate any nonsense about my practice.

"It doesn't keep me anything of the sort," I said, "but I like my breakfast in peace."

So after a little preliminary skirmishing while I tried to finish my breakfast, they started to business.

Maxwell began by saying that he wanted to clear the ground, and to do it he meant to speak quite plainly.

"If we say things you don't like," he added, "remember we no more mean to be rude than you do. Indeed, our intention is complimentary."

"How do you know I don't mean to be rude?" I remember asking. "It's the only way to get rid of some people."

But Maxwell laughed and said they knew, and went on.

"You've told us you're not a busy man," he said, "and we think you're comparatively poor. Now this will be a professional matter, and we want you to deal with it on that basis. We're comparatively rich beggars; aren't we, Percy?" and Perceval nodded and admired his violets.

"We're going to take up a good deal of your time too, till the job is finished."

"What job?" I asked.

"It has to do with Scrymgeour, and D'Aurelle, and the Mummy."

"I'm in that matter already, on my own account," I said. I didn't think it necessary to add that I didn't know exactly where I stood in regard to it.

"You won't get far alone," Maxwell said, "and if you try alone you'll make things very unpleasant for us, and for other people to whom it matters a good deal more. Now look here! Perceval and I were at Dene Court, and we made them call you down."

"Why?"

"You were mixed up in poor Scrymgeour's affair, and we liked the way you behaved in that, didn't we, Percy?"

Percy nodded, and I stared at them both. I was considerably surprised at this statement, but I merely stared and grunted.

"Now, I fetched you for poor Scrymgeour," Maxwell reminded me, "and we made them fetch you again the other night. We want you to hold yourself in readiness to go again to any patient whom we ask you to see, say during the next six months, and to take such hints as we may suggest for helping you to understand the cases. We propose offering you a retaining fee of five hundred pounds."

"Guineas," Perceval suggested.

"I forgot. Of course, you doctors always count in guineas. I beg your pardon. Guineas it is. Have you studied Egyptology, and do you object to meeting a few of the Plain Speakers who have been studying such things?"

I sat back in my chair and considered them both attentively before I answered. They were quite serious.

"I know practically nothing about you two men," I said at last.

"You'd know a good deal if you used your wits," Maxwell insisted, "and you can learn more if you make inquiries. Besides, hang it! we aren't trying to *borrow* five hundred guineas, are we?"

"No." I allowed that. "But I don't see why you're trying to make me take them."

"I give you my word," Maxwell said, "that if you stick to the job and try to explain certain things, even without succeeding, you'll most likely have earned the fee twice over before you've done. Perceval here agrees"; and at this point Perceval fished out a cheque-book and began to write an order on Coutts. But I refused it for the time, saying that, though I wouldn't promise anything definitely, I agreed to act for a day or two on their suggestions, always reserving my right to stop at any point I chose. Then they went away.

Now I'm quite old enough to have met blackguards in all ranks and classes; but wealthy blackguards of good family don't work in couples, according to my experience. So I hunted up the genealogist and *flâneur* of my club, and mentioned Perceval's and Maxwell's names casually.

Maxwell he knew slightly, and said he had been recommended for the V.C., "and no one except the War Office quite knew why he didn't get it. Don't suppose the Johnnies up top know either," my young friend opined. Perceval he hardly knew at all. "Not easy to know, either, don't you know. A trifle exclusive, like most of these quiet fellows with a peerage ahead of 'em."

The result of my deliberation was that as far as the *bona fides* of these two were concerned I was safe. There was no attempt at bribery or deception at any rate. I decided to let matters rest until I had heard what more they meant to tell me.

A couple of days later I had a note from Perceval telling me that the "Open Minds" would meet at his house on the following Saturday evening at nine. They had already told me that a little section of the Plain Speakers called themselves the Open Minds.

"The name was the women's notion," Maxwell explained, "and the men didn't care what they were called."

I sent a note to Perceval saying that I would be there.

CHAPTER X

THE OPEN MINDS

It was now late in February, and the weather was so bleak and damp that one's own fireside at night was more tempting than any outside engagement.

Sitting at dinner the night of the meeting, and listening to Mudge's casual conversation as he served me (for I dined at home), I was tempted to let the Plain Speakers and the Open Minds go to Colney Hatch or the devil *en masse*, without my company. It seemed to me, looking at Mudge's pale, expressionless face while he carelessly referred to some fabulous adventure of his with a *mousmé*, that the ways of the Plain Speakers were foolishness, and that if I tried to learn anything through them I was a fool too. I'm not sure whether it was a thought of the Mummy or of the red-haired girl that drove me out into the street that night.

I remembered I wondered about it while I waited for the taxi-cab that Mudge whistled up. But I decided that since I was fifty it must be the Mummy.

I was specially reminded of my age that night, because the post had brought me the prospectus of a new scheme for the assurance of income in cases of total disablement. I read the confounded thing attentively, and then discovered, at the end, that fifty was the precise age at which the company refused fresh clients. Confound them!

I went out into the dirty night dreading rheumatism, but quite ready to prove to myself that mind and body were not crippled yet.

I found Perceval alone in a tall, narrow house, in Park Lane. In the room where he received me were a good many cut flowers, and hyacinths in quaint glass vases. I liked Perceval, but was inclined to wonder why. His politeness seemed almost exaggerated, his dress over-careful, his tastes feminine. On a white rug lay, as if posed, a fine black Persian cat.

"One seldom sees that," I said, nodding at it, "in a man's room," and Perceval looked at me with the faintest of smiles.

"You don't keep a cat?" he asked. "Let me introduce Bhanavar the Beautiful," and, stooping, he took the animal in his arms, where she rested, purring softly.

"You like them?" I asked, seeing her satisfaction.

"Not particularly," he said, smiling faintly again, "which makes it easier to have one. Dogs are different, and I won't have another. They die, and you are miserable; or you die, and they are miserable, and perhaps neglected too. If Bhanavar the Beautiful died to-night I should be sorry that a beautiful beast was gone to dust, but I shouldn't mourn overmuch. If I died she wouldn't miss me. Being a valuable beast she'd find a new master—or, more likely, mistress, and the luxury she is meant for, to-morrow. So neither of us would suffer in any case. I hope you appreciate my philosophy."

I didn't. I thought it too elaborate.

"You seem to have a fancy for them, dead or alive," I said, and nodded at a very fine tiger-skin that was stretched in front of a settee. "You didn't kill that, I suppose?"

"A present from Maxwell," he said indifferently. "He is always giving things away. It's quite out of place here, but he would be offended if I moved it"; and then, asking me if I cared for the format of my books, or only for what they contained, he showed me one or two from the Kelmscott Press, and we were talking of Morris and the Pre-Raphaelites, of whom, apparently, he knew a good deal more than I, when a couple of the Open Minds came in. Others followed, till there were fifteen or sixteen in all. The last to come in were Miss O'Hagan and Professor Maundeville, who arrived together.

I was standing near Perceval, who introduced me as a new member to each guest as they came to greet him. I was introduced to these last two in the same way, but Miss O'Hagan had noticed me directly she entered, and I was conceited enough to fancy she looked pleased. She said nothing, however, though, by the by, I had not got the letter from her which I had been led to expect. Maundeville looked surprised when he found me at Perceval's side, but merely nodded in friendly fashion, and then limped away. I have seldom seen any other man carry a limp so jauntily.

He proceeded to read a paper that evening on Dreams. More accurately, he talked on them, for he had nothing more to help him than a half-sheet of note-paper, and spoke of recurring dreams, of the curious stimuli which in certain cases have been obviously responsible for dreams, of horrible dreams, and of those in which the imagination takes one to heights of ecstasy, never in all one's days reached while waking. His words were wonderfully charming and persuasive. No; persuasive is not the right word, for he was so far reminding us merely of what everyone, even the dullest or most matter of fact, has probably experienced at least once or twice.

I looked about me, and thought I could see the memories of old dreams in the eyes of half a dozen near me.

He turned whimsically to abuse the man in the street, who uses "dreamer" as a term of reproach—the man who is always asking of every other man, "What does he *do*?" and whose highest form of virtue is to be "busy."

"If it weren't for dreamers," he said, "the fool wouldn't have

the motors and aeroplanes into which he is now anxious to put his
money. But these work-a-day dreams and their fulfilment aren't
what I have in my mind just now, though the man who never
dreams of the impossible never reaches the highest possible."
He went on to speak of the inconsequence of dreams; of the
surprises in them which our own brains spring upon ourselves;
of dreams when we know we are dreaming, and try to wake or
to dream on, as the case may be; of dreams which we would not
repeat for a million, from which we hurry, to escape alive; and
of those other dreams, more vivid than waking, for a return of
which one would give all one has. Then said he:

"As a matter of fact, it is at any rate as easy to return to the
track of a dream as to follow a known road. The track is there,
the impression on the brain-cells is there. You can, with intelli-
gent effort, go over the old road, which is easier every time you
attempt it.

"The region of dreams becomes astonishingly vivid if you
frequent it. A great deal of what one experiences while waking is
comparatively vague."

He smiled, limped across the room—he had talked standing
with his back to the fire—and sat down, picking up the black
Persian from where she slept on the white rug.

The chat became general, and interested me because of its
frankness.

Trance, sleep-walking, hypnotism, and other abnormal conditions of the brain were touched upon, seriously and otherwise;
and some queer, some laughable, experiences were given.

All the time I noticed that the red-haired girl listened, sometimes with obvious interest, sometimes with none, but never
spoke. Yet it was clear she was much interested in Maundeville's
theory about the power of the will in dreams.

Presently someone referred to the topic of second-sight, and
to my surprise Maundeville turned to Maxwell.

"Tell them," he said, "what happened to you in India," and
Maxwell spoke, not very willingly, and with very little detail.

He had been one of a large pig-sticking party, having a fortnight's hunting, and living under canvas. "We rode hard, and did
ourselves pretty well at night," he said.

One night at dinner he noticed a curious appearance of mist about the man sitting opposite. He confessed that he thought it was liver, or that he had taken more wine than he had intended. He noticed, though, that everybody else was quite clearly seen.

The next night his *vis-à-vis* was more obscured. The third night, the concluding night of that man's leave, he was wrapped in what seemed like a fog, up to his mouth. That night he was stabbed by his native servant as he entered his tent after leaving mess. Maxwell didn't recollect any other experience of the same kind happening to him, and he had no theory about it.

"Perhaps a touch of the sun," he suggested; "I'd been riding hard. It was the season I held the cup," which apparently was a pig-sticking trophy he thought the most important thing in the trip.

Informal chat went on for a while longer, and then people began to leave. Perceval asked me to stay. It was now about half-past eleven.

CHAPTER XI

HOW TROUBLE BEGAN

When the last of his guests had said good-night, Perceval turned to me and, with apologies for making me mount to the stars, took me up in a lift to his smoking-room.

This was a fair-sized square room, with a very large window on one side. We were so high up that, lying back among the cushions and looking out, I saw nothing but the stars in a black sky.

The room was pleasantly warm, and the floor was covered with a heavy Persian rug. There was practically nothing in the place but lounges and smoking materials of all possible kinds. The walls were of a smoky grey, and at first seemed blank. But while we lounged and talked I found that they were covered with the faintest possible suggestion of face and figure. They were alive with those delicate things you may sometimes fancy you see in a smoke-cloud. Perceval told him it was the fancy of a man who often sat there with him. It was Maundeville's work, I found out afterwards. I was looking at this queer decoration when Maxwell rejoined us, and we turned at once to things that seemed to me quite as fantastic. Perceval began by asking if I had any objection to staying the night there.

"Your man can send things round, you know," he suggested. "Then you can get straight to your bed when we've done with you. There's a room ready, and Max, you can have a room too."

To a bachelor of fifty it doesn't much matter when he sleeps or where. I said so, and Perceval telephoned instructions to the servants' quarters. Then I settled back among the cushions to smoke, opposite my two companions, who began to tell me about the Mummy.

"Perhaps you will not think these explanations worth the name," said Perceval, "but we are now able to tell you what little we know, and you will help us to find out more."

He began with the "Plain Speakers." This club was started, said he, with no serious object. It was at first merely a quaint diversion of intimates who moved in a somewhat artificial and conventional set. It had developed useful possibilities, but the members steadily avoided taking themselves seriously.

Plain speaking, or silence, being the generally well-kept rule, members now and then were sure to reveal unexpected opinions or knowledge, and discover unsuspected sympathies. This led to the occasional meeting of the Open Minds, for which the only necessary qualifications were that one should already be a Plain Speaker, and interested in what one may conveniently call the "occult" or "supernatural," and ready to speak quite frankly thereon, even at the risk of unsparing ridicule from other members.

"Some of our finer spirits," said Perceval after a pause, "were, or are, really interested. Some of us, I, for example, go because friends go. Maxwell here was asked to attend a meeting because I had spoken of one or two things which he had come across abroad."

I glanced at Maxwell, and he shrugged a shoulder apologetically.

"I had to knock about a bit among the people in the Soudan,

and on the Indian frontier," he explained. "I was in the Intelligence Department. Had to hear and see all sorts of things. Played the fakir once for a month, and couldn't wash, by gad! But I learnt to hold my tongue and sit still. Go ahead, Percy!"

"Maundeville comes, as you see," Perceval went on, "but says that his interest is altogether psychological. But it was a story of his that began the trouble.

"Maundeville had been several months in Egypt, and turned up at the Open Minds one evening, when the 'Evil Eye' was discussed. No one present had the slightest belief in it, except that they agreed harm might be done to the superstitious through suggestion. But some had queer stories of the superstitions in places as far apart as Sicily and the Highlands of Scotland."

After the discussion was ended (Perceval said) half a dozen men went to Maundeville's house for a smoke, and got him on to talk about his discoveries. He showed them a few small things, and then was reminded of the evening's discussion.

"Come to think of it," he told them, laughing, "I need your prayers. I'm not 'over-looked,' but I'm under an awful curse, which I suppose is just as serious. It's a pity I didn't remember that earlier. I could have made the ladies' flesh creep," and he told them about the finding of the Mummy.

"He had found it," he said, "while excavating a hundred miles or so East of Luxor. His men had fled, and he had opened the tomb with a friend. On the floor of the burial-chamber lay the bodies of four young girls in perfect preservation, though they crumbled at a touch. Probably they had been poisoned in the tomb, and the poison was some powerful antiseptic. The sarcophagus was not remarkable except for the firmness with which the stone was sealed down and the warning curses inscribed on it which showed that a priestess of Amen-Ru lay buried there. Inside the sarcophagus lay a wooden coffin with the figure of the priestess in her robes painted on it. At each of the four corners of the coffin lay a canopic jar, and on the top was a papyrus roll on which was written:

"'Thou who hast disturbed me, a dead woman, and broken the seals, and weakened my Ka—behold my Ka shall follow thee, and shall see Justice through a woman; thou shalt know Hell before Death; and the hand, that broke the seals of Sleep and of Silence, shall bring Death to thee also.'"

Asked what he had done with the Mummy, Maundeville acknowledged it was there in his house; and presently under pressure agreed to show it. He got Scrymgeour and young D'Aurelle, therefore, to go with him into another room and carry the mummy-case to the dining-room, where the other five men were sitting.

The Mummy was not in its coffin, but in the unopened inner case. They put it on the dining-room table, and when Maundeville refused to open the case, saying scoffingly that he meant to do so with an expert, and not before a set of ignoramuses like themselves, they sat round and smoked, and speculated about the Mummy, its probable appearance, its age at death, and other possibilities connected with it.

One or two of the younger men chaffed Maundeville about his guest, and Scrymgeour offered to entertain "it" or "her," and so possibly to lighten the curse for him.

"Scrymgeour was a bit above himself that night," Maxwell said. "A Highlander would swear that he was 'fey.'"

"His head was turned," Perceval remarked in his high tenor. "You remember, Max? It was not to be wondered at," and Maxwell nodded.

"What was his head turned about?" I asked, naturally enough.

"He thought he had gone one better than the rest of us that night, poor chap!" Maxwell said, and explained no more, but went on with his story.

Young D'Aurelle, too, was excited, he said, and inclined to annoy Scrymgeour.

"Why?" I asked again.

"Because poor Scrymgeour was so pleased with himself," Maxwell explained (but it was no explanation to me then), and continued the story thus:

When Scrymgeour offered to house the Mummy for him, Maundeville became unusually solemn.

"Everybody who has had to do with it since I started to disturb it has had bad luck," he declared; "everybody, at any rate, except myself."

"And why not you—the chief villain?" Scrymgeour asked, helping himself to more liqueur.

But Maundeville couldn't say. He knew how the Arabs would account for that, but it wasn't a good enough explanation to satisfy him or anyone except themselves.

Then somebody asked how the Arabs would account for it, and Maundeville said he did a little service to an Arab, who knew about the Mummy, and he had been rewarded by a charm.

Then Scrymgeour (Maxwell went on), who had drunk a good deal, reiterated his offer with a lot of sneering laughter.

"Maundeville told him that he wouldn't advise him to test his luck with the Mummy. Indeed, he said he thought that less than ten days of the Thing's company would make Scrymgeour wish he had never looked at it, and Scrymgeour got annoyed. 'I'll lay my Vandyk against your Japanese armour,' he said, 'that I house the lady for a fortnight without asking you to take her back,' and when Maundeville objected, he was a bit insolent, and suggested that Maundeville was backing out, and challenged the rest of us to join." D'Aurelle at once offered to do so, others followed, and at last apparently Maxwell and Perceval got drawn in, being twitted by everybody else.

It ended in the small hours with a queer scene. The men there joined hands round the table on which the mummy case lay, Maundeville still protesting, and agreed each to entertain the Mummy for a fortnight in turn, the order being decided, at Scrymgeour's suggestion, by the cards, Maundeville to be the dealer. The Ace of Spades was suggested laughingly by someone as the appropriate card for the Mummy's chance host.

It fell first to Scrymgeour, and in the morning following the last night of his term, the morning for which Perceval and Maxwell had accepted his invitation to breakfast, he was found dead under the conditions I have already told.

A few nights after Scrymgeour's funeral the men met again, discussed the matter, and again tried the cards. The Ace of Spades went to D'Aurelle—"and you know the result," Maxwell said.

"I know what followed," I allowed. "But you've got to remember the difference between *post* and *propter*. Still, it's a queer business. What am I supposed to do in it?"

"The business has to go on, of course," Maxwell said. "We want you to watch it and solve it, if you can."

"At best it's a silly affair," I said, "and in my opinion it's more than a bit brutal. You've no right to be playing tricks with a woman's body, whether she has been dead an hour or ten thousand years. Why should you go on?"

"I should be sorry to speak offensively," Perceval replied, after a moment's hesitation, "or I might ask whether you break your word when it seems inconvenient to keep to it. I don't think that the point you raise needs any consideration. Indeed, unless that is quite plain to you I think you shouldn't go further into the affair."

"I shall certainly go further—with you or without you," I said angrily, "but if you like to leave me to do so independently, you can."

I think Perceval was ready to answer sharply, but at this point Maxwell, who had sat watching us both, interfered.

"Stop there, both of you!" he said. "If you don't, you'll be saying more than you intend. Percy, we asked the doctor to speak out! Doctor, we've told you the most important part relating to what you know already. But I'm going to tell you more, at once, without bothering to ask for any promises of secrecy. What Perceval and I are really anxious about is that Miss O'Hagan has got mixed up in this miserable business. That's one reason for bringing you into it, and, at any rate, it's the best possible reason for keeping things quiet."

At that, Perceval leant across and said he was sorry if his manner had been offensive, and that he agreed with me the thing was brutal; and I said I might not have put the objectionable question if I hadn't felt very much interested.

"Now, what about Miss O'Hagan?" I ended.

"She was the first," Maxwell answered, "to find Scrymgeour after his death. No one knew about it but Perceval and I, and Scrymgeour's man."

"It is since then that she has stammered," I hazarded suddenly, and Maxwell said "Yes" again.

"Miss O'Hagan," he said, "is very impulsive, and is quite unable to understand the ordinary point of view, or, at any rate, to bother about it. She had an idea, she told us later, that Scrymgeour was in danger, and she immediately after breakfast went to see that Mummy to reassure herself. When Seymour said that it was past Scrymgeour's usual time for rising, but told her he had strict orders not to go into the room until he was rung for, she knocked several times, uselessly, of course, and then opened the door, telling Seymour there must be something wrong. She found Scrymgeour lying dead, and a few minutes later we came in. We persuaded her to go home, got her away without anyone noticing, and then I went to fetch you. Now you know all about it."

I suppose that very few stories can seem absolutely impossible to a medical man who has been long in practice, unless they involve, or seem to involve, the supernatural. Even then one must keep an open mind—the only scientific attitude. What seemed supernatural yesterday is possible to-day, and will be commonplace to-morrow.

The part apparently played by the Mummy was the only part I jibbed at. The vagaries of the Plain Speakers and Open Minds I was ready to accept.

Stay! there was another point that surprised me. I asked: "Why do you let me know about her now? It's a private matter, which doesn't seem to concern me."

"That's quite true," Maxwell said. "Well, for one thing, we have her leave to tell you; but that's not enough. It was quite easy to get that. But we, Perceval and I, thought you ought to be told, because we don't know what may be important in the puzzle. Besides, you would be sure to hear of it all from her anyway, some time or another."

"You will understand now that we're not likely to keep anything back, having told you that," Perceval added. "You must feel that you have our confidence."

"You can't help yourselves very well," I reminded him. "I don't want to be offensive, but it's best to see things as they really are."

Maxwell grunted a half-laugh, and Perceval, who was now smoking, seated with his legs curled under him on a divan, blew a couple of rings and waved them aside before he answered.

"We brought you in at the beginning," he said, "and I don't regret it. We are glad you've taken an interest in solving the mystery. But unless you're very dense you ought soon to be convinced that the best and safest way is to trust us as we trust you—not as a genius, but as an honest man."

"Do you mean that you expect me to report everything I know or suppose, as I go along? I'm not prepared to promise anything, except that I will do my best as a merely honest man to find out whether the Mummy had any connection with these deaths."

"You don't understand at all," Maxwell said. "We know you'll do your best, and we don't care what you choose to tell us, or not to tell us, in the meantime—or, at any rate, you must please yourself about that. The only point we insist on, is that as soon as possible you make up your mind about ourselves.

"Then you'll be able in your work to rely on this—what we tell you is what we believe; and further, that what you choose to tell us won't be misused."

"Very well," I agreed. "At present I don't see any reason not to believe you. I'm not going to say more than that, for I don't know enough.

"Now, if I'm not keeping you too late, I should like to sit up a while, but to drop this Mummy business altogether," and they agreed to this, and entertained me very well till I chose to go to bed. I had to acknowledge again to myself when I left them, that they did not seem either knaves or fools.

CHAPTER XII

MAUNDEVILLE CALLS

The next morning, after breakfasting with those two, I walked to my flat. When I was within a few yards of it I saw a man turn out from the door, a card-case in his hand, and limp jauntily off the kerb to cross the street.

It was Professor Maundeville.

I suddenly wondered why he limped. It was obviously a very slight shortening, or something that at any rate did not prevent great activity.

Apparently he had been leaving a card on me; but I watched

him cross without trying to stop him. It happened that I had one or two people to see that morning, mostly in neighbouring mews, coachmen's children and the like, and after that I wanted time to myself. I saw him avoid a stylish motor with a jump, smilingly snap some one word at the occupant, which apparently made him furious, and then reaching the opposite side he turned, saw me at my door, and at once crossed again.

I waited, thinking that if he followed me up the stair it might be some time before I could get rid of him; and he joined me in the street doorway.

"What a beastly morning!" he said cheerfully, directly he was within speaking distance. "Only a Plain Speaker can do it justice. How do you keep warm? Let us get a little farther in."

The wind certainly was cutting, though the morning was rather bright, and I saw that he was wearing a fur-lined coat.

If I put on a thing like that I feel like a fifth-rate actor. It suited Maundeville quite well, though.

He looked at me, and then up the stair.

"I left a card for you," he said. "I wanted to see you. But perhaps it's inconvenient to have me up now? Gad! that's good."

A private door connecting the passage in which we stood with the provision-dealer's shop under my rooms swung open for a moment, and a gust of warm air, scented with coffee, cloves and, I suppose, a lot of other things, drifted past us.

Maundeville sniffed with enjoyment.

"If a camel would only grunt!" he said, "and if one only got a whiff of the mews mixed up with this, one could almost forget this brutal English spring. It smells of the bazaar and the caravanserai."

I was amused, though I wanted to be rid of him.

"Isn't it said that our climate makes us what we are?" I asked him.

"Yes! and what are we?" he retorted. "A dull, pig-headed, self-satisfied lot."

He sniffed again, as it were reminiscently, with a regretful shrug, muttering a word or two under his breath, which I thought might be Arabic, and then put the matter away from him briskly.

"Well," he said, "I see you're not going to ask me up the stair just now. Certainly it's not the right time to call on a new acquaintance. But I find we have friends in common" (he mentioned two or three names), "and I fancy we may have some common interests too. Will you dine with me to-night somewhere—say at eight? Plain Speakers can afford to dispense with a little ceremony, can't they?"

I considered. If I were left to myself for the rest of the morning, and for the afternoon, there was no reason why I shouldn't dine out. I said so, and he nodded approvingly.

I watched him away, as I wished to follow the same direction alone and think things out as it seemed likely we should talk about the Mummy at dinner.

Deeply I considered what Perceval and Maxwell had told me the night before, and tried for a little while to build some theory thereon. I soon stopped that, though, for I hadn't much evidence, and I found myself suggesting theories which I could neither prove nor disprove. I ended by hunting up a clean note-book that afternoon, putting a big M. on the cover, and jotting down facts as they occurred to me. I say "facts," but in the note-book I carefully separated what I had seen from what I had heard.

Then I locked the notes up before I dressed to go out. I didn't want Mudge's studies of human nature to extend so far.

I never met with a better host than Maundeville, or a more entertaining. From the time I entered the hall of "The Scribes" until we lit our cigars before leaving he was admirable.

"Life *is* short," he said casually at one time, "even if many men have said so. Preliminaries waste time between men who understand one another;" and without being at all familiar he took a certain amount of intimacy and sympathy for granted.

What helped to make him a good host was no doubt the obvious fact that he was enjoying himself and wanted me to. He bubbled like a glass of champagne, was ready to talk or to listen, but kept an observant eye on the dinner and the service all the time.

Our oysters reminded him of pearl-fishing, and he told me that I must see one or two fine pearls he had bought at a south-sea fishery.

Sherry set him for a moment on Spanish affairs. That suggested a flick at Church and State, and our own powers of accommodating our religious views to circumstances, and incidentally he spoke of Don Carlos, whom he, as a boy, had seen at Madrid.

Our table was near the fire. I sat with my back to the wall, and he at right angles to me. So I saw everybody who came in, and his occasional comments on his fellow-members were amusing, though he professed to know so few.

He interrupted a witty criticism of a "serious" novelist who sat near, to tell the waiter that there was a piece of cork in my sherry.

He ended what seemed to me a comprehensive criticism of the German Emperor, by sending his congratulations to the chef on the freshness of the salmon. It might have been taken that day, he said. Ice couldn't preserve that perfect flavour. And the chef sent back an equally polite message to the effect that M. le Professeur was right as usual, and that he happened to be able to guarantee that the fish was taken by a club member that very morning in Wales, and sent by express from the Wye. Maundeville nodded, and sketched for me a fortnight he had spent on the Wye, when he seemed to have been equally keen on angling and archæology.

Then he amused me with an account of his first day's fishing far up the Nile, where, as he put it, he didn't know whether to expect a rise from a hippopotamus or an alligator. He fell silent for a minute or two after that, staring blankly at the table. When he roused up again he looked about him as if wakened. "Well, a hippopotamus steak isn't half bad if you're hungry," he said, "but neither is a Wye fish," and he chatted and made me chat till we reached the sweets. Then he suggested having coffee and liqueurs where we were, to avoid interruption in the smoking-room; but we found that, according to club rules, it would be still too early to light a cigarette.

"All this," he said, "makes a good excuse for finishing the evening at my place."

He beckoned to the waiter and scribbled a couple of messages for the telephone, then chatted on, turning his conversation to medicine.

"I studied it," he said. "I even took degrees. But thank heaven I hadn't to get my living by it. The study is fascinating, but the practice is repulsive to my mind. A general practitioner is a gen-

eral servant, with no certainty of regular wages. Theoretically
he is an angel of mercy; practically, as you know, he may be anything between a soft-hearted incompetent fool and a first-class
tradesman."

"You're talking to one of the profession," I said.

"I defy you to say you make more than a living by it," he
laughed; "plain speaking is a luxury which can only be supported
by an independent income—though a philosopher may manage
it on a small one if it's a luxury he sets much store by."

"At fifty," I said, "one wants an occasional luxury."

"Fifty?" he looked me over; "I congratulate you. I should
have taken five or six years off that. A wise man (which means
a healthy man) of fifty has tremendous possibilities. He knows
what he wants. He knows what isn't worth bothering about. He
has possibly half of an enjoyable life still before him."

"Oh! oh!" I laughed. "I congratulate you on your youthful
optimism. *You* can't be fifty!"

"Never mind what I am!" He waved that point aside with a firm
brown hand. "Half of an enjoyable life, I say. See how the centenarians increase! Look at the *Times* announcements, and notice
what a number of men are eighty, ninety, and over, at their deaths.
Old sailors, old soldiers, old fox-hunting squires. How many of
them do you suppose have given Life any scientific consideration?
An occasional pill. Whisky, perhaps, sometimes, instead of port.
That's about all; and yet they've lived. But I bore you?"

"Not at all!" I laughed. "You encourage me."

If that was not absolute fact, at least I was amused. It was
impossible to be bored by a man so very much alive. We had
finished dinner, and he laughingly went on with his whimsical
argument, stopping to crack a few filberts, which he did reck-
lessly between his teeth.

"For one thing," he said, "you will agree that when you are
fifty you haven't lived fifty years."

"I agree to nothing till you've proved it," I retorted.

"Well, you won't pretend that a man begins to live directly he
comes into the world, will you?" he asked. "The first years are the
life of a parasite."

"Continued, perhaps, indefinitely," I suggested. "But what

about the last—'Sans eyes, sans ears, sans teeth, sans everything'?"

"I deny that, too, as a necessity," he said. "Look at Lord——!" and he named one of the marvels of our time. "Look at Lady——!" and he mentioned one of the *haute noblesse* who had just given convincing and, for some of her peers, unpleasant proofs that her memory (or imagination) and her enjoyment thereof, were quite unimpaired.

"At fifty, too," he went on, "one's blood has cooled. One no longer acts on impulse. One concentrates more easily, achieves with less effort. A boy's illusions——"

He broke off and seemed to consider.

"—are replaced by a man's," I added for him.—"Different, often, but always illusions."

He was on the point of retorting, but checked himself. "Come," he said, "my tobacco will put you in a better frame of mind. I did something useful once for a tobacco merchant in Cairo, and I actually think he sends me pure tobacco. It's rather rash to rely on a man's gratitude, though, isn't it?—unless he is expecting something more of you."

"Who is cynical now?" I asked.

"I don't pretend to be anything else," he retorted. "I have faith in Nature, if you give her a chance, but not in human nature. Let us be going!"

He led the way down, softly humming an air.

CHAPTER XIII

THE MUMMY RESTS

A motor-brougham stood at the kerb, and we entered it. We slipped away west, quietly, through a drizzle of rain which made the streets and pavements shine with reflected lights. Maundeville hummed as he went, in a soft baritone. But in less than ten minutes we stopped. He made me wait until a man, evidently watching for us, threw the house-door open.

"This rain," Maundeville said, "is soaking. But it's soft, and really means spring. It's a west wind, I'm sure I can smell the buds bursting in the country lanes," and he ran up the steps humming again. A minute later I was lounging before a wood fire, while Maundeville discoursed learnedly on liqueurs, of which an embarrassing variety stood on the table with Turkish coffee and Egyptian tobacco.

The room, lighted more by the fire than by a couple of shaded electric lamps, was very comfortable, and warm in colour. The walls were dark red, and the large rug covering most of the polished floor was dark red and blue. There were half a dozen paintings of desert scenes on the red walls; beautiful things they seemed to me. Maundeville, when he saw that I noticed them, told me they were the work of one man, a corporal in the Foreign Legion.

There were a few foreign weapons and queer odds and ends of foreign manufacture, hanging here and there about the mantel-piece and between the pictures.

"Many not worth tuppence," Maundeville explained, "but they're all reminders of queer times here and there."

I crossed the room to look more closely at one picture of a night scene in the desert, lit by a camp-fire, and then went back to Maundeville, who was now jibing gently at the Plain Speakers and their eccentricities.

"These coteries remind me of some Japanese boxes," he said. "You open one, and there's a smaller inside. You open that, and you find a smaller still. You go on opening if you've nothing else to do, and you find the boxes getting smaller and smaller, till at last you reach the smallest—with nothing in it."

"Nothing?" I said, with no particular intention, but Maunde-ville looked at me attentively.

"Nothing, I think," he answered. "If you spent a while opening the Japanese boxes (the notion serves well enough) and had a nightmare the night after, you couldn't swear that the nightmare was let loose from the innermost box." He considered me. "If I only knew how much I could say to you without breaking one of our idiotic promises!" he added; and then suddenly, "Have a look round the house! I've some more pictures upstairs, and a sort of a little museum or curiosity shop in the back room there," and he nodded at a door in the far end of the room.

He led the way out into the hall while speaking. There the chauffeur, and the servant who had let us in, sat by the fire, rising as we passed up the stair.

"Am I keeping you?" I asked Maundeville.

"Not you! What suggests such a thing?" he asked.

"The motor is waiting."

"Oh, is that all! Pierre always hangs about till eleven or so when I'm at home. If you got tired of me and went away early I might take it into my head to go somewhere for an hour or two. I've no special occupation to keep me in this week. But there's nothing to take me out either, as long as you will keep me company."

He led the way up a broad stair, switching on a light here and there as we went. It seemed a large house for a bachelor to occupy. There were rooms on both sides of the hall, and the main stair opened at the first floor on to a little gallery hung with a good many pictures, and containing one or two bronzes. In spite of Maundeville's taste for archæology and antiquities generally, all the paintings seemed modern, and a large proportion of them French. He stopped to point one out here and there, and then threw open a door at the gallery-end.

"There are no pictures in here," he said. "I think bindings are sufficient decoration, don't you?" and he switched on a couple more lights. The room was rather long and narrow. A wood fire burnt at one end. In the centre of the floor was a heavy round table, with writing materials, a typewriter, and a few scattered books and magazines. Near the fire was a high desk at which one could write standing. The walls seemed panelled with dark wood, but it was hard to tell, for they were practically covered with books, and the air was scented by leather and morocco bindings.

I stepped in and looked about me, envying the man his money for the first time. Here one could read or write in absolute comfort. The carpet was like moss, the walls of the old house were solid, the windows were double; there was a leather-covered door inside the one that opened on to the gallery. The noise of the West End was unheard.

"May one explore?" I asked, stretching out a hand, and Maundeville nodded.

"A mixed lot," he said. "I've no one's tastes to consult but my own."

I took down the first book my hand fell on. It was Colonel Peter Hawker's *Wildfowling*, first edition. By it stood Scrope's *Deerstalking*, Millais's *British Wildfowl*, and a little favourite of my own, *A Book of the Snipe*, by Scolopax. On the shelf below, choosing at random, I found Lang's *Ballades in Blue China*, the *Ballades* of François Villon in the old French, an Elzevir Dante, dated 1600, and apparently all the modern poets.

I saw Sir Richard Burton's *Book of the Sword* on one shelf, his translation of the *Arabian Nights* on another; while the three or four shelves nearest to the high desk seemed crowded with books on Egyptian, Greek, Roman, and Indian antiquities, great books, profusely illustrated with photographs and drawings; and the one or two which I opened had autograph inscriptions in French, Italian or English by the authors.

"Take me away!" I said more than half seriously. "At last I know what covetousness can be. When we get outside you had better search me—though evening-dress fortunately . . ."

"My dear fellow!" He laughed heartily, and I suppose touched a bell unobserved by me, for the man-servant at once showed himself in the doorway. It was as though he had waited in the gallery outside, just as he had waited in the hall downstairs.

"Bates," Maundeville said, "this is my friend Dr. Armiston. I hope he is going to use the room often. You'll see that he is comfortable when he comes."

The man looked at me for a moment and bowed; then disappeared before I had got over my surprise.

"He's an expert at tea and coffee," was Maundeville's only answer to my thanks. "Try him! The beggar doesn't get half enough to do," and he led the way out into the gallery again.

"Here's another room," he said, throwing open another door, "but there's nothing to see in it."

The room was almost empty, except for a large easel with some covering over it, a throne or dais, and a few empty frames, and canvases turned to the wall.

"You paint," I said.

"A little. I use the room quite as much for the foils," he answered carelessly. "My bedroom's in there," he nodded at another door. "That's about all up here."

He led the way downstairs again, past his man and the chauffeur, who were still by the hall fire.

Leaning his shoulders against the mantelpiece in the dining-room, he looked thoughtfully across at the door which he had already pointed out before going upstairs.

"Are you going to show me your museum?" I asked.

"I was wondering," he said, in a lost sort of way, and then rousing up. "Well, why not?" he added briskly, and leading the way down the room, took me in.

The electric lights showed a room perhaps twenty-four feet by eighteen. In the middle, littered with papers, was a large plain deal table, over which lights hung.

A papyrus roll lay there, and one or two well-worn books. The only one I happened to pick up was the Egyptian *Book of the Dead*. On the walls were a few large photographs. One I happened to recognise as the Taj-Mahal; others were of ruins, pyramids, one of a Sphinx; others again of interiors, perhaps sepulchral chambers, taken, I suppose, by flashlight.

"That only reached me yesterday from Orkney," Maundeville said, nodding at a flint arrow-head. "Now, given the remote possibility of a thing like that being absolutely shielded from exposure —this one lay among bones in a stone coffin—how long could a bloodstain remain on it?

"This is an *omnium gatherum*, isn't it?" he asked, strolling slowly down the room. "It sends specialists into fits. But most of 'em find something interesting, mixed up, in their opinion, with a great deal of rubbish. Yes, that's a lasso. I've seen it used very effectively; and, indeed, at one time I could shy it decently myself. This hoard reminds me of the way a Parisian palmist once damned me with faint praise. The dear lady said my talents were so diffuse that she feared I should never make my mark. To revenge myself I cast her horoscope (oh, that's easy enough in a way) and showed the shocking results she might anticipate by having been born under Mercury."

While talking, he moved slowly on with his jaunty little limp, but I suddenly halted.

Standing upright against the wall was what I had indeed known I might reasonably expect to find there—a mummy-case. And yet, happening as it did, to be in a little recess between bookshelves, I came upon it with a start.

I stopped dead, and Maundeville presently turned, and seeing me stare at the thing, watched me just an instant, and then asked whether I was interested in Egyptology.

That question, you may remember, had been put to me before.

"I'm interested in this," I said, nodding at the mummy-case, for I saw, by the curious dark stain on the front, that it was the same thing I had once climbed to the top of a motor to examine.

Maundeville came slowly back and stood looking at it with me.

"Yes, I thought you would be interested in that," he said. "Have a good look at it if you care to, and then we'll go back to the other room."

I looked it over carefully, more, of course, from mere curiosity than because I expected to see anything very illuminating.

"One would like to open it," I said. "Haven't you thought of doing so?"

"My idea is to burn the whole thing soon," Maundeville said. "It will burn like a torch, but we will open and examine it first. If you care to help me when I do so I shall be delighted. Have you finished? Let us go back then. You can come in here and look at it again some other time, you know, if you want to," and leading the way back into the room we had first sat in, he pushed an easy-chair to the fire for me and put a box of cigars at my elbow.

"Now," he said, stirring up the logs, "I wonder how much I may tell you."

"What about?"

"About Scrymgeour, and D'Aurelle, and that thing you've just been looking at."

I was choosing a cigar, and I picked one out, pierced it, and lit up before I said anything. I reflected that even if he knew no more than did Perceval and Maxwell, still, if he chose to chat freely he might speak of something they had overlooked or forgotten.

"I suppose you're free to tell me what you choose," I said, "and a good cigar like this makes a good listener."

"Well, I'm not sure about my being free." He helped himself to a whisky-and-soda, pondering the matter over.

"You're a Plain Speaker," he said, "so one could discuss that lot freely—if there is anything to discuss, which there isn't. You're also an Open Mind (silly label!), but I've nothing particular to say about that. The question is, if you don't mind my asking, Are you going any further? Remember, I don't assume any right to be answered. But if you chose to answer, and said no, then we could drop a queer business altogether and talk of something more amusing. If you said yes—that, for example, you intend to join in a foolish experiment for which I'm partly responsible, I venture, since I *am* partly responsible, to suggest consideration before you commit yourself. If you understand, then I'm speaking clearly enough. If you don't, then so much the better. We can drop it."

"I think there's no room for misunderstanding," I said. "But I've seen your Mummy before, and, as far as I'm concerned, I'm curious about it. I'm committed, in fact, already."

Maundeville nodded, and his good-tempered, clean-shaven face looked concerned, but he evidently wasn't surprised.

"It seemed likely," he said. "Well, you're in it with the rest of us! Those two fellows haven't broken the letter of the law, at any rate, by bringing you in. Perhaps they thought it the surest way of keeping you quiet. You're bound by the same promises as the rest of us now, you see. Such an easy thing, to make a promise!"

He lapsed into silence again, lying back in his chair, his cigar forgotten and burnt out.

Then he roused himself and sat up briskly.

"Well, I am sure it's no use giving you vague warnings," he said, "even if I could make them definite and credible, which I can't; you're not the man to draw back."

"No, I'm not," I said.

"And after all, there are great advantages to us if you come in," he went on, as if thinking aloud, "though I should have warned you. You bring a fresh eye to it. You're not likely to have any bias. Well, we'll talk the thing over again soon if you like."

I rose to go, saying that I envied him his library more than anything else.

"Use it! Use it!" he begged me. "Let me find you there some

afternoon pretty soon, and we'll compare notes about this insane affair. Have another look at that too." He nodded towards the door behind which the Mummy stood. "I'll remember to put on the top of the case my notes about the inscription."

We passed out into the hall. It was then after one o'clock in the morning, but the chauffeur and valet still waited by the fire, and Maundeville insisted on sending me to my rooms in the car. The rain was still drizzling down in the glistening, almost empty streets.

CHAPTER XIV

THE PRESIDENT OF THE PLAIN SPEAKERS

Undoubtedly spring had fairly opened upon us with that night's rain, as Maundeville had said. I felt that to be settled next morning, when Mudge came to pull up my bedroom blind and brought in a pair of new light grey trousers, and suggested a new hat, as I passed out after breakfast.

One of Mudge's aphorisms is that "Folk judges more by the houtside of 'ats than by the hinside of 'eds—bein' heasier to see."

So I went straight to my hatter, lest otherwise I should forget it, had a top-hat "moulded" (I think that's the word) for me, and heard as usual that my head is a very remarkable shape.

Passing the Army and Navy Club, I recognised someone at the top of the steps, just outside the porch. It was the distinguished personage whom I had met as President of the Plain Speakers. He stood there drawing on a glove, and looking down on the passers-by, while he chatted to a younger man who stood at his elbow. I suppose that, for a Londoner, my ignorance of the proper obser-vances towards these elevated personages is phenomenal.

I assumed, however, that since I had never seen him except as President of the Plain Speakers, I was not expected to recognise him in any other capacity.

Although I was under the impression that he happened to see me, I therefore passed on without any sign of recognition, and had got some yards past the club when I was lightly touched on the shoulder.

Turning, I found the younger man of the two had followed me.

"Pardon me," he said, "but I am sent to ask whether you can spare a few minutes without inconvenience."

He smiled affably on me, showing a well-trained moustache and faultless teeth; then turning his head a little, glanced back significantly at the steps where the older man waited.

"I suppose that's a command for me too?" I said. "Is that what it comes to?"

The young fellow, who was very good-looking and had an open-air complexion, seemed amused.

"I don't think I can put you under arrest if you refuse," he said; "but you'll come, won't you?" and I followed him back and up the steps.

Men were coming and going, passing in and out of the club doors. Those who noticed the man who had sent for me lifted their hats as they passed, and got a lifted forefinger in return. I imagined it correct to raise my hat as I went frowning up the steps, and was pleased to remember that it wasn't my old one. This struck me as distinctly snobbish, and I felt more sulky than ever.

The President nodded to me, smiling, and his messenger moved across to the other side of the porch, and, lighting a cigarette, gazed placidly down Pall Mall. I imagined him to be of a most equable and philosophic temperament. He looked prepared to stand there all day, if need be, and to enjoy himself placidly all the time.

"Well, Dr. Armiston," the President said, looking hard at me, "the sight of you passing reminds me of something. I want to have a chat with you."

He stopped and continued to consider me. I said nothing, but waited. I thought, however, that Mudge was an excellent fellow to have insisted on the grey trousers and new hat. I composed a casual remark to be thrown at him during dinner that evening, "When I was chatting to the Duke at the Army and Navy this morning," etc.

I then discovered that the President was leading the way into the club. The door flew open before him, held by a saluting commissionaire.

Directly we moved, the younger man found that he had just grown tired of his cigarette and of the passers-by. He dropped both, so to speak, and turned to lounge in after us. The President considered a moment in the hall, and then leading the way into a smoking-room chose a quiet corner, and invited me to sit near him, offering me his cigarette-case. A couple of men smoking near by glanced at us, and presently seemed to find seats more to their liking a little farther off. The young fellow who had summoned me lounged in, and became interested in a paper. Of the thirty men or so in the room, no one took any apparent interest in our quiet corner or came near it.

"I think it most likely, Dr. Armiston," the President suddenly began, watching me closely, "that you know who I am."

"Well, sir," I said, not having time to pick my words very nicely, "I believe I do. But when we met before I was merely told that you were our President, and that night I asked nothing. The fact is, I was occupied with more important things. That is——" I stammered, stopped, tried to improve upon my explanation, and failed altogether.

"I hope you understand what I mean," I ended lamely.

"It seems quite obvious," he said, with a certain suggestion of dryness. "Of course, it is only as President of the Plain Speakers that I venture to ask your attention for a few minutes."

What the devil was I to say? I hadn't meant to be rude, but I wished I had expressed myself differently.

"We understand on both sides, then," the President went on, "that we meet as Plain Speakers. I imagine that rôle wasn't unfamiliar to you, doctor, even before you joined us. For the time please understand that I, too, am going to say precisely what I mean."

I bowed, and said nothing, but wondered whether he was going to take advantage of the occasion to tell me what he thought of my manners.

"I said just now," he went on, "that I suppose you know who I am. I wanted to remind you of that for various reasons. For one thing, you will know that it is comparatively easy for me to get reliable information about any man I am interested in for the moment. I know you, therefore, probably much better than you know me."

"There is nothing worth knowing, I fancy, Mr. President," I said, still feeling rather sulky, and altogether puzzled, "even 'for the moment.' "

"We needn't discuss that," he said. "Leave that to me. Now, what really matters is that there are things going on among the Plain Speakers which I know little or nothing about."

"Not even with your special facilities for getting reliable information, Mr. President?" I began to wonder whether I was going to be pumped. He slowly looked me over with a cold stare, which even at the time I wished I could cultivate for the occasional control of Mudge.

"I shouldn't suppose there would be any need of reminding you," he said presently, "that among gentlemen private affairs are respected." He stopped, and I sat sulky. If he didn't want to get information out of me, what did he want? What would happen if I suddenly remembered I had an engagement, and got up and walked out? Should I be allowed to reach Pall Mall unhindered? Or would all these quiet, well-groomed, well-set-up men rise at a word of command between me and freedom? I don't know what feelings expressed themselves in my face; but the President, who was watching me, suddenly began to laugh quietly.

"I know something of you from Captain Maxwell," he said, "and something from Mr. Perceval. I got enough information elsewhere to serve my purpose. Since I have this advantage I can talk to you freely. It will simplify things if you understand that I mean precisely what I say. No more, no less."

He waited a moment, but I said nothing, and he went on.

"It's easy to see that there are inner circles in the Plain Speakers. I'm there only as a private individual, for my private amusement and possible edification. I've no particular privilege, no particular rights. On the contrary, for fear that I seem to trade on what happens to be my position outside, I cannot question members as freely as any other member can.

"It is quite possible, too, that because of my position outside this little society, members, out of pure consideration for me, avoid entangling me in any troublesome affairs, which might conceivably some day become public."

He stopped again, and still I said nothing.

"Apparently you're able to hold your tongue, Dr. Armiston, as well as to speak plainly," he said, smiling. "Evidently you're not going to help me at all."

"As you know, Mr. President," I said, "I am the most recently elected Plain Speaker. But even supposing I knew anything of troublesome affairs, as you call them, I dare say I should try to imitate the other members out of pure consideration for you— or for other reasons."

"I dare say you know the Scottish word 'dour,' " he said quietly. "Well, I will tell you what I know, what I think, and what I want. Then perhaps we shall understand one another.

"To begin with, I know, of course, that two of the Plain Speakers, Scrymgeour and D'Aurelle, have lately died. They both died suddenly, and apparently alone. You knew neither of them, but you certified one death and countenanced the certifying of the other. You then joined the Plain Speakers, and one or more inner coteries of which I know very little. That is what I know.

"What I think is that these two deaths were suspicious, and that you are partly responsible—since you certified—for the fact that there has been no further inquiry. I think, too, that you joined the Plain Speakers because of those deaths, and that you have those certificates on your conscience."

"I certified what I believed to be true," I said angrily.

"Would you sign them now?" he retorted. "I know you acted honestly at the time," and he went on without even troubling to wait for my answer. "I'm going abroad to-morrow," he said, "for three weeks—perhaps four. I shall be moving about, but Captain Hext there will be in constant communication with me." He nodded slightly at the young man so thoroughly wrapped up in his paper. "He can be found here from twelve to one on most days. He shall also give you a private address. Now I have no idea of asking you to give me information which involves any breach of confidence. But I have certain responsibilities. If any other mysterious death occurs—let us say the death of *any* member, mysterious or not—find my whereabouts from Captain Hext, and let me have all details possible at once."

"All public details," I suggested.

"Everything public to the Plain Speakers," he amended. "Further, in this society you're an—an——"

"Outsider," I suggested.

"Well, yes, if you like, in no derogatory sense," he said. "The words I was hunting for were 'impartial observer.' You don't know one of us practically, except as members. Many of the others meet me elsewhere; and perhaps it isn't easy for them to forget it. I don't suppose you have any very exaggerated idea of my importance."

"I think much more of you than I did, sir," I blurted out, and immediately discovered that this was not altogether so complimentary a statement as I had intended; but the President thanked me gravely, saying he was quite sure that I meant it, and went on:

"You would be more likely than most of the others to tell me, I think, without my insisting on information, if I could be useful. Tell me in any case if there is any more trouble, and give me all details possible without breaking any pledge."

He rose, and the man he had spoken of as Captain Hext rose too, and at a sign came towards us.

"Hext, I have told Dr. Armiston at what times you're likely to be found here," the President said, "and I want you to give him your card as well. He may wish to communicate with me while I am away. Give him all the help you can."

He nodded genially enough to me. "Take care of yourself," he said, "I suspect you're thoroughly mixed up in this silly business, whatever it is. But you've an older head on your shoulders than the rest have. I hope you'll use it. Hullo, General! How is the rheumatism, now that we're getting a little sunshine?" and he turned away to a tall, thin man who had just come in, leaning on a stick.

"Let me see you out, doctor," Captain Hext said, and we passed together into the hall.

There he fished out a gold card-case and gave me his card. I was hunting for one of mine, when he told me not to trouble.

"I happen to know your address," he said. "Remember, I'm put at your disposal."

He walked with me to the door, which swung open before us, and there he shook hands most cordially.

"Now remember!" he said, as though to be of service to me would be a privilege to him; then I passed out, and stood on the steps again, looking down upon the passers-by.

It was about midday, and everybody seemed to be enjoying the sunshine. March might have stolen a day from May, and nobody seemed in a hurry. I loitered in a corner of the porch, out of the way of the clubmen who passed in and out continually. I wanted to think for a minute or two, and it was easier to do so where I was, than moving in the crowd on the pavement; and my own quiet club was some way off.

I thought I had not promised anything too much or said anything compromising; but I had been taken by surprise in meeting the President (who can be spoken of just as well by that name as by any other). I stood there in the porch then, smoking and trying to recollect all that had been said. Just as I had decided that, at any rate, no harm had been done, and thought of moving, a passing victoria was checked by the traffic, and one of the two ladies sitting in it looked up at me and bowed. It was Miss O'Hagan. I lifted my hat, and at the same time felt a touch upon my shoulder, and turned. It was the President, who had just come out again, and who stood by me, while Hext, a little apart, was once more appreciatively surveying the sunshine and movement of Pall Mall.

"In thinking over those two deaths, by the way," the former said quietly to me, "one naturally considers points of difference and of similarity. Both these poor fellows were bachelors, and both had independent means. Perhaps you don't know where their property went? Ah! that is Miss O'Hagan, is it not? It's said they remembered her." He lifted his hat, glancing at the spot where the victoria waited close by the pavement. "Well," he said, "you're a bachelor too, I understand, though perhaps not so well provided as they were with this world's goods. You're an older man also. Well, take care of yourself, doctor, and let me hear from you if there is anything to report. No news will be good news."

He went away down Pall Mall, with Hext at his side. I waited a moment and then followed down the steps. The victoria was still waiting, and Miss O'Hagan leant forward and beckoned me to her. When I went forward she bowed, stammering an apology for having failed to write (as she promised when I first met her). She introduced me to her friend, an old lady with a placid face, who bowed with great politeness, saying that she had much pleasure in making my acquaintance, and seemed to me to inspect me with more interest than I am accustomed for women to show.

Could I come and see her that afternoon? said Miss Hagan, giving me an address in Cadogan Square. I had to refuse, but arranged for the following afternoon, and they drove on.

As the victoria passed slowly down Pall Mall, I saw a good many men turn their heads to have a second look at it. The dark bay horse was a fine stepper, and perhaps some turned to admire his action. I thought it more likely, however, that they were attracted by the girl's pale face, very handsome, or so it seemed to me, and very sombre, and overhung by the heavy masses of dark red hair.

CHAPTER XV

MISS O'HAGAN EXPLAINS

I spent the evening of that day at home, shuffling the loose bits of paper on which I jotted down my occasional ideas about the Mummy, and looking through the rather more coherent notes in the book I had marked "M."

I made a note about the President, and decided not to discuss that chat with anybody. Indeed, it was then that I definitely resolved to be very chary of repeating to any one Plain Speaker what any other might say; and I decided to apply this rule, so far as I thought proper, even to Maxwell and Perceval.

"But," you may object, "what about their fee? Doesn't that make confidence necessary?" Well, to that objection I had several answers. I hadn't the fee. I hadn't promised to take it. Besides, if I thought I could help at all by holding my tongue, then I owed it to them to do so.

And all the time I was frankly uneasy at being mixed up with the business at all.

Why hadn't I sent these fellows to the devil, said distinctly what I knew and what I didn't know, and let the coroner and the police have a free hand?

So not at all in the bland mood suited for an afternoon call upon a young lady, when late in the day I walked into Cadogan Square. I nearly walked out of it again at once, for I was told that Miss O'Hagan was "not at home," and I was moving off, furious with feminine inconsiderateness, when it suddenly occurred to me to say who I was. That altered matters altogether, and I was taken upstairs to a little boudoir where I found Miss O'Hagan and her *dame de compagnie.* Tea was brought in immediately after, and Miss O'Hagan seeming nervous, I found myself talking the most amazing society twaddle to the gently twittering Mrs. Vavasour. Her very name brought to mind Dundreary whiskers and my mother's crinolines.

Some unnecessary admission on my part shook her confidence sadly. She left the room with a puzzled air, and for the first time I heard Miss O'Hagan laugh. I was not at all sure whether the laugh was against me or Mrs. Vavasour, or both; but it had a very pleasant sound, and I did nothing to discourage it. I found myself thinking that I was fifty, and she twenty-three or twenty-four, and that if things I needn't talk about here had prospered when I was twenty-five, I might have had a girl of my own to laugh at me like that, and to keep me polished up a bit—instead of being a lonely, ill-mannered bachelor.

I suppose I began to look sulky at that, for she stammered an apology. (We must take that unfortunate stammer for granted, if you please, for some time. It was less frequent when I became less of a stranger, but it did not leave her altogether until after a good deal had happened.)

"I'm afraid it's my fault," she said, "that you've had so much Court news inflicted on you, Dr. Armiston. You looked so bored and puzzled that I couldn't help laughing."

I muttered something about being pleased to be the cause of laughter in others, and she went on:

"My cousin is a very loyal woman, and takes a great interest in all the royal family. When she was a child she lived at Windsor, and I suppose used to have them all pointed out to her. She has watched their lives ever since, and knows them all by sight still."

I listened, and didn't see how this concerned me, but the girl went on:

"Mrs. Vavasour saw you two standing outside the club and pointed you out—and wondered who *you* were. She supposed you must be a soldier. I said you were a doctor and that I had been wanting to consult you, so we waited. She is very glad that I should see anyone obviously so high in his profession as you are."

"I didn't know I was here professionally."

"You're here as a nerve specialist," she said, smiling, but watching me anxiously. "You're recommended to me by my cousin Charlie Perceval, and by Captain Maxwell."

"I don't think these young fellows are competent judges," I said more carefully. "That is what I mean. For instance, if they told you that I was a specialist, you're misinformed. I'm a general medical practitioner, a sort of 'Jack of All Trades, and——' You know the rest."

I stopped, and she looked at me very distressfully, though one could see that she was doing her best to keep cool. I dare say I didn't feel any the less sympathetic because she seemed to me extraordinary beautiful, and much too proud a young woman to ask for anyone's advice in general.

"They told me I could trust you," she said dolefully, but very quietly.

"I don't know how they could tell, but so you can," I replied. "You can trust me not to trade upon your ignorance. Tell me what you can about your trouble, and I think I can tell you where to go for the best advice."

"I suppose you think, like Mrs. Vavasour," she said, "that it's this stammering I want to see you about. It isn't the stammer, though that's horrible. It's the cause of it that I want to talk of. What does it matter to me whether you're a specialist, as long as you're an honest gentleman, and someone I can talk to quite plainly?"

I clumsily tried to treat the matter in an off-hand way. "Among so many Plain Speakers——" but she interrupted impatiently, as if in desperation.

"You must not laugh at me," she said. "You must not!" and then hurriedly, "Hear me! I have two dead men always on my mind, always before me, sleeping or waking. For God's sake help me, that there may be no more!"

I sat and stared at her, doubting my own ears. "You!" I said.

"Yes, I!" she repeated defiantly. "I did not mean to tell you that, in that way; but I don't care. You won't laugh any more, at any rate."

Laugh! I certainly didn't feel like laughing any more.

I leant back in my chair and considered her critically. The afternoon sun was shining straight in upon her. It lit up the coils of red hair, and shimmered upon her face and neck. She was a picture of youth and vitality. Two dead men on her mind! The idea was absurd.

"Tell me what you mean," said I.

She sat looking first at me, then away from me, as if still in an agony of doubt. One could not help being very sorry for the girl.

"Remember, I'm old enough to be your father," said I.

"Yes," she said quite simply. "you're old enough to be my father, and that makes it easier, but it's very hard," and she sat looking at me with a little frown for a few seconds, as if considering me, before she spoke again.

"The beginning of these things," she said presently, "was when I saw you first in the Albany, on the morning Mr. Scrymgeour died."

"What were you doing there?" I asked. "Why were you at the Albany? Remember, I've no authority to ask questions. But you invite me to."

"It's not easy to answer your questions," she said at last, "but it will be harder to tell you everything without being asked. I was at the Albany because of a letter that I got the night before from Mr. Scrymgeour. Some months ago he made me an offer of marriage, which I declined. That night he wrote saying that in case he died he would like me to know that his feelings had not changed, and that he had left me most of his property."

"You went round before breakfast to thank him?" I suggested, with some attempt at irony. Really, one must not believe everything one was told, just because the teller happened to be a beautiful woman. But if she saw my intention she paid no apparent heed to it.

"Mr. Scrymgeour was a man for whom I always had a very great liking," she said. "After I had refused him I liked him better than ever, because of the way he behaved to me. I suppose I'm impulsive, and I'm not responsible to anyone for what I do. If I make mistakes, no one is likely to suffer except myself. I knew that it was the last night for him to keep that horrible Mummy in his room. I couldn't sleep; and between seven and eight I suddenly made up my mind to go and make sure that all was well. I am often out round the Square before breakfast. I had a couple of books he had lent me. I meant to leave them with his man, and learn somehow that he was well without seeing him."

"You went alone!"

"Is there any danger in going from Cadogan Square to the Albany between eight and nine in the morning?" she asked angrily. "Yes, I went alone. Mr. Scrymgeour's servant told me he was not up yet, but expected Captain Maxwell and my cousin to breakfast at nine. I said he must be dressing, or would like to be called; and I made the man knock at his door, while I waited on the stair. But when he came back saying he could get no answer I was frightened. I insisted that he must open the door, and because he hesitated, and talked of waiting till Captain Maxwell and my cousin came, I knocked, then threw the door open myself and looked in. The door was the one opening directly on to the lobby, and at once I could see him lying on the rug. I've seen dead men when with my father in South America and other places, and when I crossed the room and knelt by him I knew he was quite dead. The other two came up just afterwards. It was then I began to stammer."

"What happened after?"

"They asked me to wait in the sitting-room; the three talked together for a little while, and then my cousin and Captain Maxwell came to me. They said there was sure to be an inquest, and that they must get a doctor. But that it was much better I shouldn't be troubled to give evidence, and that I had better go and say nothing."

"Why didn't you go?"

"I did. But when I had gone some distance I found that I had left my muff behind. I met you after I had fetched it."

I sat and considered the matter—as well as I could without a cigar.

"You went to Mr. Scrymgeour's rooms because you were afraid something had happened. Why were you afraid?"

"Because of his letter."

"Can I see it?"

She flushed up. "No, I burnt it."

"When?"

"When I knew you were coming."

"You thought I might ask to see it?"

"Yes, it seemed likely."

It seemed to me that I was dealing with a young woman of some decision, in spite of her stammer. I made no comment on her admission, but felt that since she was so frank on this point she was not likely to be untruthful on others.

"Well, I suppose you had a right to burn the letter if you wanted to," I allowed.

"I certainly had," she said. "Please don't imagine that I have any doubt about it."

"But did your friend say he thought he was going to die?" asked I.

"He didn't say so. But he told me that sitting there as he did sometimes at night with the Mummy near him, and remembering it sometimes when lying awake, he had thought about the beginning of the matter a good deal. He thought he was wrong to have made a joke of it, and he wished to tell me so."

"Why?"

"He knew what I thought of it. To make a bet on the body of a dead woman, who had done all she could to make sure of being left quiet! It was a coarse thing to do. A callous, cruel thing. I found out something from my maid through Mr. Scrymgeour's servant, and I guessed a little more, and spoke. This was before Mr. Scrymgeour's death. Of course, if they had really thought there was danger, they wouldn't have let me in. I told them, my cousin and Professor Maundeville, that I was under no obligation to keep silent, having found it out for myself, and that if they didn't let me join I should speak about it openly. I was sure there would be trouble of some sort."

"Maundeville is most to blame," I said. "He's old enough to know better, at any rate; and he is responsible for the Mummy being here."

"They agree that he tried to stop the thing," she said, "but the others, Mr. Scrymgeour especially, told him that he had challenged them and couldn't back out. He protests to me he is very sorry about it, and owns that the whole affair was in bad taste. But he has been so accustomed to mummies that he didn't think of this one as I do. I call it sacrilege. I said that trouble must come of such callousness. But, of course, they will keep to their agreement, which affects their word of honour, and take the consequences."

I listened and asked no more questions, and soon after I left her. It was not until I sat smoking alone that night I remembered I had suggested no treatment for the stammering. I wondered whether Miss O'Hagan had noticed that. I didn't think she had. I decided to see her again, or write to her when I had thought over this queer business of the Mummy.

But by the first post next morning I heard from her briefly, and will give the letter in full:

"DEAR DR. ARMISTON,

"I must see you again soon, and I will write later making an appointment.

"In the meantime I beg you to treat as confidential *whatever* concerns our interviews, however trivial it may seem. I mean even things that you would not think in any way professional. I acknowledge that I am nervous, and that my ideas, which I am ashamed of, may be hysterical. I hope they are. But to be silent can do no harm, can it? I even ask you, if you mean to end this ghastly business of the Mummy, to give your ideas to no one, and to repeat to none of us what any of the others may say to you, or what you may suspect or learn for yourself."

I read this note three times over, and then decided to burn it. I was struck by her use of the term "hysterical." Now an hysterical patient never seems to think that she is hysterical. For a girl even to admit to herself the possibility of such a thing is enough to make me doubt it. At any rate, to be silent could do no harm, as she said—a most unfeminine attitude of mind. I began to form a complimentary estimate of Miss O'Hagan's mental powers, as well as of her physical charms, and replied that I would do as she wished.

CHAPTER XVI

IN MAUNDEVILLE'S MUSEUM

Three or four days after I had called on Miss O'Hagan I went to Maundeville's house, and buried myself for an afternoon in his library. Once in it, indeed, I didn't think of time at all. I roamed about the room trying to get some general idea of the books there. Remembering what Maundeville had said on the subject of middle age, I was amused to see that he had several books dealing with the prolongation of life. There were the works of Metchnikoff, Brown-Séquard and others, with one or two scrap-books of press-cuttings relating to centenarians. The shelf ended with works on occultism, and I wondered whether Maundeville classed the two subjects together, and whether he considered both seriously or otherwise.

I passed on to other shelves, dipping into a book here and there, and I was deep in one on Egypt, most beautifully illustrated with drawings and photographs, when Maundeville's man, without asking if I wanted it, brought in a tea-tray. The result was that I stayed on, without seeing anything of Maundeville, until about eight o'clock. Passing down the stairs I met the servant again, and asked whether I could go into the museum without disturbing Maundeville. He said that his master would not be home at all that evening, and that his orders were to admit me whenever I came to any room I wished. He switched on the lights in the museum for me, and I sat there perhaps a quarter of an hour looking idly at the mummy-case, and speculating vaguely about it and its contents.

Intentionally I did not try to think hard, but just looked at it and let my brain work or play as it would.

As I was strolling absent-mindedly out of the room I kicked against something hard, and nearly fell. Looking down when I had got my balance, I saw that I had come on a large tortoise, which was half-hidden under a table.

In the hall I spoke of this to the man, who was lounging there, saying I hoped I hadn't injured the beast, for I had really kicked it severely. This provoked the only smile I ever saw on Bates's solemn visage, but he merely said he thought the thing could stand more than that, and very likely had stood more, since he had heard his master say he knew it to be older than any man.

I told him to let his master know of my visit, and went off to dinner.

I dined at home that evening, and alone. Mudge explained to me when he had brought in the coffee, that I had left most of a sole, which he thought an uncommonly well-cooked one, and had let a cutlet grow cold before I began it. The fact is that my few minutes in Maundeville's museum had possessed my mind with that mummy-case. I imagined it waiting there quietly in the darkness, till it should go out to find another host. The painted face was heavily malignant, and sitting alone in my room I could not get rid of it, although I knew quite well that it might not be a recognisable likeness of the woman whose body it covered.

Unless a man is a poet or novelist by trade, to have an imagination at fifty is merely ridiculous, and I felt this acutely. But you will agree, I think, after due consideration, that two such long-enduring things as a mummy and a tortoise do seem quaint, taken together in a London house. One imagined the tortoise now slowly crawling about in the darkness of the museum, the Mummy looking down on it with blind eyes.

Really, it's no wonder that I didn't do anything except fancy ridiculous things that evening—and all because of that miserable Purveyor beneath me. His trade was increasing (confound him!) and he had lately started an extra-sized coffee-mill, which was worked at night, grinding coffee for the next day's sale.

When it began it lifted me clean out of my chair. A Twopenny Tube under the floor couldn't have been worse, and it went on continuously for a solid hour. I sent Mudge down to remonstrate, but all doors were locked, and of course the rascals were wrapped in their own thunder.

The next morning I got myself into a quiet and reasonable frame of mind, and went in myself to interview the Purveyor. It was troublesome that I had ceased, after a very short trial, to get my coffee there, because, as I had told the Purveyor plainly, in a little note, I disliked chicory, and in any case wouldn't pay the price of coffee for it.

At this interview about the coffee-mill we were both very polite till near the end. When I found him quite obstinate and intending to have that row every night (coffee, he said, must be fresh roasted and fresh ground to please *his* customers), I said that in that case I must appeal to our landlord, and he laughed. It wasn't polite to laugh, and I said so plainly, whereupon he laughed again. I then told him to read the Adulteration Act and mend his ways lest a worse thing come upon him, and I left.

I went from him direct to our landlord, but fared no better. He was polite too; but when I said that unless things were put right I must consider the question of giving notice, I got it straight from the shoulder. That, my landlord said, might certainly be the easiest way out of the difficulty—especially as my troublesome neighbour would take the flat at once if he could get it.

That shut me up at once. I hate bluff, and I'm bad at it. I knew I didn't want to change, and couldn't pretend plausibly that I did. I left my landlord in disgust. How the devil was I to do anything at night with that infernal racket going on under me? I should be all on edge before it began and long after it had finished. To be at the mercy of a confounded grocer! To have one's peace and one's problems muddled by a wretched wrapper of sand and sugar in whitey-brown paper! I was frantic, and all the time I was jeering at myself and saying, "You're an elderly cross-grained bachelor of fifty. A young man or a wise man wouldn't notice such a trifle, or he'd see a way out. You're not only elderly, you're incompetent." I was still fuming when I went back to my flat in the late afternoon. The smell of freshly-ground coffee from the shop made me savage. I wished one could smell the chicory too, which I knew was there.

"Here," you will say, "is a most egotistical and long-winded

bore! What on earth do I care about his flat and his petty grievances with grocers and coffee-mills?" Be patient! This is, if you
are interested in any part of this affair. I acknowledged that I'm
not a skilled *raconteur*; but I tell my story as well as I can; and
remember, if you please, you can't possibly say what does and
what doesn't concern it, unless you hear me to the end.

I let myself in, on reaching my door, after interviewing my
miserable landlord, and I found Maundeville limping airily about
my consulting-room, surveying my bookshelves. "You read
German?" he asked. "That book is most scandalously mistrans-
lated," pointing at one on my table, "I'll lend it to you in the
original. Listen! I want you to dine with me to-night, or have me
to dine with you. I don't care which. I want to talk about that
wretched Mummy. It must pay another visit soon. Have you been
thinking of it?"

"I was looking at it yesterday," I said, "and I nearly broke my
neck over a tortoise."

"Ah! Methuselah," Maundeville chuckled. "Lively company,
isn't he? Do you know, I've good reason for thinking him older
than the one at St. Helena, and that's known to have been almost
as big a century and a quarter ago as it is now. That comes, I suppose, of having a low temperature and a slow circulation. What
do you think? Methusaleh won't burn out, will he? He doesn't let
himself go! He isn't enthusiastic about anything, and never wor-
ries, as far as I can see. I imagine his mind is as slow as his body.
When I sit alone and look at him, as I do sometimes, he suggests
all kinds of idle speculation."

"For example?"

"Oh, well, he has the secret of longevity, hasn't he? But he can't
give it away, and I don't know how to steal it from him. What
does he get out of his existence? Which is the more desirable, the
long-drawn-out or the concentrated? Which is the more fortu-
nate, Methuselah or, say, a Mayfly?"

"We don't know; and if we did, we can't choose," I said. "We
can only cut the thread. We can't spin it out much."

"That's shockingly unscientific," Maundeville declared dog-
matically. "Have you decided that we're to learn no more? Why,
there's plenty forgotten that's worth learning over again. We

think ourselves very wise. But who knows what knowledge was drowned with Atlantis?"

He was limping springily to and fro before my bookshelves as he talked, half to me, half to himself.

"We need dinner to-night, at any rate," he said suddenly, laughing. "I haven't learnt to do without that while I can get it. Have you?"

"You must dine with me, of course," I said, "but I must look at my engagements first. I think it only means making dinner a trifle late."

"We'll dine here," Maundeville said. "Your man looks competent for anything. A steak and a bottle of claret, eh?"

I was on the point of agreeing—ready to show that Mudge's resources went further—when I suddenly remembered the infernal coffee-grinding. I expressed my feelings on the subject freely, and Maundeville listened sympathetically.

"You could read at my place, of course," Maundeville suggested; "but a man doesn't like being ground out of his own arm-chair. Let me look over the flat, will you?"

Of course I was ready enough to do that, though I didn't see how it could interest him, and I showed him over everything, even Mudge's cock-loft and kitchen.

Maundeville's idea was to beat John Smith by "deafening" the floor and walls. He explained that he had got it done in his own library, "and I hope you've noticed how quiet that is," he said. "I've a patent deafening of my own," he went on, "and a patent way of getting it under the flooring without much upheaval. Which room do you particularly want quiet?"

"This one," I said.

"Well, I fancy the mill isn't directly under this. It's under your bedroom probably. But I expect a joist or two conduct the vibrations. You may need to break the continuity of one," and he dashed down on an envelope a diagram of the probable relation of upper and lower rooms, and the joists as he had mapped them out by percussion.

"I promise you it will only cost a trifle," he said, "and will increase the value of the house. Your landlord won't object. We'll talk to him."

He was diverted from this subject by Mudge, who brought in a tea-tray, together with some letters.

There were two or three notes of no pressing importance, and the usual number of samples of patent medicines and patent foods, including a French preparation for injecting youth into old bodies, and two or three cultures of the sour-milk bacillus—each, of course, the best.

I pushed one or two across to Maundeville.

"Look at these!" I said. "Man will always wish to prolong his troubles, I suppose. You had better make a vital extract of your Methuselah and put it on the market. 'Tortoisine,' or some name of that sort. It would sell like hot cakes."

Maundeville began debating the suggestion half seriously, not so much from the financial point of view as from the physiologist's. He told us that he also had a parrot then in his house, almost featherless, "who became so wise that he stopped talking years and years ago," and a raven at a little place he had down in Hampshire. "A grey disreputable old warlock," he called him.

"I'm making parallel observations on the three," he said, "to determine any points that I can of likeness and unlikeness."

"Mix 'em in one concentrated essence," I suggested flippantly, helping myself to tea. "Boil 'em down!"

But Maundeville rose from his chair, and began restlessly to limp up and down the room.

"Death is nothing," he said. "One goes to explore a new country—which is always interesting. Or being tired, one sleeps. But the gradual decay! The growing old! The ceasing to enjoy, or to be enjoyed!"

He stopped and looked at me whimsically. "Garrulity is a shocking bad sign, isn't it?" he asked. "But sometimes I think that this very revolt against the generally accepted course of things is promising. Discontent is the root of research and of knowledge. Inquisitiveness, too, is youthful, and keeps one young. I have found out some curious things already."

He broke off, and went tapping about the room, suddenly changing his mood.

"We must certainly get this deafened," he said, chuckling softly. "We know, at any rate, that a quiet mind is an aid to longevity. But a disputed point is—may we dine well with impunity?"

"We mayn't dine here at all," I said sulkily; and I gave him the name of my club and practically turned him out, as I had a couple of letters to write and two or three people to see.

We dined comfortably enough that night; for the learned men who admitted me to their circle on insufficient evidence, at a time when the committee wished to increase the membership, do not altogether despise the science and art of gastronomy. Besides, there are a few retired Army men, Indian colonels and other connoisseurs. Maundeville was most amusing and erratic, though he noticed everything, and threw in very discriminating comments on the menu. He said he could always make sure of properly appreciating a good dinner, by calling to mind the many occasions on which in different parts of the world he had been unable to get any at all.

"Reversing the 'Sorrow's crown of sorrow' attitude," he said flippantly, "the height of comfort is only reached if in the midst of it you can think of hard times."

He refused to discuss the Mummy in any way while we dined, and turned the conversation, how, I don't remember, by giving me a ludicrous account of the way in which he got his limp.

Some of his student days had been spent in Paris; and there he became somewhat smitten with a certain *midinette*, who lived on the same stair above him.

"Mamzelle was pleasant enough," he said, "and sometimes smiled on me. But a fellow-student thought I was poaching on his preserves, and challenged me. I chose swords, with which I was fairly good, and believed I could bleed my passionate friend gently. But he jumped about so much, and poked at me so outrageously, that I thought there was a risk of killing him. It suddenly occurred to my vivid imagination that I should be awfully bored by the plump bone of contention—and while I considered this the clumsy fellow literally fell on me, and skewered me at the hip-joint. That comes of looking too far ahead; but I still have that failing," and so he rambled on, scoffing sometimes at others, and often at himself, until we settled in a quiet corner of the smoking-room.

"Now," he said, "we're fortified and steadied by an excellent dinner. We shall take common-sense views of things. To take fantastic views one must fast. The saints and such folk always did, before they saw visions and dreamed dreams. After those turtle flippers one's imagination is well under control. Let us put the Mummy on trial impartially."

And then he said he didn't believe in any danger in the beginning, and didn't now—unless, possibly, through imagination. "I may have pretended to at the time," he continued, "but I didn't expect to be taken seriously. If I had thought there was any danger, how could I have allowed such foolishness? The silly business began in smoking-room chaff, and was expected to end in the same way.

"The thing had stood in my curiosity shop for some weeks, and I was none the worse. How, indeed, could I possibly be? Though I've sat at all hours alone with it when I was working out the inscriptions on the case, and comparing them with those I had copied from the passage to the tomb and from the sarcophagus. Awful things they were, too—in a way. If the lady devised them herself she must have had a lurid imagination."

I wanted to hear all that he could tell me—nonsense or otherwise.

"I think Maxwell or Perceval told me," I said, "that there was some story of a spell a woman gave you."

"So there was! I had forgotten having mentioned that. I suppose I needn't say that I attach just as much value to such things as you would—and no more. But it's true enough, as far as it goes. The woman's child was doubled up with cholera, poor little beggar, and everybody had bolted from it except herself. I saw to it for a couple of days, and she was absurdly grateful. She was a woman with a tremendous reputation among the Arabs for uncanny knowledge. She told me of a lot of queer things, some of which proved true enough, and she pronounced a sort of charm over me." He stopped to laugh. "There were several unpleasant features in it," he said. "I had to swallow something horrible, I remember. If I knew it all we might try its effect as an antidote on the next host of the Mummy. But let's argue the matter seriously—though that's difficult to do."

"One thing is serious enough," I said. "There have been two

deaths. Were they in any way connected with the Mummy? And is there any chance of more?"

"Find the answer to the first question," Maundeville retorted, "and the second will be easy. But who knows more about that than you do? I understand that you investigated both cases, and that there was no similarity between them, except that both might be considered to a certain extent accidental, and both men were entertaining the Mummy at the time. I really believe the thing to be probably merely a very remarkable coincidence. I think the jury's verdict in poor Scrymgeour's case, and your certificate in D'Aurelle's, to be the common-sense explanation. Their time had come, and the Mummy could neither help nor hinder. They would have died then if she had still been lying where I found her."

He spoke with obvious conviction. Their time had come, and that was all about it, though regrettable enough.

"It may be so," said I. "But excluding the supernatural, which we both refuse to admit, of course, let us consider whether anything about the Mummy could give these results by natural means?"

"How is that possible?"

"I don't think it is possible," I said, "but we're trying to consider the puzzle from all sides. Could the case, for instance, or its contents, be so prepared that contact or propinquity might injure any meddlesome person?"

"How, again?"

"Well, by dulling their senses? Or by lowering their vitality?"

"Theoretically it might, I suppose," Maundeville allowed; "I hadn't considered it. But it hasn't affected me in my house."

"In fact, practically there are a dozen arguments against it— quite so," I said, and for some time again we both puffed away in silence.

"There's another point one has considered, of course," Maundeville said at last. "Could these two deaths conceivably be due to malice? Does anyone in any way profit by them? Have you any opinion about that?"

"No one profits so far as I know," I said. "But——" and then suddenly checked myself.

"But?" Maundeville repeated after me.

I had suddenly remembered the remark made by the President of the Plain Speakers—that property had been left by each of these men to Miss O'Hagan. Strange that my sudden impulse was to say nothing about the girl's position! No doubt you have noticed how very often, if you are thinking intently of any person, a companion will bring up that person's name. Probably, in many cases, what has already been said has naturally suggested the same line of thought in both minds. Sometimes the connection is far to seek that it seems as though one had thought aloud. Maundeville observed.

"You've met a good many of the Plain Speakers now, I think: the President, of course, and Lady Havers and others?"

"Yes."

"I'm not sure if you were introduced to Miss O'Hagan. She was at the Open Minds too."

"I remember. We chatted a little," I said.

"The poor girl has developed a stammer quite lately," he said thoughtfully. "These nervous disturbances are queer things. One would like to know the cause in this case."

"Queer things, as you say," I agreed, and no more for the time being was said about the Mummy.

Although it was late when Maundeville and I parted, I spent some time afterwards in looking over my notes and adding a few more.

The result seemed to be mere exasperation. I had no theory worth the name, and I was inclined to believe that if ever I discovered a clue it would lead merely to a mare's-nest. I jeered at myself as an elderly busybody, with a talent for interfering unduly with matters which didn't concern me, and for which I had no capacity. I envied Mudge his stolidity, which at the same time was exasperating. I don't think a dozen mummies could rob him of a minute's sleep.

CHAPTER XVII

THE BANYAN

In a quiet back street some three minutes' walk east from Piccadilly Circus, if you have curiosity enough to search diligently for
it, you will see a gilded sign hanging over first-floor windows. You
might puzzle for some time (always supposing you thought it
worth while) before you would discover what this gilded sign was
meant for. It is a banyan, and The Banyan is the name of the place
at which I dined with Maxwell that night.

The place is not a club, but an eating-house, with rather
a special *clientèle*. It's run by a retired quarter-master, who
somehow made his little pile in India. He works it with Indian
servants, and caters for Anglo-Indian tastes. If ever you go there,
try the fowl-curry, the chutney, and the fruit. It's the first place
where I was given a spoon for my curry. Men have been known to
come home cursing India and all its ways—and yet turn up at The
Banyan within a month. Maxwell said that he went principally to
keep up his Indian vocabulary. Among the staff there are generally half a dozen presidencies represented, and the proprietor can
speak Persian and Burmese.

It seemed to me that whatever crazes might possess us, as Plain
Speakers, Open Minds or private individuals, we had one element
of sanity in common. We were none of us so desperately infatu-
ated with the affair of the Mummy as to insist on discussing it at
dinner. I said as much to Maxwell after we had dined, and while
we smoked alone in a sort of private smoking-room where there
was just space enough for us to stretch ourselves comfortably on
a couple of brown-holland-covered divans.

He smiled faintly, and said every student of the art of war
knew the importance of the commissariat department. "But
now," he said, "dinner is over. Let's get to business. I've things to
ask, and something to tell you."

"I suppose you can ask what you choose," I said, "but at the risk of seeming uncivil to my host I warn you that I don't feel bound to answer."

Maxwell stiffened visibly, and sat considering me for some time, but I endured his stare without discomfort.

"There was a small matter of a fee," he said at last; "I merely mention it."

"There's not the least need," I assured him. "I haven't forgotten the offer. Be good enough to remember that I haven't accepted it yet, at any rate," and we sat glowering at one another over our cigars, till at last I burst out laughing.

"Come," I said, "I'm, alas! much the older man, and I've no wish to stand on my dignity—a precarious footing, perhaps, at the best. I know nothing whatever worth telling to or hiding from anyone, so far as I see, in any way concerning this infernal Mummy."

"Then why make such a mystery of it to me?" Maxwell asked sulkily.

"I don't," I said; "I think I owe you frankness. In common honesty, therefore, when you say you're going to question me, I warn you beforehand that I mayn't feel bound to reply. There are three or four of you talking more or less confidentially to me (the Lord and you alone know why!), and if you want one another to know what you tell me, why, you can tell one another! I'm not going to circulate your confidences, that's all. Hang it, man! You gave me to understand that you came to me because you heard I was honest. Doesn't the quality please you on closer acquaintance? I find it most confoundedly inconvenient myself, at times."

I stopped, thinking that I had gone far enough to meet him, but Maxwell still smoked on and said nothing. He had stopped staring at me, and now sat cross-legged on the divan, with his eyes fixed upon the floor immediately in front of him. He seemed to be smouldering like the dull ash of his cigar.

He was looking extraordinarily thin about the face, and I had noticed that he had merely played with his food at dinner.

"I'll try a bit of thought-reading," I said. "You're thinking, 'Here's a wooden-headed chap who has a reputation for honesty because he's uncivil. When he holds his tongue it's merely to cover his ignorance. What's the good of him?' "

"What would you have me think?" he asked, without troubling to deny that I was near the mark.

"Well, there's an alternative," I said. "Here's a man who knows he is growing old without having done anything worth doing. Maybe he envies his juniors, who have already made a name, and got honours. But till now he has always been able to keep some self-respect—self-conceit, if you like. Now it's possible that he has put his name to a lie, and he knows it."

"Well?" Maxwell was watching me again.

"Well, that's my case from my point of view," I said; "I take no more risks. I'm going to see this thing through—with you or without you. And if I think it is proper to hold my tongue at any time, I shall do so."

"You believe there is something, then?"

"Yes," I said, "I do, though I haven't an atom of proof. But if you object to my general method, which is to hear as much as I can, and tell as little as possible, why, you must leave me to myself. I shan't drop it."

Maxwell's eyes became dull again, as though he had ceased to look out through them.

"I see more trouble coming," he said. "Do as you like."

"What trouble?" I asked, "and how do you see it?"

Maxwell said nothing, but clapped his hands, and an attendant pulled aside the curtain over the doorway, and salaamed.

Maxwell spoke to him in some foreign dialect, and the man brought writing things. He wrote a word or two on a half-sheet of paper on which the banyan was stamped, slipped it into an envelope, which he sealed with his signet ring, and handed it to me.

"Later," he said, "it might be useful if you trusted me more. Meanwhile I trust you. Put that away, and don't open it till you know the result of the Mummy's next move."

"And if it doesn't move again?"

"But it will," he said. "We needn't discuss that. You've met Miss O'Hagan lately?"

"Yes," I said. "She asked me to call, and herself told me why she stammers."

I heard him sigh, but he asked no more about that visit, as I had been afraid he might do.

"Just now you spoke of yourself as growing old," he said, after a long pause, during which we both puffed away and thought our own thoughts. "I'm accustomed to size men up, and to me you seem very fit—or I wouldn't have worked you into this job. Still, you don't call yourself young?"

"No, I don't call myself young," I agreed.

"If one thinks of you as a grave and reverend signior," Maxwell said, with another faint smile, "that makes it easier to talk. Perhaps you've forgotten the fancies of a young fellow?"

"Perhaps," I said.

"Or never had any in particular?"

"You're at liberty to think so if you choose," I said, my mind leaping back to the time when I, too, was under thirty. "Still, if you think it will in any way help our business, or make it easier for you to talk, I'll try to remember, or to imagine, that I was once a young fellow."

Maxwell looked at me curiously.

"Yes, anything to help our business," he agreed. "I don't know where I'm prepared to draw the line when that is concerned. I'm ready, you notice, to be tolerably rude, at any rate. But I'm ready, too, to give you a pull on me. I think it's as well you should know that I'm very deeply in love with Miss O'Hagan."

I wasn't surprised to hear this. I sat wondering a little why I wasn't, and what I had noticed to prepare me for it. After all, what did that matter? Nothing at all.

"Why do you tell me?" I asked. "What has that to do with the Mummy?"

"Everything. Haven't you been told already that she found out about our insane agreement, and insisted on being allowed to join? What if she got the Ace of Spades?"

"Oh, this is ridiculous!" I said. "It must be stopped at all costs."

"Tell me how—short of breaking our word," Maxwell said, "and to double your fee is the least I'll do for you. But, remember, you're bound equally with us."

So I was, and for the time, at any rate, and for an altogether improbable danger to anyone, I wasn't prepared to perjure myself any more than the rest of them.

"Why on earth did you let her join?" I asked angrily. "You who pretend to be in love with her!"

"Pretend!" Maxwell said softly, and laughed, and nothing more. But he might have protested a good deal and made less impression on me.

"Well, assuming your devotion to the lady," I said, "you'll allow that was a queer way to demonstrate it."

I was quite intentionally brusque with him. I thought in that way we were more likely to understand one another. Even if I vexed him it wouldn't particularly matter, provided it made him talk; but he took my impertinences with surprising patience.

"You don't seem to realise things as they were at the beginning. She took us by surprise, and made us ashamed of ourselves, before any of us had any notion of danger. The thing was merely a poor joke then. It may be nothing more than a ghastly coincidence now. But in any case men can't go back on their word because a thing proves less of a joke than they expected. Hang it! Even in the twentieth century decent folk still keep to their word!"

"It will be carried through, then."

"Confound it, man! What else can we do? Assuming the apparently impossible, the worst—that those poor chaps, Scrymgeour and D'Aurelle would be alive now if it weren't for the Mummy. Are we to be less plucky than they? Are they to stand to their word and die, and are we to break ours to live? I don't want to rant—but that's impossible."

"And if Miss O'Hagan gets the Ace of Spades?"

"I'm ready for that, as far as I can be," Maxwell said. "My plan would need her consent, and I might fail, of course. But till she gets the card and till my plan falls through, it's no use to think about any other way."

"You'll report to the police if she gets the card?" I said. I wanted to draw him as far as I could.

"I would do nothing of the kind," he declared. "She knows now, as far as any of us do, the risk she runs. She would never speak to me again if I did such a thing."

I had my own doubts as to what a girl might or might not condone of things done for her sake, but I held my tongue. It was safer to show doubt about Maxwell himself.

"Does she know you're her lover?" I asked, and added some sort of an apology for the question. "I don't think I'm generally inquisitive," I said, "but I fancy the more you can tell me, the better. It goes no further."

"I don't know whether she does," he said simply. "I've said nothing, except to you. I've sometimes thought she must see it. But so many men are in love with her—she mightn't notice."

Here was refreshing modesty—if genuine!

"This attitude is hardly *nouveau siècle*," I remarked. "Why haven't you spoken plainly to her?"

Maxwell shifted uneasily where he sat cross-legged on the divan, and looked more like an awkward schoolboy than anything else.

"I don't know," he said. "It's not easy to talk about. I only tell you because I'd like you to see how much I'm concerned. My idea is to do something worth doing—to get my name up—before I say anything. Look here! I'd rather not discuss it any more unless we've some particular reason for doing so."

"You tell me you're rich?" I remembered.

"Oh yes, I'm rich," he said indifferently. "So is she."

"With the rank of captain and the D.S.O.," I added.

"Yes, that's all," he said. "If I had only had the V.C. now! Fellows said I was going to get that. I think that might have made a difference. She's a soldier's daughter, don't you know."

" 'He either fears his fate too much,' " I quoted.

" 'Or his deserts are small?' " Maxwell finished the tag. "Small enough, God knows!" he added; "but if I had a chance of getting my name up!" and I sat and contemplated this phenomenon, an officer of the Engineers who apparently did not think much of himself.

"Well, it may be useful to know what you've told me," I said, "and I don't know that I'm justified in catechising you any more on your private affairs. I won't repeat anything without your leave—and I think, if I were you, I wouldn't repeat what you've told me to anyone else for the present." I added something about feeling rather surprised and flattered by his confidence.

"I haven't done anything yet to show that I deserve it," I acknowledged, "and I don't know when I shall."

"Oh, that's all right," Maxwell said, dropping his sombre mood. "We said what we meant to one another from the start, didn't we? Besides, it's easier talking to a man so much my senior." I admitted that probably I hadn't taken that sufficiently into consideration.

He was quite right. We had begun by saying what we meant to one another, and we seemed likely to continue that healthy practice. Really, I liked the young fellow, even if he did sometimes touch one upon the raw!

CHAPTER XVIII

MEDITATION AND THE MUMMY

I have no doubt that I mention a great many things neither interesting nor important except to myself. But in referring again to that confounded coffee-mill, I am dealing with something which really had an ultimate result affecting the affair of the Mummy. The noise drove me frantic for three or four evenings. Either I forgot to go out, or I came in too soon. The thing was additionally annoying because it was so ridiculous.

I finally mentioned the matter again to Maundeville, when I met him one afternoon in Piccadilly, and reminded him of his suggestions. He very kindly took up the question at once with his usual energy. We went to his house, and he demonstrated outside and under the library and museum how perfectly sound had been cut off.

It was done by double doors and double windows, with a very thick fibrous material, something between wadding and felt, worked in under the flooring, and between the opposed ends of joists. The patent was his own, plotted out in the first place, he said, for his own comfort.

It was demonstrated to my landlord that the work would improve his property without expense to himself, and the job began at once—the whole flat being done, one room at a time.

Maundeville dropped in three or four times when passing, to see, as he said, that the British Workman didn't spoil the reputation of his patent; and at his repeated invitation I made pretty free use of his library during the eight or ten days that my flat was under treatment. Mudge kept a fish-like but vigilant eye on the workmen, merely remarking that in times past he had often done sentry-go while his ship coaled. This present operation, I gathered, was not so arduous or so dirty.

I went to Maundeville's one afternoon to consult his library—more particularly the pile of books, always increasing, in the museum. We were both interested in some really reasonable and well-conducted correspondence contributed to British and foreign scientific magazines at that time, on the phenomena of Life and Death, Growth and Decay. There was something new by Metchnikoff, which Maundeville wanted me to look at.

Near his door I met Perceval and Maxwell, coming away. They said he was not at home, and Perceval suggested that we should both go with him to Park Lane for tea.

I excused myself, on the ground that I wanted at once to run through this book, which I understood Maundeville wished to pass on to some correspondent of his, and I happened to mention the author and the subject.

"At the Service Clubs," Maxwell said, yawning, "it is thought that Metchnikoff, if that's his name, should be shot. Men with field-rank sit drinking sour milk, and talking hopefully of not being too old at eighty. The subs watch 'em, and take too many nips, to keep their spirits up."

"Maundeville must be an Altruist," Perceval decided. "He's investigating solely for the good of the race. I imagine it would take more than a dairyful of sour milk to protect his vitals against women and needles. You recollect, Max?" and Maxwell said he remembered, and they both seemed amused.

"What's that about women and needles?" I asked.

"A small joke against Maundeville," Perceval explained. "One of his Egyptian prophetesses told him if he wished to last as long as the pyramids, to beware of women and needles. We chaffed him one night about being a hardened and selfish bachelor, and he told us that yarn. I wonder whether he thinks it could protect him against the Ace of Spades?"

"Well, the Mummy was a woman," Maxwell reminded him, and that ended the chat.

They might chaff now and then about the Mummy, and they did. Standing in Piccadilly in bright sunshine, the pavement gay with the ridiculous women's hats of that season (you may apply the adjective to the hats or the women or both, as far as I am concerned), the gutter absurd, too, with sandwich-men advertising the latest musical comedy, one felt the Mummy was altogether out-of-date. One was bound to think of it as beneath contempt. Still, it always suggested unpleasant memories or vague possibilities—and the mention of it was always enough to turn or throttle any ordinary conversation. I nodded to them and went on—my business at Maundeville's house not being affected by his absence.

I went straight to the museum, saying casually to Bates in the hall that I understood his master was out. I read for an hour or so, and then grew fidgety. Methuselah, the tortoise, seemed almost restless, and kept moving about the place. Now and then he distracted my attention by the faint rattle of his carapace on something against which he blundered. I sat and watched him for a time, wondering whether any sense of spring really stirred him; for that afternoon was quite warm, and all along Piccadilly flowers were being hawked in the sunshine.

Methuselah's wanderings brought him at last against the mummy-case, and there he stayed quiet at the feet of the painted figure whose eyes stared across at me, seeming to follow when I moved, as painted eyes will.

I wondered, as I had done before, whether the somewhat malevolent face bore any faint likeness to what lay beneath. I wondered what did lie beneath now, and decided to suggest to Maundeville an experiment with X-rays, which could, of course, be repeated any number of times before the Mummy was exposed to light and air.

As a trio, this Mummy, Methuselah, and I, suggested some grim comedy to my mind. Here was I, quite well aware that the better and greater part of my life was of necessity past, and nothing particular done in it. Here was I, searching, perhaps as an Altruist, probably as an Egoist, for what modern *elixir vitæ* might yet be found. Here was Methuselah, who certainly had the secret of prolonged life, but who could not yield it to me, or tell me if he found it worth having. Looking down on us both, there was the Mummy, dead but incorruptible.

The wisdom of the Egyptians could keep everything but life in the body. Even hate seemed to have lived in it, and revenge, deadly for those who disturbed it.

This room did not get much daylight, and electric lamps were plentiful. But as I was no longer reading I did not trouble to switch them on, and sat there in the shadows, staring at the mummy-case and going over its history again.

I was constantly trying to determine whether there were any possible means by which the dead woman could ensure that those who troubled her rest should suffer for it. I don't, of course, refer to any "supernatural" power. As far as I defined a possible source of danger, I thought of it as something like a poisonous exhalation, set free from the case or the Mummy on exposure to the air, and affecting those who stayed long near it. For example, I fancied it was a part of this insane compact, to use no stronger adjective, that the Mummy should be in its host's sleeping-room at night. Now, could that conceivably so affect a man's vitality as to cause fatal syncope? It seemed most unlikely; but then no likely solution occurred to me. The answer to the riddle, indeed, if there were a riddle and an answer, was, if I may put it so, likely to be unlikely.

In my ordinary matter-of-fact state of mind the Mummy often seemed a bugbear, a scarecrow, and the deaths of its two hosts mere unpleasant coincidences. Here, watching it in the shadows, somehow——!

Well, I shrugged my shoulders and got up from the books, conscious that I was fanciful, and deciding to quit the room, since in it I couldn't use my wits to any practical purpose.

In this little museum, you will understand, not a sound reached me from beyond the door. If one dropped into a ridiculous train of thought, as I had, nothing from outside broke in to interrupt

it. Hence, probably the attention which I had given to the slight
occasional noise made by the tortoise's slow movements.

I compared this with my own flat, now at the workmen's
mercy, and it occurred to me that I would go upstairs, and determine whether the library and the studio, both facing north, while
the museum faced south, were equally silent.

I loitered for a few minutes in the library, which was empty
and undisturbed by any echo, and then I passed on to convincing
proof of Maundeville's success with the studio. I was in the room
before I realised that others were there already, and before they
knew I was near. I stood in the doorway stuttering a clumsy
apology, and so much taken aback that I didn't know whether
to bundle and go at my quickest, or wait to hear whether my
excuses were accepted.

There were three people in the room—Maundeville, Mrs.
Vavasour, and Miss O'Hagan.

CHAPTER XIX

"SHE IS FAR FROM THE LAND"

It was Miss O'Hagan whom I saw first, and who first saw me. She
was sitting upon a throne, as I fancy artists call the raised platform
on which a model poses, and was listening, bent a little forward,
to Maundeville, whose back was turned to me and who stood at
an easel, painting while he talked.

Mrs. Vavasour was placidly occupied in some fancy-work, a
knitted silk purse, I believe, and near her was a tea-table, with a
tray, cakes, cups, et cetera. My clumsy entry broke the spell and
disturbed everybody. Miss O'Hagan naturally changed her pose,
and looked over Maundeville's shoulder at me. He wheeled
about, to see who had disturbed her, and Mrs. Vavasour dropped
her knitting and raised her glasses to peer at me.

Maundeville was the first to speak, and greeted me as though I
were not only welcome, but expected.

"*Ben venuto!*" he called out, coming to meet me. "Just the man
we wanted. An impartial critic and a Plain Speaker!"

"I was told you were out," I stuttered. "It's true that was some time ago. The deafening—I heard nobody."

Maundeville beamed upon me and cut short my apologies.

"You give an unsolicited testimonial to my invention!" he said. "Of course you heard nobody. Can I help being pleased to see you? Don't run away! You've met Miss O'Hagan, I remember. Dr. Armiston—Mrs. Vavasour. Have you had tea?"

I said Bates had offered me some, but I had refused.

"Oh, you've been among the books?" Maundeville went on, picking up a brush again. "Now, Miss O'Hagan, there's a good half-hour of light left, and I know that a spectator won't trouble you."

While Maundeville fiddled with his palette, I looked across at Miss O'Hagan, trying to decide by her face whether she wanted me to go or to stay. She smiled faintly, as if she had at any rate no objection.

"We have now been caught in the act," Maundeville said airily, stepping back a little from his easel and looking to and fro between it and Miss O'Hagan. "We can't humbug the doctor, I'm afraid, Miss O'Hagan, and we can't execute him. I propose swearing him to secrecy, after owning to everything."

"Honestly, I haven't looked at the easel," I said, "and I don't want to be told anything. I promise to forget."

"Uncomplimentary to the sitter and the artist," Maundeville declared, getting back to the canvas, which only showed its edge to me as I sat near the tea-table.

"Oh, but you must see the picture, doctor," Mrs. Vavasour added, "it's lovely."

"The fact is," Maundeville went on, speaking slowly, and in disconnected sentences while he painted, "you have lit upon a terrible conspiracy. Look a little more downward please, Miss O'Hagan!" Maundeville then gave all his attention to the canvas, while I chatted to the old lady, or rather listened to her, and looked at Miss O'Hagan more closely.

She sat on a stool, one elbow on her knee, her chin on her hand. She wore a low-cut dress of green silk and queer make. I said to myself at the time that it might have been her grandmother's. As a matter of fact, she told me afterwards that she had a portrait of her great-grandmother in that dress, which she had routed out a few months before, and used at a Fancy Ball. A little pattern of shamrocks was on it in another shade of green. Emeralds were in her red hair and about her neck.

Placed as I was I could not see much of her face, but I saw the curves of cheek and chin, youthful neck and rounded arm, and it suddenly struck me that she was very beautiful. I had known her to be good-looking, but this was something more. It was a very long time since I had seen anything so apparently faultless as her form. The little ear turned towards me, the wrist and hand beneath the rounded chin.

Really, I said to myself, any mere elderly anatomist was justified in staring. As for artists—whether painters or sculptors—if they could do her justice, they should be "justified."

Knowing that she could not notice and be annoyed by my critical inspection, I continued to watch her, while Mrs. Vavasour twittered gently about various exalted personages, and I interjected a "Yes" or "No," as occasion seemed to require—and once, at least, gave the wrong answer.

"—and I was considered a good-looking girl at that time," she ended one of her reminiscences of a time when royalty had kissed her, or something of that sort.

I felt the need of being more attentive, and turned to face her directly as I replied.

It suddenly struck me, as I looked, that what she said was well within the mark. She, too, must have been a very good-looking girl at one time. She was a pleasant-looking little old lady now.

"*Bien entendu!*" I said honestly, though no doubt awkwardly enough. "My eyes tell me so."

The dear woman smiled and positively blushed—she still had a charming complexion—and asked me where I had learned to pay such compliments; but I replied at random, having already turned again.

Meanwhile Maundeville was hard at work, sometimes talking a little to Miss O'Hagan, often merely looking at her intently, putting in a touch here and there on the canvas, his mouth pursed in consideration, his quick grey eyes roving, sometimes discontentedly, sometimes with a look of satisfaction, from sitter to canvas and back again. Even in this room, with its big north lights, evening was now coming on. But he worked away, anxious, one supposed, to fix and finish some particular pose or expression. Suddenly he threw down his brush.

"I've done!" he said. "You can come down from your throne," and Miss O'Hagan, after sitting for a moment longer quite still, as if absorbed in something, stirred, slowly rose from her seat, and taking the hand Maundeville stretched out to her, stepped down on to the floor. It seemed to me that she was even more graceful in movement than when still. Tall as she was, it was only by comparing her height with her surroundings that one realised it. She moved across to the tea-table, and holding out her hand, stammered a few words to me, and I repeated my apologies for having come in on them.

"But you're going to justify yourself," she said. "Professor Maundeville wants a critic," and she half turned to Maundeville, who had dropped into a chair in front of the easel and sat looking at his work. His mood seemed unusually serious, for him, and he neither spoke nor paid us any attention for some few minutes, but sat quite still, all his thoughts apparently concentrated on what he had done. His head was silhouetted against some piece of white stuff that hung on the wall beyond him. His close-cut, thick grey hair didn't hide the fine shape of his head. His well-tanned face, rather prominent aquiline nose, and bold chin, stood out finely against the white background. Undoubtedly he was a modern scientific man, but sitting there he didn't give one that impression.

"Are you an artist?" I asked Miss O'Hagan softly; "if so, there's a sitter for you in your turn."

She looked, and looked intently at him, but shook her head. "It's beyond me," she said. "What would you call the picture?"

It seemed unimportant. "I don't know," I said.

"Nor do I," she agreed; but something in her voice made me turn to look at her. She, however, had moved towards Mrs. Vavasour, who put some question to her and then spoke to me.

"Do you think birthdays should be kept, Dr. Armiston?" she asked me.

I answered something silly while looking at Maundeville

again, and trying Miss O'Hagan's suggestion of fitting a title to the picture he made.

The head, somehow, was not modern, if you took it alone. It was Middle Ages, and all-round, action and thought mixed. I shrugged a shoulder at my own fancifulness, and turning my attention to Mrs. Vavasour again, found she was giving me an invitation, to which I listened with some astonishment. It seemed that two days hence would be her birthday, her seventy-seventh, I think she said; and she had been accustomed for many years— "ever since I was an old woman," she declared, smiling—to give a party to her child friends—mostly, she said, the grandchildren and great-grandchildren of her own contemporaries. Would I join? Maundeville and I would be the only men.

I join a children's party! Me!

I'm afraid of children, and I said so; but Mrs. Vavasour seemed to think that was another attempt at a joke. It's quite true, though. I respect them and many of their ways, but I'm sorry for 'em when I think what poor creatures most of them will turn out. And Maundeville! *Que diable allait-il faire?*

I said "Maundeville too!" without any attempt at concealing my amazement, and I got a mild snubbing.

"You are old enough to understand children," Mrs. Vavasour answered me. "Professor Maundeville does, perfectly. If you doubt it, come and see for yourself. Young men can't be expected to understand or to have patience, and I don't invite them. But you ought to. A doctor, too!"

And Miss O'Hagan adding a word, I said I would, though it seemed to me that an elderly medical man was likely to go as far as anyone towards spoiling a children's evening. They would surely be wondering what brought me, and would be seeing grey powder in every spoonful of jam, if once they heard I was a Medical. Still, I promised, and just after that Maundeville stirred, took a last long stare at his work, and then joined us.

"You may as well have a look," he said to me, and all of us moved across the room and stood in front of the picture, Maundeville lounging by the side of the easel and facing us—perhaps to judge by our faces what the opinions were.

I was certainly very much astonished by what he had done.

In the picture Miss O'Hagan sat before us as if she lived and breathed. I have put down the first emphatic phrase that comes, and it can stand. Though how the deuce she could live without breathing is what I don't know.

She sat on the stool she had used on the throne, facing us directly, but with her eyes downcast. One hand half held a harp, the other hand fell at her side.

It was as though trouble had swept over her while she played, and left her stranded. In the background was nothing but a few shadowy faces—mere ghosts. The red hair was beautifully done, the loneliness and melancholy of the figure were wonderful. Maundeville, to do a thing like that, must have, I thought, a more sympathetic nature than I would have given him credit for.

"Well, what do you think about it?" he asked presently, half-laughing.

What I said pleased him, and he smiled upon me, openly charmed, though my opinion on the average picture isn't worth twopence.

As the two ladies were leaving the studio Mrs. Vavasour suddenly remembered that she had left her purse on the tea-table. I was moving to get it when Maundeville forestalled me. He limped quickly to the table, picked up the purse, and began to return.

Half-way between the table and the doorway where the two ladies waited, he startled us. With an inarticulate sort of cry, he jumped at the girl like a cat across the remaining space between him and the doorway, the force of his onset driving Miss O'Hagan into the gallery outside. Directly he had struck against her he half stumbled, half threw himself sideways on the floor, and at the same moment a bust, which had stood above the doorway on a small bracket, fell with the bracket, grazing his shoulder, and smashed on the floor. He lay for an instant, then rose, looking very white and shaken.

"See if I've hurt her," he said to me, and dropped on to a settee close by the door, where he sat with his head down between his hands.

Outside in the gallery Mrs. Vavasour, wonderfully like a ruffled hen, was quite needlessly begging Miss O'Hagan not to be fright-

ened. The girl had been flung against the wall on the opposite
side of the gallery, and was sitting on the floor half-laughing. The
coils of her red hair had got loosened, and hung about her face.

"Are you hurt?" I asked; "Maundeville wants to know."

"No," she said. "Will you give me a hand?"

I helped her to rise while Mrs. Vavasour chattered and fluttered about her, twisting the hair into order.

"Something fell, didn't it—and he saw it coming?" she asked,
leaning against the wall and looking through the doorway at the
débris on the studio floor. "Where's Professor Maundeville? Was
he hurt?"

She moved in as she spoke, and we found Maundeville sitting
where I had left him. He rose with a laugh when he saw us,
though he still looked extraordinarily pale.

"I have to thank you," the girl began, "I do, very heartily." She
looked upwards, and evidently realised then, as I did, that the bust
had fallen from a considerable height.

"It might have been pretty bad, I see," she said quietly. "I'm
very much indebted to you, Professor Maundeville. I hope you're
not badly hurt. Please sit down again!"

Maundeville sat down, but did his best to treat the whole
matter lightly.

"If you're sure you forgive my way of speeding a parting
guest," he said, with a whimsical smile, "I'll try to forgive myself.
Oh yes, I'm all right—only frightened."

"You're not looking all right," Miss O'Hagan persisted, watching him. But Maundeville refused to answer seriously.

"Without attempting to put a valuation on your imperilled
brains," he said, "think of the threatened damage to my reputation for hospitality!"

The girl stood looking at him with a curiously uncertain air,
but Mrs. Vavasour now joined in.

"We must leave the Professor to rest after his great effort, my
dear," she said, and then added, with a certain stiffness, "and you
must remember you've had a very bad shaking too."

It was so obvious that the dear lady somehow thought the
affair should have been more decorously managed, that we all
three smiled.

"A very bad shaking, I'm afraid," Maundeville agreed. "I was shockingly rough. I can only plead inexperience!" and with that we all laughed, even Mrs. Vavasour, though she did so with some uncertainty.

Then the ladies said good-bye again, and this time got clear off, and I with them. Maundeville saw them into their carriage. I left him on the kerb, watching them away, and though he persisted that he was all right, he still looked very pale under his tan.

CHAPTER XX

MANY-SIDED MAUNDEVILLE

I went round the next morning to ask for him, and found him much the same as usual, trying some chemical tests for alkaloids in his museum. He was not very willing to say anything more about the accident of the previous evening.

"I've been busy this morning," he said, "and couldn't go out. But I sent Bates round with my card to inquire for Miss O'Hagan. You'll be glad to know that Mrs. Vavasour allows she is apparently none the worse for her fall. Indeed, they had intended to do me the honour of calling to ask after my welfare, but Bates told them I was engaged."

"He ought not to have let me in," I said, looking round for my hat, but Maundeville stopped me.

"This is mere mechanical work just now," he said. "Besides, you're different. With ladies one has to be more punctilious and less honest. They won't accept a divided attention, will they?"

But I know very little about women's vagaries, and I said so.

"They're queer creatures," he said thoughtfully, working at his test-tube while he talked. "They can't understand themselves half the time. The other half they take care no one else shall."

On such matters I was out of my depth altogether, and I made no comment.

Maundeville then changed to the subject of the coming children's party, to which he seemed to look forward with as much pleasure as if he had still been a child himself. He talked of nothing else till I left him—still working at his test-tubes and alkaloids. One thing he said just as I was leaving rather annoyed me.

"You'll call to inquire for Miss O'Hagan this afternoon, I suppose?" he suggested.

"I didn't mean to. Why should I?" I asked.

"Why shouldn't you? You know that she had a shaking last evening."

"I knew at the time that she was none the worse," I said, "and, besides, you've told me so just now."

Maundeville began to laugh, somewhat unreasonably, I thought. I went away wondering whether he laughed at me, and whether I deserved it.

When I looked back on Mrs. Vavasour's party I am inclined to wish that I had more chances of attending such functions. As it was, for want of practice, I was the shyest person there, and the most awkward. Soon after arriving I heard one child ask another who I was and what I was doing there. No one seemed to have any doubts about Maundeville, and he had none about himself.

One or two of the elder children greeted him at once with questions about some performance of his dating a year back; and in a few minutes he had the whole crowd about him, the smallest nearest, the eldest hanging on the outskirts, while he surveyed them all with the utmost nonchalance, and sipping his tea told them a wonderful history of a white mouse which he had found in the pocket of one of the boy-guests.

The mouse, it seemed, was an enchanted prince, who had since come into his kingdom. He was now looking for a princess, who must not be more than eight years old, and who would have a silver coach drawn by eight white horses in silver harness.

The children flattered him by their breathless attention, Mrs. Vavasour beamed upon him, telling me aside that his stories always had a happy ending, and Miss O'Hagan listened and watched with an intensity which seemed unnecessary.

I felt awkward and *de trop* until I found myself quite forgotten by everybody. After that I watched and listened, and really forgot myself too.

After we had finished tea the children had games, in which

Maundeville joined like a boy. When the ladies thought a rest was necessary, he began performing all sorts of conjuring tricks to keep the youngsters still.

One small child amused us by explaining to her still smaller sister that getting things out of jugs was the proper and original juggling. Maundeville asked her gravely if she knew what "saucery" was, and when she said she wasn't sure, but supposed it was juggling done with saucers, he said she was quite right, and that he would show us some.

He demanded a saucer—"your biggest and most beautiful," he said, and he got one of a very beautiful blue and gold.

This he turned upside down on a small bare table, and began waving his hands over it, talking to the children about spring.

"After these warm days," he said at last, "there should be butterflies about. Has anyone seen any yet?"

One or two had—most had not.

"There should be some," said Maundeville, looking up towards the ceiling. But no one saw any there.

"They don't live in houses," one boy observed.

"Oh, don't they? Quite sure?"

"Quite," said the boy sturdily.

"Didn't I hear one?" Maundeville asked, and lifted the saucer. There were half a dozen scattered butterflies of various colours.

"They're dead," said the authority on butterflies.

"Maybe! Maybe!" Maundeville agreed. "It's not easy to say always what's dead and what isn't. They all look dead before they're butterflies, anyway. Let's give them a little air!"

A very dainty Japanese fan lay on the table where nothing but the saucer had been at first. Maundeville took it up, and began waving it very gently to and fro.

"If we wake them up ever so slowly," he said; and one, a pretty yellow one, began to stir, fluttered up, and settled again. Then a blue one floated off and returned. Then the two began to chase one another; and soon Maundeville was following the whole lot of them about, talking nonsense, pretty nonsense, all the time, and looking as if they led him more than he drove them.

He followed them round while they danced through the air, now high, now low, till all, except a blue one, were lost in a lot of flowers I had brought. The blue one fluttered across the room to where Miss O'Hagan and Mrs. Vavasour sat side by side.

"Why can't you follow the crowd?" Maundeville asked it, and drove it back towards the flowers, but it fluttered off again, and settled on a white shawl which Mrs. Vavasour had thrown over her shoulder.

"Now I have it! Keep still, please!" Maundeville said, and laid his hand on it. "It stings!" he cried, and drew his hand sharply away.

"Butterflies don't sting!" shouted the boy, who had posed as an authority before.

"Come and try!" Maundeville suggested. "Gently now, or you may be sorry."

The boy drew near, put a hand out and pulled it away with a howl. The butterfly had turned into a small brooch.

"It had better stay there," Maundeville said.

Mrs. Vavasour was as delighted as the children.

"It looks as though it might fly away again," she protested.

"Ah! we must prevent that," Maundeville said, and snapped on the thinnest possible gold chain.

The thing was prettily done, and I turned to Miss O'Hagan, saying something about it.

She didn't notice me, but was staring at Maundeville as if fascinated. He had laughingly accepted Mrs. Vavasour's thanks, and was busy in consoling a small damsel who wept because she wanted another butterfly to settle on her too. He got wonderful sugar-plums out of the child's hair to supply everybody; and a few minutes later the party was over, the last of the children had gone, and Maundeville and I had said good-bye and left together. The evening was fine, and we walked away down Regent Street and turned into the Haymarket.

Although I was ready enough to have Maundeville's company, I hadn't much to say. The fact is that I had been forced, or at any rate tempted, to compare myself with these fellows, of whom I had lately seen so much. The result was humiliating, and I felt sulky. Here, now, was Maundeville, equally at his ease with men, women and children, learned, accomplished, witty, playful, debonair. I envied and admired him, and was to have another sample of his quality that evening.

I had appointed to meet a journalist friend of mine in the Strand, and Maundeville said he would walk with me part of the way.

Then suddenly I remembered that I ought to have had another document in the packet of papers I was carrying; and since no conveyance was handy, we took a short cut by back streets to my flat, Maundeville always observing and commenting as we went.

He was just speaking of the grace of movement shown by a bare-legged girl of ten or so, who slipped ahead of us with her news-sheet and bundle of evening papers, when the child came to grief.

A swarthy fellow, looking like a foreign sailor, lounged suddenly across her path; she ran against him, knocked a pipe out of his hand, and it clattered and broke on the pavement. He stared at her for an instant, then struck her heavily on the side of the head just as she was darting on. She fell in the street with a scream, and I, being nearest the gutter, managed to drag her by her scanty skirts from the wheels of a passing lorry. But by the time I had straightened myself again the man was sprawling. Maundeville had knocked him off the pavement into the street, where he lay stretched for a few seconds as if stunned, and then raised himself on one elbow.

The fall of the child had stopped the near traffic, and the fellow was safe enough. He staggered to his feet an instant later. I saw his right hand go to his side, a woman shrieked from a window above our heads, and he ran in at Maundeville, no one interfering. The child was still hanging a dead weight on my hands, and I wasn't quick enough to do anything, but Maundeville seemed quite able to take care of himself.

Something in the fellow's right hand flashed towards Maundeville's throat, but he slipped to the left, at the same time striking the man's right arm with his own right. Twisting forward, he caught him at the back of the neck with his left hand, and his left leg with his right hand. He fell on one knee and seemed to toss the rascal forward. I heard a crash as the man's head whirled against a plate-glass shop-window, and then he lay still on the pavement.

At once there was a crowd, but Maundeville pushed quickly

through it, reaching the child, whom I still held, but who was now standing.

"She's all right, isn't she?" he asked at my ear. "Here, child! Could you run if I gave you half a sovereign?"

The child looked up, considered an instant, then nodded, casting a glance about her.

"Here, then! Cut when you see your chance. Here's my card. Come to-morrow and let me see you're well."

I saw the girl stoop and bite at the coin, and then felt her tug under my hand.

"But——!" I said.

Something pressed between my knuckles, and I could not keep my hold. Someone stumbled against me, and the crowd was pushing and shouting all around. The child, a small eel of a thing, in any case, had disappeared altogether. Maundeville's back was towards me, and presently I saw he was pushing to the shop doorway, where a policeman stood over the beaten man, who was now sitting up and staring stupidly about him.

"'E tried to knife the gentleman," said a shrill voice in the crowd; "I seed 'im!"

"Nonsense, surely not," said Maundeville. "I think the lady's mistaken, constable."

"I seed the lamplight on it."

"A bangle, I think," Maundeville suggested. "The fellow wears one."

The constable looked and found one, but wasn't quite satisfied. At this a second constable, who had come up, searched the lascar's clothes, and found nothing except a coin or two and some sort of an amulet.

"The fellow's sobered," Maundeville said, "and the child's more frightened than hurt. Why, where's she gone?" He looked about him, but naturally saw nothing of the girl. "Well, that shows she's none the worse, and I refuse to prosecute," he said; "I'll give the chap a lecture."

He spoke sharply to the lascar for a minute or so in a foreign tongue that the man quite evidently understood, and answered humbly enough.

"Better let him go, I think," he ended. "Come along, Armiston.

We shall be late," and he turned away, the policeman letting his man go after a moment's consideration.

Maundeville chatted on, until we reached my rooms.

"You had better take a look at my shoulder," he said then, and I turned on him and had his cloak and dress-coat off in a jiffey. There was a grazing wound over the insertion of the deltoid on the right arm, and the shirt and silk vest had stuck to it.

"Then——" I said, sponging it.

"The bangle had a sharp edge presumably," Maundeville suggested gravely, and then began to laugh. "It didn't occur to those muddle-heads to search *me*," he said, drawing a long sheath-knife from an inner pocket, "or we should have had to attend at the nearest police-station to-night, I suppose, and the police court to-morrow morning. Better give that scrape a good antiseptic scrub, I expect. Probably the man used that knife for everything. My fur cloak saved me, but it also made me devilish slow."

CHAPTER XXI

I AM INVITED TO A CARD-PARTY

The next night Perceval wrote asking me to dine with him at Park Lane, but I refused. I knew I had been growling to everybody about that confounded coffee-mill, and I thought that his invitation was merely a charitable attempt to make me less discontented for a night.

His man, a haughty, pasty-faced individual, who brought the invitation, took back my refusal and thanks; but came again with another note, in which Perceval wrote that it was very important he should see me, and begged me to make an appointment with him for any time after dinner that suited me, either at my flat or his house, as I pleased.

When I found that he really wanted me, I was rather disgusted with myself for having refused his invitation. However, I had done so finally. I sent word that I would look him up at about nine, and as my reward I had a shocking bad dinner alone at the club.

I cursed the Mummy several times that evening before I remembered that it couldn't possibly be held accountable for my present grievance.

Obviously I was becoming—had, in fact, become—a fine specimen of the crusty, crusted elderly bachelor. As I walked to Park Lane I wondered whether a little real hardship or danger, instead of these petty grievances of mine, would not probably do me a world of good.

Well, I was soon to have plenty to occupy me.

Perceval was sitting alone in his dining-room, with fruit and decanters on the mahogany before him. He rose to welcome me, took me to a chair placed ready near his own, and thanked me very warmly for coming.

Really I liked the young fellow more and more, in spite of a certain air of fastidiousness and formality which I thought affectation.

"I think," he said at last, "that if you don't mind we will have the decanters brought up to the smoking-room. Not only will there be less risk of eavesdroppers up there, but also I always fancy myself more reasonable nearer the stars. Nothing," he added, smiling, "seems to matter quite so much up there."

We accordingly mounted to the smoking-room I have already told you of, and it being late we found a few stars overhead, and a great many twinkling lights below.

Here Perceval explained abruptly to me why he had pressed for my company that evening.

"I asked you to come," he said, "because I want to warn you that in four days we intend to have another deal of the cards. This will give you time to consider what position you intend to adopt," and he leant back in his chair and watched me curiously.

"I need no time," I said. "I shall insist upon being one of your card-party; and I don't think I can be prevented from joining it."

He made no reply to this announcement of mine for some little time, but lay back in his chair staring out at the sky.

"I think," he said at last, "it is only fair to say that neither Maxwell nor I can claim any right, as part of our bargain, to make you go so far."

"I suppose not," I said, after some consideration. "I hadn't thought about it. Neither can you prevent me from going as far as I choose."

"There's always some satisfaction," Perceval said, smiling, "in finding that one's first impression of a man is correct. You will continue to be obstinate—I am really inclined to say pig-headed—even to your own disadvantage, and at a certain amount of risk?"

I nodded.

"I have no idea," Perceval went on gravely, "of trying to influence you in this matter one way or the other. You know as much about it now as I do—more, perhaps. But I want to remind you, before the cards are dealt, that we understand you accept our conditions—the conditions that bind us all. Whoever gets the Spade accepts it without calling in outside help to avoid the consequences. Any public inquiry would inevitably end in my cousin's name being dragged in. That would matter comparatively little if her part in the matter were known as it really is. There is nothing discreditable about that to any of us—and least of all to herself. But the mere truth wouldn't suit either the newspapers or their virtuous readers at all. I leave you to imagine the placards and the headlines for yourself. That view of the matter will never occur to her; so it's our business to protect her interests, and we're all quite clear about it."

"Meanwhile, at any rate, you're letting her run another risk," I persisted. "What if she gets the Spade? Maxwell seems to have some idea of what he would do under those conditions, but he didn't tell me."

"Has he?" Perceval asked. "Well, I can guess what it is—and I don't see any reason for not telling you. I should propose marriage in order that I might be better able to look after her. I'm sure he would do the same."

"How on earth can you be sure? Has he told you so?"

Perceval looked at me with some amusement.

"Maxwell and I have known one another," he said, "from the time we fought together over a couple of toy soldiers. We don't need to tell one another everything. We should both propose. Nora would refuse me, as she has refused a dozen or more of other men. She would accept Maxwell—unless she thought that she put him in danger by doing so."

"What on earth do you mean by that?" I asked. "How could she put him in danger?" and Perceval, who seemed now to be talking half to himself, looked up surprised.

"What did I say?" he asked. "Oh, I remember now. I didn't mean anything particular. I don't know why I said that. Now are you going to be one of the card-party? I think it altogether for you to decide."

"Yes," I said. "If I thought there were any risks I should keep clear, I suppose. But it's all rubbish. I'm coming to prove it. Tell the other men that they must admit me, or I'll somehow make it hot for everybody."

"Oh, I don't see why anyone should object," Perceval said. "I'll see to it and let you know. Only remember! The same considerations that bind us must be binding on you. You must take your chance with the rest, and whatever happens you must keep it to yourself."

No one did object evidently. A couple of days later I got a note from Perceval of the time at which the cards were to be dealt at Maundeville's house.

CHAPTER XXII

WHO GOT THE ACE

I hate the east wind as much as any fairly healthy man can, and to tramp in the east wind under a dull sky to take my chance of being made a victim to a confounded Mummy seemed absolutely insane.

As it was fixed that those concerned should meet at five, and settle the matter without any elaboration or delay, I reached the house about a quarter before the hour, and saw Perceval and Maxwell coming down the street together before the door was opened to me. Perceval, dressed as usual point-device, in grey, had a very fine orchid in his button-hole. When I said something about the east wind and the vindictive hag (I was sure she was a hag) about whom we had met, he refused to consider either, and begged me to give my attention to the orchid, as quite as curious and far more beautiful. I went in growling at his levity. I suppose the east wind had got on my nerves. At any rate I was in a shocking bad temper, and knew that quite well.

Bates showed us into the little museum, where Maundeville was ready, with a young fellow to whom I had not spoken before, but whom I remembered seeing at my introduction to the Plain Speakers. He was tall, dark, thin, and looked decidedly consumptive. He was talking fast and excitedly to Maundeville, but broke off abruptly at our coming, and crossing the room, very closely examined the mummy-case, which stood in its usual position against the wall.

We chatted for a few minutes, and then Maundeville looked at his watch.

"Five minutes to the hour," he said, "and we agreed to be punctual. Who else is to come? Only Lethredge and Miss O'Hagan, I believe? Well, we must give them five minutes' grace, I suppose, but, I think, no more."

I said nothing, but the other three men agreed to this at once—even hurriedly, I thought.

A couple of minutes later Bates brought in a letter for Maundeville, who opened and glanced over it, then turned to Bates.

"Let the messenger wait!" he said, and then, directly Bates had left the room, "Listen to this!" he went on. "It's from Lethredge.

"'DEAR MAUNDEVILLE,

"'I was schooling a polo pony this afternoon. He crossed his own legs and broke one of mine. I can't well join you. Put a chair for me and deal to that. Keep the messenger, and let me know by him whether I'm to have the honour of entertaining the Lady. It might break the monotony of my cure—or make it unnecessary! Yours,

"'GUY LETHREDGE.'

"Well," he added, "I suppose we must do what he asks. What do you men think?"

I gave no opinion, being quite ready to let the others settle as they chose. Maxwell nodded his consent. Perceval, considering his orchid, yawned slightly, apologising for doing so, and said he imagined poor Lethredge to be within his rights; but the other young fellow protested hotly. From what he said I inferred that, incomprehensibly enough, he wanted the Ace of Spades, and saw that the smaller the party, the greater his chance of getting it. He was quite rude to Perceval, who merely shrugged his shoulders and became silent.

"Votes are against you," Maundeville said, and the young fellow stopped arguing to cough.

A pack of cards lay on the table, and Maundeville took it up, and then went to the door with it in his hands. "I forgot," he said, "a Frenchman is to bring me a letter of introduction some time this afternoon. I'll make sure that Bates keeps him."

He spoke to Bates at the door and came back.

We had seated ourselves round the table, I happening to be with my back to the Mummy.

Maundeville took a chair opposite to me, and there were then two empty—for the man Lethredge and for Miss O'Hagan.

"Now," he said, shuffling the cards, "I'm going to speak plainly before I deal. I'm sick of this business. I'm ready to stop it and declare all bets off if you fellows are. The joke has gone far enough."

Maxwell looked at him oddly and said nothing. He told me later that he was sure the thing would go on, and therefore it was useless to talk. Besides, he wanted the cards dealt and the matter ended before Miss O'Hagan could come.

Perceval said, "It has gone too far to stop." The other, his name was Steyne, laughed.

"Whatever the rest do, I hold you to your bet," he said. "I hope I've as much pluck as D'Aurelle and Scrymgeour. I'm going to see it through."

Of course I still said nothing. I hardly felt more than a looker on.

"I'm in your hands altogether," Maundeville said politely, "only I don't like it. Indeed, I protest against it. But if you choose, of course, I'm tied."

He looked at his watch again. "Five past," he said. "Does anyone think we ought to wait for Miss O'Hagan?"

All said no at once.

"Cut, please!" Maundeville went on, pushing the pack across to me, and then suddenly changed his mind.

"Cards are queer things," he said. "I've dealt each time before. Let us ask Armiston to do it to-night for a change. I'm sure he won't refuse, will you Armiston?"

The rest turned towards me, no one speaking, and I hesitated, not knowing what to say. I had an intense objection to taking such an active part in a transaction which I thought altogether detestable. I was there practically to make an end of it, and although somehow I couldn't realise that there was any appreciable risk to myself, I disliked letting my hand decide, or even show, who was to be the next man threatened. I was on the point of appealing to them not to ask me, when another point of view made me hesitate.

Having of my own accord taken this affair in hand, I had absolutely no right to shirk anything connected with it merely because I didn't like it. Further, though I listened to everything anyone of these people had to say about the Mummy, I tried to keep an open mind, but not to be too credulous with any. Now if I myself dealt the cards, I could at least be sure that no one had previously determined who should get the Ace of Spades.

"Very well," I said, "I'll deal if I may do it in my own way. How do you do it, Maundeville?"

"I begin with the man on my left," Maundeville said. "I deal slowly, and each man is free to turn up his card if he chooses, directly he gets it. I don't suppose any one of us cares how it is done."

"Only be quick about it," Maxwell added.

"Very well," I said, "I hope the holder of the card won't blame me. Don't touch them, please, till I've finished the pack." And beginning with Maundeville opposite me, I dealt next to the empty chair for Lethredge on Maundeville's left, and so round. Someone shifted Miss O'Hagan's seat from the table just as I began, and Perceval asked Maundeville whether, since there were no ladies present, he might light a cigarette.

I dealt in a dead silence, and dealt slowly. Once I confess to stopping altogether. There was a loud rattle behind my chair, where I knew the mummy-case to be, and to my disgust I had stopped dealing and turned to look over my shoulder before I knew what I was doing. It was only Methuselah, the tortoise, blundering against the wooden case in the course of his wanderings. I cursed him and my own silly nerves, under my breath, and went slowly on.

In those few seconds I noticed all sorts of trifles, all my senses seeming powerfully stimulated.

I heard young Steyne breathing quickly, I smelt Perceval's Turkish tobacco. I saw that Maundeville, leaning back in his chair, looked straight before him at me, drumming noiselessly on the table with his finger-tips while Maxwell watched him. The cards dealt before the empty chair slid and scattered a little, though I never had heard falling cards sound so heavy before. Perceval had to draw his heap together to prevent them from getting mixed with those for Lethredge. I was determined not to hurry, but I seemed to deal those fifty-two cards through all time. When the pack was ended I sighed, and watched while the men picked up their hands, wondering to which of them I had given the Spade. It never occurred to me to look at my own little heap.

"Trump!" said Perceval softly, and held up the Ace, and then began to settle the orchid more securely in his buttonhole, while the rest of us stared at him awhile in silence.

It was he who spoke first, passing his cigarette-case across the table to me. He asked Maundeville at the same time what hour on the following day would be convenient for handing over "the Lady" if he sent round his motor to fetch her.

"One may as well speak of her respectfully," he said, "though apparently one can't speak *to* her with any hope of making friends; and I suppose I can't entertain her in the ordinary sense of the word."

"Why wasn't it dealt to me?" Steyne muttered. "Oh, the cursed contrariness of things! Perceval, be a good fellow and pass her on to me. It would be the greatest possible favour."

"My dear fellow," Perceval remonstrated, "would you have me inhospitable? It's a sort of royal visit, don't you know. Not precisely by invitation, but hardly to be avoided—and, of course, a great honour. Really, I can't give the lady up."

Steyne turned angrily away, muttering something quite audible about d——d affectation, but Perceval didn't heed him.

"Send for the thing when it suits you," Maundeville said. "But to-day is Thursday, and I happen to remember you talked of spending the week-end in Hampshire. Now, as far as our wager is concerned, as I understand it, you keep strictly to its terms if you send on your return."

"That's very nice of you," Perceval said. "I meant to wire, telling my friends that an unexpected visitor prevented me from keeping my engagement. But I know they would be annoyed. I think, do you know, Maundeville, that I'll accept your interpretation of our agreement, if you're sure it doesn't inconvenience you."

So it was arranged that he should send for the Mummy on the following Tuesday, and Maundeville suggested a move out of the museum into the dining-room, where he said there was tea for anyone who cared to have some.

Meanwhile Maxwell had been sitting quiet, saying nothing since Perceval had shown the Ace of Spades. I looked and saw that he sat frowning a little at the table before him. As far as his face expressed anything, it seemed to show some bewilderment. I wondered why.

I was concerned that I had dealt the card to Perceval, but I couldn't bring myself to say so easily. I reminded myself that I had dealt merely to be quite certain of fair play—and yet—if things went badly by any chance I knew quite well how I should feel about my share in it.

But how could they go badly? What could possibly happen?

Perceval was the first to pass through the double doors which ensured quiet for Maundeville in the museum. Steyne followed him, talking querulously in a high-pitched voice about his luck, and I was next.

I heard Perceval say "Nora!" immediately he passed into the dining-room. Steyne broke off short in the middle of his complaint, halting in the doorway; and I, looking over his shoulder, saw Miss O'Hagan standing before us, with one hand resting on the dining-room table. She was very pale, and seemed startled at our sudden appearance—paying no attention to some trivial remark Perceval made, but looking at each of us in turn as we passed into the room!

CHAPTER XXIII

MAXWELL IS SURPRISED

"You've waited for me!" she said, without any attempt at greeting us separately.

"To pour out tea for us? Yes," Perceval answered her, but she paid no attention, looking past me at either Maxwell or Maundeville who followed.

Maundeville, who entered last, ejaculated her name and went forward to her, but she barely noticed him.

"I'm late, I know," she said, "but you've waited. I've been here ten minutes."

"Ten minutes!" Maundeville echoed. "You should have come in at once."

"Your man said you were engaged."

"So we were—but not for you," Maundeville said. "You had a right to be there. But I never heard you."

"You *have* dealt," she decided, looking from one to the other of us. Then there was an appreciable interval before she spoke again, her voice quite unrecognisable.

"Who——?" she began, and stopped. It was Perceval who answered.

"I have the honour," he said. "Now won't you give us tea?"

He pushed a chair up for her, and she sat down without another word and began to fumble with the kettle of boiling water and the tea-caddy. It was quite obvious that she didn't know what she was doing. I counted eight spoonfuls of tea going into that teapot, and then I just put a hand out and moved the tea-caddy. I wanted a cup myself, and I didn't want my nerves jangled more than they had been.

My action roused her and made her think what she was doing. She looked at me, smiled queerly, and paid more attention.

Perceval made a casual remark or two to me, and then softly,

"I shall be back in town on Monday night. Can you come and give me a thorough overhauling?"

"Why?" I asked. "Do you feel ill? You seem all right."

"I feel all right," he said. "My point is that I want you to certify me as sound before I take in this blessed Mummy—or else to know definitely what other cause might account for any trouble after she comes."

This seemed a very reasonable step to take, and I agreed to it. "Fix your own time," I added, and he smiled whimsically at me.

"Dinner at eight," he said. "You wouldn't come two nights ago, but this is a professional engagement. Besides, you can hardly refuse me any reasonable request just now. I might accuse you of being responsible for my position."

This remark worried me. "I did what I thought best," I said. "It enabled me to be quite sure that pure chance decided the matter. I didn't like the job," but Perceval laughed outright.

"You surely don't think I'm such a fool as to hold you responsible?" he asked. "There's even an advantage. I guessed why you agreed to deal. You've always looked with suspicion on the whole lot of us. Now I suppose you'll allow that I, at any rate, am not a criminal."

A few minutes later we said good-bye to Maundeville, and the three of us, Maxwell, Perceval, and I, saw Miss O'Hagan into her carriage, which was waiting for her with Mrs. Vavasour, and then walked towards my place together.

"Did you hear what your cousin told me?" Maxwell asked suddenly. "She was late because just about the time she should have started, a woman, practically a beggar, came to see her."

"She needn't have seen her unless she wanted to," Perceval pointed out.

"Well, the woman came by appointment. She wrote beforehand saying that I had told her to call. As a matter of fact I knew nothing about it till Miss O'Hagan told me."

"Was that what you were looking so puzzled over?"

Maxwell gave no answer for the time, but stopped and looked across the street.

"I'm going through the park," he said at last. "Look me up directly you come back from Hampshire, Percy. Did I look puzzled? Well, if you must know, I was taken aback when you got that card. I would have been ready to lay odds that I knew the man who would get it."

"Complimentary to me!" I said, pretty much nettled. "If you thought *you* knew, I suppose you were sure *I* did."

"Sounds like that, doesn't it?" Maxwell allowed quietly. "I ought to have thought of it before I spoke, for I'm not going to explain just now. I was wrong, any way, you see. Good-bye, both of you. Mind you keep fit, Percy," and he crossed the street and disappeared.

Perceval watched him go, and then turned to me.

"We're all quite mad," he said gravely. "Don't you think so? And Maxwell seems as bad as anybody. Ready to give odds that he knew who would get the spade, was he! Now I wonder where my cousin's opportune beggar came from?"

"That was a mere chance," I suggested. "If Miss O'Hagan is a rich woman, as I suppose she is, she must be constantly liable to have callers of that kind."

"Using Maxwell's name as an introduction? I don't fancy so," Perceval said pretty dryly; and then, having made me promise to dine with him on the Monday night, he left me.

I stayed in my flat that evening, in spite of the workmen's half-completed jobs and the demoniacal coffee-mill.

As a matter of fact, all these mysteries so much kept my attention that night that I didn't remember the embarrassments at all.

CHAPTER XXIV

PERCEVAL IS PHILOSOPHICAL

It was on the Sunday morning of that week-end that instead of going to church I visited a friend of mine, who has a couple of surgical wards in one of the London hospitals. There was a case he wanted to show me.

Cases may be of importance to a surgeon, but simply gruesome to others. There's no need to speak of that one therefore. But to see it I went into the Male Ward, and on leaving it

I suddenly recognised a man in another bed—the lascar whom Maundeville had upset so scientifically near the Haymarket.

"What's wrong with that chap?" I asked Sparratt, nodding towards the fellow's bed.

"Nothing but a very bad shake and a fracture of the surgical neck of the humerus," Sparratt said. "But for a day or two I thought there might be a fracture at the base"—he meant the base of the skull. "The ruffian must have got a most awful wallop. I believe he was under the influence of bhang or some other of their concoctions at the time. I daresay it lessened the shock, but it obscured symptoms."

"How does he account for his condition?" I asked.

"He doesn't. He can't, or won't."

I chuckled, rather amused. "Perhaps I can help you," I said. "Perhaps his English isn't good enough." I thought it would be a good yarn to give Sparratt over one of his Cubans presently.

"Why? Do you know Malay," Sparratt asked, "or whatever he talks? But you wouldn't get anything out of him."

"Oh, I believe I could explain things, if you liked," I said, still grinning internally.

"Then you'll go one better than about the brightest man I know," Sparratt said, grinning in his turn.

"And who may he be?"

"His name's Maundeville," Sparratt said, moving across the ward to the lascar's bed. "I don't suppose you've met him, but he has the gift of tongues, and he talked to the chap the other night for me."

"What happened?" I asked, rather taken aback.

"Oh, he could make him understand, and he scared him a bit," Sparratt said, looking at the shoulder-splint while he talked, "but he couldn't get any explanation. It seemed to follow some drunken row—though with lascars we find that generally means knife."

The situation was amusing, and I was greatly tempted to explain the case to Sparratt, but I actually refrained.

"Well, if your friend who can talk to the man in his own tongue can't help you, I suppose I can't either," I said.

"Knew you couldn't," Sparratt assured me. "Pity I didn't take you on for a box of cigars," and then led the way back to the balcony, where we talked of other things.

On the Monday evening I dined at Park Lane with Perceval, and later I overhauled him thoroughly, as he had wished—as thoroughly, in fact, as though I were acting for an insurance company with which he wanted to insure heavily. I found nothing wrong with him that I considered of any serious importance.

I finished my examination by telling him that the very light defects which were all I could find were accounted for by what he had already told me about himself. As a boy, he said, he had been troubled a good deal with asthma. The attacks were now only occasional; and he found that the ordinary stramonium cigarettes always relieved them.

I do not recollect that anything else of real importance was said or done that evening. Perceval, who seemed altogether at his ease, got me to witness his signature of three documents, which I did, together with his butler.

I cannot say that I myself was so unconcerned. I referred to the Mummy more than once. I remember asking him to believe that I was sincerely doing what I thought best for our investigations when I agreed to deal the cards, and I said, though clumsily enough, no doubt, how much I regretted that the Ace had fallen to him.

He listened patiently, blowing rings of smoke across the room while I talked. We had gone after dinner to the queerly decorated smoking-room at the top of the house, and we were facing a gorgeous sunset, which Perceval seemed to think more worthy of our attention than the Mummy.

"My dear sir," he said at last, gently stroking Bhanavar the Beautiful while he talked, "if I run the risk for a moment of boring you, with references to my affairs and my sentiments, you must forgive me. All that I intended to ask this evening was a medical examination, and that is done."

"I'm here to listen to anything you choose to tell me," I said, "but especially if it bears upon the matter of this accursed Mummy."

He thanked me formally, but lay back in his long chair stroking the cat, and apparently giving her all his attention for some moments before he said more.

"You will, of course, understand," he said at last, "that I recognise my personal feelings and opinions to be of no importance except to the owner. I do not often, I trust, inflict them on anyone. Just now, however, I believe you may be glad to hear them.

"First of all, with reference to your having dealt me the Ace. I repeat emphatically that I understand your motive in agreeing to deal; and I approve of it completely. You can't possibly do me the injustice of imagining that, nevertheless, I blame you for the result. Indeed, I shall be seriously offended if you allow yourself to suggest that point of view again. It assumes even a lower intelligence than I possess."

I muttered something about not intending to suggest that, and promised to say no more.

"I fancy your intelligence is quite as likely as mine to settle this question of the Mummy," I said; and I remember his ambiguous reply perfectly.

He said, "I'm hoping to help you in the end," and then he went on:

"Just now it seems advisable to speak quite plainly. To be frank, I've no great liking for life as I find it. This is a matter of personal taste, personal idiosyncrasy, personal losses, and some disappointments. Though life is quite endurable, I don't think it can ever be enjoyable—and I see no reason for me to make a fuss about any risk there may be of quitting it."

He paused again, apparently picking his words with care.

"Circumstances for which it would be ridiculous to blame anyone," he went on, "have prevented my life from being happy for several years. Things have so arranged themselves lately, that when I began to think happiness possible I found myself mistaken. Life, therefore, while quite endurable, as I have said, isn't a thing I cling to at all. I'm ready to drop it—just as I drop this cigarette, which isn't drawing properly."

His manner was so quiet and composed that I checked myself from answering angrily.

"Your attitude doesn't seem particularly heroic," I said. "In fact, it's pretty slack, if no worse;" but he smiled at me, with no sign of irritation.

"I have sometimes fancied," he said, "that, it being the business of medical men to keep others alive, they often end by valuing life extravagantly. One can't depreciate the value of the commodity one deals in."

"At any rate, it can't be restored or replaced," I pointed out.

"Ah! Who assures you of that?" he asked me. "You're speaking a trifle at random, aren't you? And at any rate I'm going to try another cigarette from a different box," which he accordingly did, and, having lit it and satisfied himself that it drew satisfactorily, he looked at me again with a somewhat whimsical smile, and went on talking.

"If things go wrong with me, from your point of view, while the Mummy is here, you must remember what I've told you. Waste no time in grieving about me, or in blaming yourself. Each death must logically make the problem easier to solve."

Even in that smoking-room there were signs of care and taste in design, with plenty of money to help them.

"It seems to me that you have more cause than most men to think life worth living," I said. "I don't understand why you should be anxious to quit it. We all think ourselves sick of things at times, but we don't give in, and soon we change our opinion about it. Try a canter before breakfast, and a tonic."

"Against the Mummy?" He smiled. "Let us suppose that I'm the spoilt child who can't get the moon and won't look at anything else." Then after a pause, "But do me the favour of assuming that I mean precisely what I say—and no more. I didn't say I was anxious to quit life. I said it is quite endurable, but that I don't cling to it."

"That's abnormal," I grumbled, and he smiled again.

"The normal apparently is to declare that you look forward to a better and happier life in the world to come," he said, "and to pay your doctor to keep you from that happy consummation as long as he can."

"Most of us know that we've done very little to qualify for the change," I said.

"I fear I shan't improve with keeping," he replied lightly. "But let us keep to our point, though I'm afraid I'm a shocking bore of a host. The essential is this. I've not said less than I mean. I'm not more sick of things in general than I have told you; and if I come to 'grief' in the next fortnight, don't let anything persuade you that I've been fool enough, putting it mildly, to settle matters for myself. I can't imagine any conditions under which I should commit suicide. I'm certainly not going to do it out of pique."

"When I talked the matter over with you last," I said, "you had no theory about this, or at any rate you gave none. Have you any now?"

"None worth the name," he said, after a little consideration. "I don't want to trouble you with mere fancies that I can't back up by evidence. If any idea occurs to me that's really reasonable, I'll let you know at once. Now let's drop the subject!"

CHAPTER XXV

PERCEVAL ENTERTAINS THE MUMMY

I left Perceval fairly early that evening. He had told Maxwell that I was going to overhaul him, and Maxwell had asked me privately to let him hear the result. I knew my rooms were disordered owing to the workmen there during the day, and I went straight to Maxwell's quarters, to tell him of my chat with Perceval while it was fresh in my mind. I found Maundeville with him, arguing hotly against any further experiments with the Mummy; and he went on with his argument, calling on me to back him up.

I said little, for I honestly felt that, fantastic as the notion had been, and in very dubious taste, it couldn't decently be dropped at its present stage.

This was precisely Maxwell's argument. As a matter of fact, he didn't argue. He merely stated his opinion, and listened with a patience that rather surprised me while Maundeville made sarcastic comments on people who knew they were in the wrong, but were too pig-headed to acknowledge it.

"I'm not going to back out just now," he said, when Maundeville stopped. "It doesn't square with my notion of playing the game. That's all about it. Otherwise, with the infernal thing going to Perceval to-morrow, I should be glad enough to cry quits. My notions don't bind you, though, Maundeville. If I thought as you do, I suppose I should chuck it at once. Why should you go on? Indeed, honestly, I believe it would be safer for you to stop."

He said this with some emphasis, and Maundeville noticed it.

"I don't understand you," he said. "I'm arguing for an end to our bets, just because it seems plain that I don't run the risk apparently falling to the rest of you. I've reminded you before that the Mummy has been with me for weeks, and I am none the worse. I can speak plainly because of that."

"Nevertheless, I think you share the risks," Maxwell persisted, staring at him curiously, and Maundeville seemed annoyed.

"Very well, my dear fellow! That closes my mouth," he said. "I ask Armiston to witness that I've done what I could to stop the Mummy's visits," and he lit another cigar and puffed away as if he meant to say no more.

"What do you think of Perceval?" Maxwell asked me. "He's fit enough, isn't he? He won't mind your telling us, you know."

"Oh, he's fit enough," I said.

"Except for his asthma," Maundeville added. "You know about that, of course. I believe he still has an occasional turn, and uses those confounded stramonium cigarettes."

"The attacks seem very slight," I said. "What's your objection to the cigarettes?"

"A mere fancy of mine," he answered carelessly; "he smokes strong ones, and I think the quality varies."

He and I then left Maxwell's together, and he refused to talk of the Mummy as we walked, saying he was altogether sick of the subject. He thought he would cremate the thing, he told me, so that no more foolery could be possible with it.

The days went by and Perceval seemed all right, which made me more cheerful, as did the fact that Miss O'Hagan often came to me, openly anxious about the results of the Mummy's stay with her cousin. She gave no reason for making me her confidant; but she begged me to keep her informed about him, and arranged to call daily for my report. There was to be a note with Mudge for her when I could not report in person. But somehow on most mornings I managed to be in at half-past ten. Well, as I say, my sitting-room and rather dingy consulting-room seemed all the brighter. After all, I dare say Mudge, who is a regular ladies' man, gave things an extra polish. I know he ran up a pretty bill in my name for cut flowers, and he stuck a flaming Japanese sunshade in my grate, without asking whether I liked it.

I grumbled to her about it, telling her I was sure she was the cause; and straightway she took the first chance of praising the blessed thing before Mudge. It was the only time I ever saw Mudge blush.

He seemed to think that on the occasions of her calls there must be no possibility of interruption. Maundeville came once while she was there, and I found afterwards that he had declared I was "not at home," and had stuck to it in spite of some argument on Maundeville's part.

The latter came again the next day, and, half laughing, told me. I treated the matter with some carelessness, but thought it was as well to say casually that she was there for such news of Perceval as I could give.

"Ah! She's interested," he remarked.

"Naturally! He's her second cousin," I reminded him.

"Of course! And she's anxious—like the rest of us," he agreed. "It should console him, eh, what? Hardened bachelors like you and me don't have young women inquiring about our healths like that. Well, we must look after him—if only for her sake."

"We're trying to do so—aren't we?" I asked him.

"I can't say I've done much," he declared. "I've had one of my fits of incredulity. At times I've forgotten about our bugbear altogether. Then I've remembered it only to laugh. But look here! Do you know, I think it's getting on Perceval's nerves. I think he wants cheering up, and I'm ready to help. Let's take it in hand, turn and turn about. 'Wine that maketh glad the heart of man,' and so forth, don't you know?"

"If he needs cheering up I'm willing to try, though I hadn't noticed anything dismal about him," I said.

"You haven't known him as long as I have," Maundeville reminded me. "He doesn't moan or whimper, but he's getting hipped most infernally. We'll take him in hand, you, Maxwell, and I, between us, and in turn."

He had seated himself comfortably in my favourite easy-chair, and while he talked his very keen grey eyes were roving all about the room. I've never seen eyes with more life and energy in them than Maundeville's. I saw now that he was taking in the details of Mudge's floral decorations—roses, that morning—that made the room sweet.

"Now if I were Mudge," he said, as though he knew it was Mudge's department, "I should sacrifice some kitchen basin for those flowers, or else let you in for a rose-bowl. They look top-heavy in those tall vases. I abominate the scentless ones, don't you? They're like a beautiful woman with no soul."

That was all very pretty, but, as I've said, he was occupying my chair, and I had some writing to do. I grunted that beautiful women, with or without souls, were not in my line.

"And as for the three of us taking Perceval in hand systematically," I said, rising, "that will need a lot of tact, or he'll turn restive. Perceval won't stand having three nurses."

"You think because I keep you out of your special chair," Maundeville said good-humouredly, getting out of it as he spoke, "that my tact isn't to be depended on? Well, perhaps you've some excuse. But think my suggestion over!" and he laughed, and limped away before I had framed a satisfactory reply. I heard him complimenting Mudge on his roses at the outer door.

To a large extent after this we did manage somehow that one or other of the three should look in on Perceval, or get him out, pretty well daily. In reply to my occasional questions, he told me that the neighbourhood of the Mummy did not trouble him in any way, day or night, except that his valet took a dislike to the thing and left suddenly.

As a matter of fact, to have a certain amount of definite arrangement about him, with Maxwell and Maundeville, suited me very well just then. An old friend of mine had been invalided home from India and was dying at Bath. I could do no more for him than any other practitioner; but he liked to see me and to yarn over old times. I used to go down once a week or thereabouts and stay a night—sometimes a week-end. I missed a visit to Bath the first week that Perceval had the Mummy. I got a rather reproachful message from my old friend, and arranged to go down two days later for the week-end.

CHAPTER XXVI

WHAT HAPPENED TO PERCEVAL

As it happened, I didn't remember, when arranging my visit to Bath, that Maundeville had spoken of going to Paris for some conference of Egyptologists. When I did remember I thought it of no particular importance, but I went to Maxwell's rooms to suggest that he should keep an eye on Perceval.

I found him in and busy. The table of his sitting-room was strewn with feathers, silks, hooks, gold tinsel, scissors and other paraphernalia, and he was fly-tying.

I told him of my week-end engagement, and he listened and considered, saying nothing until he had finished off a black gnat, at which his long fingers worked most surprisingly quickly.

"I must think what I can do," he said at last. "Thanks to Maundeville, I've had leave to fish some of the best water on the Test, and I've made all my arrangements. Of course, it would be simple enough to drop it."

"Well?"

"Well, the fact is that I was particularly keen about the business, and I've been telling Percy of it. If he finds me in town he'll want to know the reason, and he won't be easily humbugged. He is getting a bit restive already about our supervision. I think Maundeville has overdone it a little and set his back up."

He added, in a grumbling sort of way, that perhaps Maundeville would be better employed seeing to the safety of his own skin.

"What do you mean?" I asked him. "I don't see that Maundeville is in any danger whatever, and if any man can take care of himself, I should think he can. What are you driving at?" But Maxwell, looking tolerably sheepish, said he thought the Mummy had got on his nerves.

"I think they'd be steadier if I had the Spade myself," he said.

"I fancied perhaps a couple of days' fishing would put me right," and he explained no further.

The end of it was that after he, Maundeville, and I had met and talked the matter over, we arranged that Maxwell should fish the Test on Friday and Saturday, returning by the last train on Saturday night, and looking Perceval up at once, with the excuse of telling him about the result of the fishing. I was not to leave for Bath until Saturday morning—staying there till Monday. Maundeville said he would take the night boat across from Newhaven to Dieppe on Saturday evening.

Of course Perceval heard nothing of these little arrangements, for which we were half-apologetic even to one another.

On Friday evening, then, Maxwell being away, I occupied his seat at the opera, sitting by Perceval, as for the last three seasons they had taken stalls together. Then we supped and I went back with him to Park Lane, and stayed there a long time without having to manufacture any excuse for doing so.

When at last I found that the time was 2 a.m. and rose to go, I asked him to let me look at the mummy-case.

He led the way to his bedroom, which I had never been in before. A curtain of Eastern work was hanging on the wall. He drew that aside and showed me the mummy-case lying flat, with a sort of a pall of tapestry over it.

I bent to pull this off, and was startled when a black shadow sprang from it into the room. It was only Bhanavar the cat, and Perceval, politely taking no notice of my momentary confusion, explained that from the time the Mummy had been brought into the house Bhanavar had been attracted by it. If shut out of the room she hung about the landing outside, and slipped in at the first opportunity. If left alone she lay curled for hours together upon the case, and even seemed to forget her meal times.

"I believe that the servants," Perceval added, "have now some of the same objection to poor Bhanavar that they have for the Mummy. To be sure that she doesn't suffer, I have to supply some of her meals myself," and going outside to the landing, he returned with a saucer of bread-and-milk, to which he called the cat. Meanwhile I had looked at the mummy-case, and of course found nothing fresh. I threw the tapestry over it again, and Bhanavar, when she had finished her meal, went back to her chosen bed.

No doubt she was attracted by the faint odours still about the case, for some scents will draw cats long distances. But the sight of the animal curled above the Mummy, just as Perceval drew the curtain across the alcove again, stirred my imagination and remained in my memory.

"I should object to having that animal in my room at night," I said to Perceval, as I wished him good-night; but he merely smiled in his politely tolerant way.

"The one's as harmless as the other, I fancy," he said, leading the way down through the stillness of the sleeping house, "and we are agreed that the whole thing is purely fanciful."

"You couldn't give me a bed here, I suppose?" I said, yawning. "I'm suddenly sleepy, and I'm sure there are no damp sheets in the place."

"I must be inhospitable for, I trust, the first time," he answered, with a little laugh. "I take it that for a few nights more I must have only one guest," and seeing that my dodge was obvious, I wished him good-night again, and went away down Park Lane, where only a policeman was visible, standing motionless on the edge of the kerb.

Perceval saw me from the door, and the last sight I had of him was as he stood with upturned face, apparently watching a star. As I tumbled into my bed to get a short rest before the early train for Bath, I hoped that he was already asleep. But even the glimpse of that drawn curtain, with the knowledge of Bhanavar and the Mummy both sleeping behind it, had made me restless, and as a matter of fact I did little but toss about, until Mudge brought me early coffee and shaving-water.

I managed to ascertain, however, by manufacturing an excuse for a message before leaving Paddington, that Perceval, who scribbled a reply from his bed, had apparently had a better night than I.

Very likely he detected my object, and sighed good-humouredly over my inconvenient attention.

I reached Bath punctually, and was very glad that I had gone.

My old friend's trouble had become acutely complicated dur-

ing the previous night, and nothing more could be done, except
to make his end as easy as possible. He was conscious when I
arrived, and pleased to see me; but he died that afternoon, and
feeling myself useless, and a mere bore to his relatives, who were
comparative strangers, I made the excuse of professional engagements to slip away up to town again that same evening.

I drove straight to my rooms, with no particular plans made
for the rest of the evening, but as I mounted the stairs I recognised
Maxwell's voice, and found him at my door talking to Mudge. I
saw at once a reasonable excuse for his visit, an artificial fly being
fixed in the side of his neck. While I cut it out, which was possible
without much trouble to either of us, he explained that the fly
had been fixed there by another angler, who, having vague fears
of jugulars, carotids, et cetera, had begged to be excused from
removing it. Maxwell, therefore, had returned sooner than he
had intended.

"I didn't expect to find you," he explained, "but I thought
Mudge could tell me who did duty for you. Now I'll look up
Perceval, after getting a change. I'm due later at a house near his."

I went with him, and we walked briskly through a fine warm
night.

We were within perhaps thirty yards of the house, when the
door opened, and a man stood for a second in the track of light
streaming from the hall. Then the door closed, and he moved
down the steps and away along Park Lane in front of us.

"Who's that?" Maxwell asked me. "Isn't it Maundeville?"

My sight wasn't good enough to depend on in the dusk of the
evening. It might be Maundeville, for anything I could tell. "But
he should be out of town by this time," I said.

"I'll see, at any rate," he said, and pushed on ahead of me.
Presently I heard him call, "Hi! Maundeville!" and in a moment
the man in front turned and came slowly back. As he came I
recognised the characteristic little limp.

"Well, this is luck!" he said. "Perceval there has turned me out.
Wants a good sleep, he says, and I was wondering what to do with
myself for a few hours. I haven't got to read my paper in Paris till
to-morrow evening, so we've been dining together."

"We were going to look him up," I said.

"Do! Do!" Maundeville agreed. "I wonder if I dare venture in with you? He gave me my *congé* quite distinctly; and Perceval, dear fellow, is a man with whom I never feel free to take a liberty. It's different with you, though, Maxwell. Rouse him up, and I'll risk a snub under your protection. You're more intimate than I."

"I shouldn't be intimate long, if I took liberties with him," Maxwell said a trifle dryly. "It's not really late yet, though."

"Of course it isn't," Maundeville agreed, "and I'm devilish thirsty. Let's go in on him and make a night of it! I start for Paris too early to go to bed. Come along! We'll give that confounded Mummy a wake. A tantalus and a couple of syphons on the case will keep the Lady quiet, I think," and he turned towards the house. "Perceval will be mad with us," he said; "but who cares? He's very misanthropic to-night—so was I! 'Comfort me with flagons.'"

"He's a bit screwed," Maxwell said to me in an undertone, dropping behind, but Maundeville heard him at once.

"So I am, dear boy, so I am!" he agreed, turning; "but most awfully thirsty. So's Perceval. His dignity makes him seek seclusion. Queer thing! I don't remember drinking much. But he was most charming to-night. 'We arena' fou! We arena' fou.'" He hummed softly. "But we're uncommonly near it!" he added gravely. "Queer thing! What did we drink? Hock! Hic, haec, hoc—hiccups. 'Faith! there must have been some stingo in the ginger!' Come along! won't he be mad?" and he moved towards Perceval's door again, and then stood looking back at us.

"If Percy's the least bit the worse, he'd never forgive us for seeing him," Maxwell whispered to me. "It's the sort of thing he couldn't stand at all."

"You might go in alone," I suggested, "though I don't know that you should. If he has gone to bed, let him sleep it off. Maundeville would probably insist on going back too."

"I'm going back anyway!" Maundeville insisted. Whether he actually overheard me, or whether he merely spoke at random, I don't know.

"You fellows are too sober for me. Perceval and I are inspired. I've a notion to-night for translating Hafiz into English verse. Perceval shall help. I foretell Omar Khayyám despised and rejected. Good-night!" and he ran up the steps, chanting rhythmically in some foreign tongue.

"Oh, this will never do!" Maxwell muttered. "Maundeville!" he called softly. "Percy's no use at Persian. I'm a much better hand at it. Come away, man! Come away, there's a good fellow! I know a place where we can have a private room as long as we want it. Look here! choose any stanza of Hafiz that you like. I'll back myself for a box of cigars—winner to choose his own brand—that I beat your translation into English verse. Yourself to be umpire."

For a moment Maundeville hesitated on the top step, a hand raised as though about to batter Perceval's door.

"Where?" he said.

"The Banyan."

"The Banyan!" Maundeville stood considering with tipsy gravity, and then began to laugh. Once begun he couldn't stop, and the street rang with his shouts.

"Oh, come along, man!" Maxwell implored him, and, getting him by the arm, hurried him into a passing taxi, and I followed them.

It was an unpromising beginning to a sort of Arabian Night's entertainment, but it ended all right.

A cup of tea made Maundeville much as usual, only even more brilliant and amusing.

He beat Maxwell at the rhyming, by Maxwell's own admission, and when the latter rose declaring that he must keep another appointment, Maundeville turned his attention to me, 'phoned for his own motor, and took me to his own house, where we sat discussing all manner of subjects till he was told that everything was ready for him to go.

He persuaded me to see him off at the station, and wasn't very far from convincing me that it would be rather an amusing affair to see him on to the boat.

As it was, his motor took me back to my flat, and I went to my bed at an hour when a good many folk are beginning the day.

I knew nothing more until I was roused by being roughly shaken, while a voice at my elbow cried:

"Perceval is dead! Poor Percy's dead!"

CHAPTER XXVII

BHANAVAR AND THE MUMMY

I sat up, suddenly wide awake, just as Mudge rattled at my blinds and let broad daylight into the bedroom. Maxwell was standing at my bedside.

I slipped out of bed, staring at him. While he went on talking, and I stood in my pyjamas listening to him, I could hear the undertone of running water which Mudge had turned on for my cold bath. I suddenly realised that Maxwell had begun his story before I was ready for it.

"Wait!" I said, pointing to a chair. "Sit down and begin again. If he's dead, we gain nothing by hurry." While I spoke, I remembered how Maxwell had come to my flat on the first occasion, and how I had vexed him by some remark of the same kind. But this time he made no objection. I suppose he understood my clumsy ways better.

"You're sure he's dead?" I asked him, and he nodded, seeming suddenly to lose his voice.

Mudge reappeared in the doorway, and I told him to bring in brandy and a glass.

"Take a nip," I said to Maxwell. "I won't be a minute," and I turned into the bathroom, splashed into the cold water, and came out feeling that now I had my wits about me. Maxwell was sipping a little brandy while Mudge stood stiffly before him, holding the decanter. He somehow gave me a ludicrous idea of a sentry presenting arms to his officer.

It suddenly occurred to me that I had no idea of the time. I looked at my watch, lying on the little table with the coffee-tray beside my bed, and I found it was a quarter past nine.

"Make coffee and bring it in directly it's ready," I said to Mudge. "Tell me while I shave," I went on to Maxwell. "But wait a minute! Have you told the police?"

"No," he said.

"The servants will be disturbing things at Park Lane," I pointed out.

"No one is there who knows," he replied. "I locked the door and brought away the key and his d——d fool of a man too. The fellow's down in the cab."

"Go on!" I repeated, and interrupted him no more.

His story was that, being early awake, he went round to Park Lane, deciding to have breakfast with Perceval. The new valet, much to his disgust, met him with a smirk of amusement, and told him confidentially on the stair that his master had been "carryin' on" the night before, and was sleeping it off.

Maxwell snubbed him sharply for his confidence, which he supposed to be accurate enough, ordered him to wait outside, and went in alone.

On going towards the bed, the first thing Maxwell noticed was that Bhanavar the cat lay coiled at the foot, her black fur conspicuous on the white silk quilt, which was tossed in a heap. Perceval lay with his face turned from where Maxwell stood, and Maxwell moved quietly round the foot of the bed to the other side, meaning to go out again without disturbing him if he were still asleep.

In doing so, he stumbled heavily over something on the floor, and only saved himself from a fall by catching at the foot of the bed.

At once he saw that what his foot had struck was the mummy-case, tumbled upon the floor. But what immediately concerned him most was that the noise he made did not in the least disturb Perceval.

He moved up to the head of the bed, pulled away the tumbled pillows and bedclothes, and saw at once that Perceval was dead.

"I called no one," he said, "and I told no one. I made absolutely certain that he *was* dead, and then I locked the door and came for you, bringing his man with me. I only told him as we came. I wanted no one in the room till we saw it together."

By the time he had finished I was ready; and without staying to make any useless comments on what he told me I led the way out, and we went at once to Park Lane. The door was opened by the butler, who had evidently not found anything wrong yet, and who stared at the valet.

"We're going to Mr. Perceval's room," I said. "You had better come up with us," and having gone up the stair, followed by him and the valet, who was now merely a flabby, abject, pale nonentity, I went into the room with Maxwell, leaving the other two outside on the landing.

I won't harrow you with more details than are needed to make you see what met my eye at the first glance, and what I thought might be really important.

The room was dusky, for, as Maxwell remembered afterwards, he had pulled the blinds down again before leaving the room.

He raised them now, and the light fell first upon the black cat, which had coiled herself again at the lower end of the bed. Then, creeping up as the blind went higher, it showed the tumbled bedclothes and the vague outline beneath. I went round the foot of the bed, and if Maxwell had not already told me, I should have stumbled, like him, over the mummy-case, which lay diagonally between the bed and the wall. I stepped over it, and past a little table that stood by the bedside, and I drew back the bedclothes.

There was nothing particularly shocking in what I saw. Indeed, at a casual glance one might have imagined that Perceval had merely been tossing about in his bed before sound sleep had overtaken him. But looking more closely, I could be quite sure that he had been ill before he slept, and that he had probably risen from the bed after lying down. Of his death there was no room for any doubt. He had been dead several hours.

Under the bedclothes, as I turned them back, I noticed a pencil lying near his half-closed hand. I then looked about me for any scrap of writing there might be.

There was a scribbling-pad upon the little table at the bedside, and there was scrawling on the block now, but I had to carry it to the window before I could make it out.

It ran irregularly as follows:

"DEAR ARMISTON,
"I said I would write if I suspected anything. But I am tipsy.

What did I drink? Let me think. Silly rhyme! I'm still thirsty. I told you—To be plain—Pen too heavy. M. . . ."

"What's that last word?" Maxwell asked me, peering at it.

"It's not complete," I said, looking at it again. "It begins with M, I'm practically sure. The next letter is *a* or *u*. Then it scrawls off."

"It looks as though he tried to write 'Mummy,'" Maxwell suggested.

"Perhaps," I agreed. "But it might almost equally possibly be an attempt at Maxwell, or Maundeville. In any case, it's meant for me. I think we'll put it away and say nothing about it for the moment. One can always produce it later if need be."

The cries of a woman in hysterics now rose on the landing outside.

"Some fool has been babbling," I said, hastily putting the paper into my pocket. "The murder's out."

"The murder!" Maxwell repeated, looking at me.

"The mischief, then—or what you please," I allowed. "We must speak to the servants and have the butler in. Perhaps in that way we can get a few minutes more to look round before the police come."

Maxwell agreed, and we went to the door. The butler was there still with the valet. There were also three women-servants, one being an elderly woman, who, I found, was wife to the butler and was a sort of cook-housekeeper, and two under-servants, one of whom was crying.

I frightened her into silence roughly enough, and bade the housekeeper and the other maid take her to her room. "You had better come in," I said to the butler; and I told the valet to stay where he was, as I should need a messenger later.

No doubt my face or manner told them what was poor Perceval's condition, though I did not mention him. The hysterical girl was led away, sobbing more quietly, and the butler, with a very grey face, followed us back to the room.

I suppose that experience in our diverse professions kept Maxwell and me from showing much, whatever we might feel. But the butler's greyness of face was so marked, though he

followed and said nothing, that I pulled an easy-chair out from
the wall and made him sit in it before we could do anything else,
or decide under the circumstances what was best to do.

The man of his own accord played into our hands when he
was able to pull himself together, speaking first to Maxwell.

"You'll bear me out, I'm sure, sir, that my poor master hadn't
the habit of it. I never saw him like that before, sir. He could take
his glass of wine and enjoy it, as you know, sir, but always like a
gentleman, and never what you might call really drinking."

"What do you mean, Dale? Who talks about drinking?" Maxwell asked him sharply.

"It's best to be plain with you and the doctor, sir, if we can keep
it from going further. Mr. Perceval had taken too much last night,
Captain Maxwell; I could see that, though I needn't tell you he
was as nice as ever. But I never knew him like it before, and I keep
count of every bottle that's opened in this house. Still, if it once
gets outside that he had taken a glass last night, folk'll say he was
a drunkard. That's as far as can be from the truth. You know that
yourself, Captain Maxwell, sir."

Maxwell looked at him for a moment and then at me.

"I know your master didn't drink, and I'm inclined to agree
with you, Dale," he said. "Dr. Armiston, what do you think?"

I had picked up Perceval's cigarette-case, which lay on the
little table beside the bed, and I was examining the cigarettes. On
one side of the case was "Dimitrinos," on the other three cigarettes marked as containing stramonium, a common remedy for
asthma. On an ash-tray were two stumps, each of the stramonium brand. I put back the case and the cigarette-stumps exactly
as I had found them, and considered what Dale and Maxwell had
said. I then remarked that it wasn't my business to supply the
papers with sensational copy, but that I didn't see quite how to
prevent it.

"A public inquiry may be necessary," I said; "I can't at present
be sure it can be avoided. There's that man of Mr. Perceval's too;
I don't believe any mortal power can keep that booby's tongue
quiet. I suppose he has chattered already."

"Then you're wrong, sir!" the butler said, with sudden passion,
sitting upright. "He's spoke to no one yet, but me and you and

Captain Maxwell. He's had no chance, and he'll have none." He half rose out of the chair, and sank back again, and with a sort of murmured apology to us, suddenly became the quiet, conventional, grey-faced butler again. Maxwell and I just glanced at one another, and then went on examining the room.

The mummy-case was the only other thing that seemed worth any attention.

"If people come in and see this thing lying about," I said openly to Maxwell, "it is sure to make them curious and give them more to gossip about. Don't you think so, Dale?"

Dale did think so, and said so with an emphasis that would have amused me at any other time.

"Can you stand it in your room till dark?" asked I.

Dale, like a good fellow, said he could stand anything that would help to keep his poor master's name out of the papers. So we moved the Mummy to his room, and then I sent a note to a police superintendent not far off, who was a patient of mine, telling him of the sudden death—asking him to meet me at Park Lane if possible, and not to say anything more than was necessary outside, until he was sure that public interests made a public inquiry advisable.

I have no wish whatever to suggest that our police, particularly those of the higher ranks, are open to bribery, or are influenced, to the detriment of their duty, by the social position of those with whom they are dealing. If any man was to blame for it, it was I. But the inspector, I fancy, was favourably prejudiced to start with, because he knew me and believed me apparently to be an honest man. Perhaps, too, the general surroundings didn't suggest anything to hide, and besides, I daresay we seemed quite frank.

I told him, before Maxwell and Dale and the valet, that there was a possibility that death had been due to an overdose of stramonium contained in cigarettes, and I suggested that the matter should be kept as quiet as possible until there had been time to examine and test the theory.

I told him plainly that Perceval had been intoxicated the night before, and that our particular desire was to prevent the fact from being generally known.

I obtained his suggestion as to the right course to follow, and told him that I would see that Maundeville, Perceval's companion of the previous evening, put himself in communication with the authorities as quickly as possible.

Nothing was said of the Mummy or of Perceval's scrawl which was in my pocket. The valet gave evidence that his master came home "as drunk as a lord," and that he left him in his bed.

Dale testified, with obvious unwillingness, to the same effect —adding that he had never seen it happen before.

I supplemented this by hinting that small quantities of stramonium might act more powerfully together with overdoses of alcohol, and said that I would get authoritative opinions on that point.

The inspector left to report accordingly. As I left I told the valet to take Bhanavar from the room, and to keep her out. I am indifferent to cats, and admired Bhanavar merely as an ornament. I didn't therefore give her any particular attention; and I went to Maundeville's house, got his Paris address, and cabled him to return as quickly as possible, Perceval being dead, and to see me immediately. Maxwell and I then went to Perceval's solicitors and gave them all possible information about what had happened and what we had done—always excluding the Mummy. I then insisted that Maxwell should tell Miss O'Hagan of her cousin's death, and begged him to come afterwards and dine with me that evening in my flat—making the best of what Mudge could do for us. I thought it as well that we should talk things over together alone, and agree on what further should be done.

He came in to dinner looking absolutely ill, but gave me no details of his interview, nor did I ask for any.

The Mummy was smuggled back that same night to Maundeville's house, and while we were at dinner Mudge brought in a wire from Maundeville, saying that he would leave Paris that night for home, and would call on me or see me at his house, whichever I preferred.

I telephoned his man to tell him on his arrival that I would see him in my own flat.

CHAPTER XXVIII

MAUNDEVILLE CONFESSES

I was sitting alone the next morning over a breakfast that I had no liking for, when Mudge announced Maundeville.

He came in looking trim as usual, but very fagged.

"This is a very bad business, Armiston," he said, "a shocking bad business! How did it happen?"

"No one knows yet," I said. "No one but his servants saw him alive after you did."

"Good heavens! No wonder you cabled me," he muttered. "What a fix!"

"You'll be asked, I imagine, to say what you know about his movements the evening before last," I said.

"Of course! Of course! Who else can?" Maundeville agreed. "And the truth is that the later part of the evening isn't much more than a dream to me—until I found myself back at that place drinking tea and talking nonsense with you and Maxwell."

"Back at what place?"

"The restaurant. The Banyan."

"When were you there before?"

Maundeville stared. "Why, man, we dined there! Didn't you know?"

"How should I?"

"Lord! I must have been worse than I thought," he muttered to himself. "Of course you couldn't know if I didn't tell you, and if you didn't see Perceval," he agreed. "I took it for granted you knew. What a scandalous business! Honestly, I didn't know that we drank much. What do his servants say about Perceval?"

"They say he was drunk."

"But that doesn't account for things, does it?" Maundeville asked fretfully. "Frankly, I thought he was. But now that I'm sure I was drunk myself, what I thought about him isn't worth anything as evidence. Good Lord! Fancy having to own to the police, and to a respectable bourgeois jury, that one was the worse for drink, and that Perceval was the same! I'm almost sure that I've met the coroner for this district too. What on earth can I do, Armiston? I'm too tired to think, man! I can't have slept two nights ago, can I? And last night I crossed again, and I couldn't sleep then. Who could?"

"Have you had breakfast?" I asked.

"Not I," he answered. "I wired for my motor to meet me at the station and came straight here. I can't eat, though. Give me something to drink."

I gave him a cup of *café au lait* mixed with egg, and with a little brandy in it.

He sipped it quickly, and presently looked less harassed and began to talk again.

"Your cable was handed to me just as I was going to answer what the fellows over there said on my paper."

"I'm afraid it upset all your arrangements," I said; "but if only for your own sake I felt you must know at once."

He gave an indifferent shrug. "What did the paper matter? They had said nothing worth reply. Have you a hypodermic you can lend me?"

"What for?" I asked.

"Just to put some life into my stupid brains, my dear fellow," he said. "I feel as if I were thinking through a blanket. My hypodermic case must be in my evening clothes." I gave him a syringe and watched while he turned down a sock and injected a few drops, fifteen minims, I think, of a colourless fluid, just above his ankle.

"Strychnine?" I suggested.

"No. I won't give you the formula yet."

He stretched and shook himself vigorously, and insisted on washing out my syringe at once with hot water.

"Man!" he said, "I can put life into myself, but poor Perceval! I can't wake the dead."

He sat quiet. It seemed to me that already, whatever the reason might be, he showed much more vitality; but, of course, I had given him a pick-me-up. His face never had much colour, and it was almost colourless still; but a certain firmness of flesh seemed to show itself, and the eyes looked less tired and lined.

"Poor Perceval!" he repeated. "Death in itself always seems to me a very unimportant thing when age has come. But he was young."

He roused himself impatiently and looked at me.

"Help me to look at things from a practical point of view, Armiston. Can we save everybody trouble by just telling everything as we know it? Poor Perceval and I dined together and drank too much. I must own to that and keep back nothing."

"You forget the Mummy," I said.

"Man alive, what can the Mummy have to do with it? It doesn't come in at all!"

"I can't tell you," I said. "I don't say that it has anything to do with it. But certain promises were made to say nothing to outsiders about the Mummy or what happens in connection with it. Perceval got tipsy. If that was against his habits and principles, what made him break them? If anything crops up about the mummy-case in his room, then it will inevitably be remembered sooner or later that there was a mummy-case in Scrymgeour's room, and that Perceval found him dead. Whatever can be told will be ferreted out then."

"Well, what then? That won't be our fault?" Maundeville pointed out, staring at me. "I rather inferred, Armiston, that you were keen to have the superstition exploded. Now's your chance. Indeed, I don't think it can be avoided. The case is in Perceval's room, and I suppose the police have seen it by this time."

"It isn't there," I said. "It was moved out of the room before any strangers were brought in. It's in your house now, I believe."

"Well, then," Maundeville said, "shan't we just openly state the facts as we know them, and not hold ourselves responsible for other people's conclusions? There's only one other objection," he added. "Miss O'Hagan's name may be brought up. I don't believe she would wish that to influence us, though."

"How would her name come in?" I asked. I didn't see any reason for professing to have any ideas on that point myself.

"Well, she is one of the party," Maundeville reminded me. "Besides—" he lowered his voice—"Perceval was very deeply in love with her. That was perfectly obvious."

"And she had refused him," I added.

Maundeville was quite evidently surprised.

"I didn't know that. On my soul, I didn't know that," he declared. "Poor Perceval—poor fellow!" He seemed curiously touched by this secondary misfortune of Perceval's. "Are you sure of that?"

"He told me so himself," I said sulkily.

"That tends to account partly for what happened," he said, after consideration.

"For example?"

"Well, he was as quiet as ever, but it might account for his not noticing particularly how much wine he took."

"It doesn't account for your making the same mistake, does it?" I asked.

"I don't think we'll try to account for my mistakes just now," he said quietly; "unless, of course, you think that would help to explain more important matters. We'll agree to let my reputation for general sobriety—or for the reverse—take care of itself.

"All the same," he added in his ordinary good-tempered tone, "I think a bottle of hock between us, and a glass of port, with a chartreuse with our coffee, and a whisky-and-soda later with our cigars will cover our liquor bill. We'll ask Samuels at The Banyan to hunt up the bills, and we'll look at them together."

I grunted something vague, for I had already meant to do that on my own account.

"We needn't say anything to outsiders about the drinking," I said, "until we see what turns up. We should have to say how extraordinary that was for Perceval, and the next question would be whether he had any particular excuse just now for breaking his usual habits. Then the Mummy or Miss O'Hagan, or both, might be dragged in."

"As you like," Maundeville agreed. "I'm naturally not keen to talk about it. Still, if you or Maxwell choose to say publicly how things were, you must do so. Are you going to Park Lane this morning?"

"I must go this afternoon," I said, "but I've no business there this morning."

"Could you come round with me?" Maundeville asked. "I should like to go and see if anything useful suggests itself to me on the spot."

Now I detested the thought of having to be there that afternoon, and I was very loth to pay an unnecessary visit. But if Maundeville went I thought I ought to go too; and besides, I wanted to be civil after answering him sharply.

I repeated that nothing necessitated my going, but that if half-an-hour would be enough for him I could manage it; and we went together, Maundeville being silent and gloomy all the way, though he looked much less tired than when he had come into my dining-room.

I only remember one question that he asked before we reached Park Lane.

"How does Miss O'Hagan take it?" he asked—and looked at me with obvious surprise when I said that I had no idea. I added an explanation that I had not seen her.

"Who told her?" Maundeville demanded. "Someone has done so, of course."

"Yes, Maxwell. But I know nothing of what passed," and Maundeville asked nothing more.

CHAPTER XXIX

THE MINIATURE

The morning was hot, and the blinds drawn down over every window of the house in Park Lane were conspicuous in the sun.

The bedroom, which looked on to a pleasant garden at the back, was a curious contrast. It was a light, airy room, with two large windows and plenty of space.

Both windows were opened wide there and in the adjoining room, and a little wind wandered about the room, stirring the pretty curtains. Flowers were everywhere. On the mantelpiece, dressing-table, writing-table, wherever vase or bowl could stand, and some white blossoms were scattered on the bed.

There was nothing in the room to suggest death, until one's eye was caught by a certain rigidity of line under the sheet.

I looked around, annoyed at disturbing the peace of the room, and vexed with myself for having consented to come.

"There's nothing to observe," I said softly to Maundeville. "You can see the room has been tidied up and everything put straight." I turned to go, and very nearly left the room.

What if I had, I wonder?

Maundeville agreed, but stepped across to the bed and laid a hand on the sheet. His nervous system must have been in most perfect order, since he showed no sign of disturbance at what followed.

When he touched the sheet I, following behind him, saw a quick movement beneath it, and I fell back a pace, with some exclamation. I heard Dale cry, "Lord, have mercy!" behind me, but Maundeville never moved. His hand was arrested for an instant, and then he turned the sheet further, and something black sprang up and leapt to the floor. It was Bhanavar, the Persian cat.

"I ordered that brute to be taken away yesterday," I said, turning to Dale.

"It was done, sir. She must have followed someone in again."

"Why should she come here?" Maundeville asked, watching her.

"She had slept here lately. She had a fancy for the—Thing that stood there," and Dale nodded towards the alcove where the mummy-case had been kept.

"The aromatics," Maundeville said, turning to me, "possibly valerian. Who knows? I rather think that at one time valerian was supposed to ward off evil spirits. Perhaps the Egyptians used it. Where is she now?"

The cat had disappeared again while we spoke, and Dale began to look for her under the bed.

"Never mind for a moment," Maundeville said. "We'll find her before we leave the room," and he stood silently looking down at the peaceful face he had uncovered.

"Well, I'm sorry!" was all he said at last, as he turned away with a sigh; but he might have said more and expressed less.

"Now for the cat," he added. "We must find her and keep her out."

"I'll speak to Simpson about her, sir," Dale said, with emphasis. "She's his charge, and he has nothing else to do now but gossip. I'll see to it."

But Maundeville and I were both possessed with the same intention of seeing the cat out of the room ourselves.

To find her was easy enough. Maundeville went straight to the little alcove where the Mummy had lain, and there she was, behind the curtain. But she was too quick for him, and darted under the bed. Dislodged from there, she ran up the little bed-curtains and squatted at the top, spitting and growling in a fury.

The racket seemed indecent, and I said so, and Maundeville agreed.

"Stop chasing her!" he said, "and bring milk or something."

Dale pulled a bell, and the valet came running up with a scared face.

"When was the cat fed?" Maundeville asked him.

"This morning, sir."

"Bring milk!" Maundeville ordered, and the fellow went away and fetched some, while Dale suggested that the animal didn't want to leave her dead master. But the moment the milk was put on the floor she came down, mewing piteously, and drank all she could get.

"More!" Maundeville suggested; and more being brought she took that too, and then set to work on her toilette before us all.

"A good appetite—after breakfast?" Maundeville suggested to the valet. "Your master would have sacked you on the spot if he had seen this. Dale, you had better look to the poor brute's needs yourself, or kill her."

Dale said he would see to that, and picking up Bhanavar, sharply ordered the other man out.

"Shall we go?" Maundeville asked me, but I excused myself, saying that since I was there I might save time by making one or two arrangements before going.

"I don't know that I have seen anything worth noticing," he said. "The room, of course, has been put straight, as you suggested. But I am glad we came, if only to feed poor Bhanavar," and he limped away.

When he had gone I turned to Dale, and told him to bring the cat to the window. Two things about her had caught my attention. When she was bolting about the room she twice missed her leap and fell, striking against the furniture to which she was jumping. Again it seemed to me that in going to the milk she struck her nose. Of course, she was famished and very thirsty. Still——Directly Dale held her up for me to look at her closely, I could not help seeing what was wrong. The pupils of her eyes were strongly dilated, and didn't contract even in the bright sunlight streaming directly in on them through the open window. She was drugged.

I had hardly time to see this when she bit Dale, who naturally swore and dropped her, whereupon she bolted under the bed again. While poor Dale alternately sucked his finger, and prayed to be forgiven for such language in such a place, I stooped to see where the cat was hidden. I saw her, crouching at the other side and out of my reach, even if I was prepared to risk being mauled. But the sunlight shone on something else within reach, and I pulled it out and rose to examine it.

It was a plain gold locket, with a very thin, broken gold chain. I opened it under the sudden impulse of mere curiosity. It held a miniature of Miss O'Hagan, and while I looked at it Maundeville limped back into the room and stood looking at me. I think if there had been time for me to hide it I should have done so, but I was sure he had seen it.

"Here's a proof, if one were necessary, of poor Perceval's feeling," I said.

He took the locket to the window, and stood there looking at the portrait in silence for a minute or two.

"It's not a bad likeness," he said at last. "Where did you find it?"

"Under the bed," I said. "He probably dropped it there the night before last. The room has been tidied in a very perfunctory way."

"What will you do with it?" he asked me.

"I don't know," I said, a little bothered. "I wish I hadn't seen the thing. If it were anything else I should hand it over to Dale, I suppose. As it is—I don't know—I haven't had time to think. I've only this moment found it, you know. Perhaps one should send it to Miss O'Hagan?"

Maundeville considered this idea, looking at the miniature still.

"I don't think so," he said at last, handing it back to me. "It would be sure to pain her a good deal just now. Keep it for a while and think over the matter. It's safe in your hands, and you can give it to her later if you still think that best."

So I put it in an inside breast pocket of my coat, and we parted at the street door.

That evening I was intolerably tired and dispirited. The man who makes friends of his patients makes for himself just so many possible extra anxieties and heartaches—and I don't know that his patients are any the better for it either.

I had spent some hours of the bright summer afternoon at Park Lane with another medical man, making further investigations, the details of which I do not intend to inflict upon any layman. But it all left me tired, tired, and so dismal that I even let Mudge talk as he chose, and barely heard him.

I believe it was with the idea of diverting my thoughts from poor Perceval by fixing them on something brighter, that I went to my bureau, and took back the locket with me to my easychair. It was the first time that I had really looked at the thing carefully.

The miniature seemed to me unlike most others—which generally tend to what I would call the chocolate-boxy, the insipidly sweet. There was plenty of character in this one. How an artist could get so much into a locket on so small a scale was a puzzle to me. I even got a lens to examine it. I wondered whom poor Perceval had commissioned to do the thing. I believe most miniatures are the work of women. This lady must, I thought, be original above the average. She had put life into the face. She had not been afraid of the red hair. Far from that, she had emphasised it, and arranged it falling as a background all about the face and neck. The proud, refined face stood out boldly against a soft red cloud of it. It seemed to me that an artist must possess more than mere technique to do such a likeness. A certain appreciation, surely, of fine qualities. A certain sympathy.

I wondered what Maundeville would think of it as a piece of work. Maundeville had done her portrait. Stop! He might even have done this for Perceval. But if so, why hadn't he told me when I showed it to him? He knew that I had seen one picture already. In some such way I wondered, vaguely, with no great attention, staring idly at the bewitching face. Then suddenly my slow brain seemed to wake with a shock.

CHAPTER XXX

I GO A-COURTING

The day after the inquest I was in better spirits, for I had decided on a definite plan of campaign—and was, I was sure, no longer fighting in the dark. But before going on with my story let me say what happened at the inquest.

Maundeville gave evidence that he and Perceval had dined together, and that he left him in his house in Park Lane, apparently perfectly well, except for a slight wheezing, for which (he had happened to say) he meant to smoke some medicated cigarettes before trying to sleep.

Simpson, the valet, took oath that he believed his master to be well when he wished him good-night. He went out afterwards, he said, to post a letter, and meeting a lady friend was longer than he intended, and did not know what time it was when he returned.

Maxwell told how he found Perceval and fetched me.

I related what I saw (omitting the Mummy and the letter), telling the jury about the cigarette stumps, and also, with more detail than I have inflicted on you, about Bhanavar the Beautiful, and my reasons for believing her to have got stramonium, and Perceval to have had the same. I explained to the jury in what way the stramonium had reached her, and I quoted a classical case in which stramonium cigarettes had been held to cause death. I added that some thought a quite moderate quantity of alcohol would accelerate the effect of stramonium, and at this point Maundeville seemed to recall some details of that evening, and asked leave to add that he remembered how Perceval, though he drank only moderately, ate even less, in fact, ate hardly anything. The stramonium, together with the alcohol, would, therefore, probably act with more power.

The young medical man who had helped me, merely corroborated my evidence, and was very pleased to be connected with the second recorded case of poisoning by stramonium cigarettes. He was (unconsciously I am sure) anxious to prove that to have been the sole cause of death. He had already asked my leave to offer an article upon it to the *British Medical Journal* or the *Lancet*.

The jury at once gave a verdict in accordance with the evidence, adding a rider about the danger of the unrestricted sale of drugged tobacco. A mixture of frankness about some things, and absolute silence about others, had prevented any curiosity or suspicion.

My preparations for action that morning, then, were perhaps somewhat peculiar. I went to a fashionable barber, and had my hair cut and my moustache trimmed. I even allowed the man to put some stinking, oily stuff on my scanty locks, and to stiffen my moustache with the least suspicion of wax. Since I was about to play the fool, I might as well look my part. I lunched in my rooms and enjoyed the stupefied air with which Mudge contemplated me while he waited table.

"The day's fine, Mudge," I said, lighting a cigarette at the end of lunch, "and I have some calls to make. I think I'll change my clothes. Lay out some things for me to choose from, and see that my patent leathers are all right."

Mudge went off in silence, and when I went into my bedroom shortly after, I found him standing at ease beside more pairs of trousers than I had thought I possessed.

I chose rather light grey trousers, white spats, and a white waistcoat, a frock-coat (which I hate), and I worried Mudge considerably before I found a tie which pleased me. In the end I made him fetch half-a-dozen from the nearest outfitter's, and I chose a grey silk tie which Mudge swore would hardly be fit to wear twice, and I ran it through a handsome tie-ring.

"If it's a weddin'," said Mudge.

"It isn't," I assured him. "But it may lead to one," I added, and then making him brush my best hat for the second time, and choosing rather a swagger cane given me by an old friend, I set forth. Mudge, I knew, watched me from the door down the stair; and on crossing the street and turning sharply to look up at my windows I found him, as I had expected, staring at me from there. He never even troubled to move when I caught him at it, but as far as I know continued to watch me until I had turned the corner.

My first destination was Maundeville's house, which I reached soon after three o'clock. Bates told me that his master was in the museum, and I went there unannounced.

I found Maundeville writing, and according to our mutual understanding he did not stop at my entrance. He merely looked up, nodded, and went on with his work, while I replaced a book which I had taken from the table two or three days before.

The Mummy, that harbinger of evil, stood in its accustomed place. I sat down before it, staring at the case and wondering, as I had already wondered more than once, how far the malignant face before me represented what stood within. It was not all fancy. The expression of the painted figure on the lid was really heavily malignant, and it was difficult to imagine that the artist of three thousand years ago had been less prone to flattery than his brother of to-day. I imagined that he had made the best of his subject, according to his lights.

The dull, steadily staring eyes had a sort of hypnotic effect upon me, and though I could not have imagined it possible, I forgot Maundeville's presence for the time. When I remembered him again, I knew, without turning to look at him, that he was watching me.

I did turn at last, and we stared at one another in silence until he broke it.

"You interest me, my friend," he said. "As far as I can see, you try as little to seem consistent as I do."

"*Par exemple?*" I asked carelessly, returning to my contemplation of the Mummy.

"Well, just now you put on fine raiment, rather festive apparel, in fact, and then you come here and sit down to contemplate a thing of evil omen, as steadfastly as though that was your sole occupation for the day. I believe you forgot me altogether."

"I did," I said, truthfully enough. "The Thing seemed to fascinate me for the moment. I don't know that I need dress in mourning before I look at it."

"Better, perhaps, not to look at all," Maundeville suggested.

"Oh, I've always had a fancy for facing up to things, and

besides, as far as I'm concerned, the Mummy has its uses."

"I can't see that," Maundeville confessed, leaning back in his chair, and considering me attentively, while he pushed his papers away. "Unless you needed a *memento mori?*"

"Perhaps I did," I allowed. "At any rate, I think it has suggested that life is short. 'Youth's a stuff will not endure.' "

"Youth?" he regarded me more curiously than ever, but I continued to contemplate the Mummy.

"Yes," replied I. "The Mummy has reminded me that life is short—in fact that 'in delay there lies no plenty.' "

Maundeville leant forward. "So," said he. " 'Then come, kiss me, Sweet-and-twenty.' That's the conclusion of the whole matter, is it? Good luck to your wooing! How can I help you? Do I know the lady?"

I looked at my watch and rose.

"She has given me an appointment," I said. "To be late would be a bad start. I must do the best I can for myself without your help. Yes, you know the lady. It's Miss O'Hagan. Many thanks for your good wishes," and I hurried away. I was anxious about what I meant to do, knowing that I was going to do it badly at the best. I went and sat in the Green Park alone, going over my plans to make the best of them, since my dull head could make out none better, and in the end I hung back so long that I had to take a taxi.

Once in the cab, curiously enough I didn't think at all about Miss O'Hagan or what I meant to say to her. I sat wondering whether Maundeville was still in his museum. I somehow thought he would be sitting looking at the Mummy, just as I had done an hour or so before.

I had parted from him with, I believe, somewhat a jaunty air. If it had seemed a trifle forced, what else could one expect of fifty trying the role of five-and-twenty? Now my spirits drooped a bit, and I met Miss O'Hagan with, I suppose, about as grim a visage as usual.

CHAPTER XXXI

Her stammer was very marked that afternoon, and I thought her eyes looked as though she were sleeping badly. Still, young tissues have wonderful elasticity, and even the deep mourning she wore for Perceval could not spoil her grace and charm. The creamy skin that sometimes goes with red hair showed doubly fair above the black ruffle about her neck.

She was alone in a room which I had not seen before, but which I guessed to be her favourite sitting-room. An oil-painting of a soldier on horseback hung on the wall opposite her low chair. It was a grim face and a thin, wiry figure, with a patch actually painted in over one eye; but there was a grotesque likeness between the rider and the girl sitting opposite, which made it impossible to doubt who he was. In a glass case beneath the picture I could see a cavalry sword, with several medals ranged around it. On the writing-desk I noticed that the inkstand was in a silver-mounted horse's hoof. A well-polished pair of gilt spurs hung over the mantelpiece under two crossed rapiers, and below the spurs were a pair of long duelling pistols, all kept scrupulously clean.

The room was not like the average lady's boudoir; but it comforted me by its suggestion of hardness, while I waited for tea to be brought in; for I had determined not to announce my errand while there was any risk of interruption; and while I waited and pondered I must have stared, for suddenly she blushed, and her blushing bothered me so much that it made me reckless. I was only keen to do my errand and get it over before I made an ass of myself. I fidgeted about, talking of matters of no interest. Then, gulping some tea down far too hot, made a desperate start.

"You should have your tea put in little bags," I said, "which can be lifted out as soon as the proper time is up. Otherwise the second cup is likely to hold less tea than tannin. I notice, of course, that this is very good China tea, with which there is much less risk. Still, one cannot be too careful of one's digestion and nerves."

Here was a pretty start! My voice sounded quite harsh and dictatorial, and Miss O'Hagan was looking more curious than pleased by this valuable information.

"I happen to speak of it," I added hurriedly, "because this miserable affair of the Mummy, and particularly the last step taken, is on my mind, and I find my nerves very irritable just when I want them steady."

She glanced down at her mourning, evidently with the idea that I referred to poor Perceval, and I blundered on: "No," I said. "What's past is ended. I'm thinking of the last move."

She had lifted a cup, but put it slowly down again—very slowly, as if forcing herself to concentrate her attention on it and to steady herself.

"The last!" she echoed. "What more?"

"Haven't they told you?" I asked. "I thought he might have called."

"He! Who?"

"Captain Maxwell," I replied. "Don't you know that they've dealt the cards again and that he has the Ace of Spades?"

I jumped to my feet immediately after and hurried across to her, cursing my own clumsy invention—for after one long stare of horror at me she had leant back and fainted.

The next few minutes were like a nightmare. I threw open a window and got her to it, though I tell you frankly that she was no feather-weight. I laid her flat on the floor and did what else I could, all the time feeling most horribly scared.

It was quite different from attending to a mere patient. For one thing, I was responsible for her really serious condition. For another, I was all the time desperately afraid lest someone should come in upon us, and in everything I did I had to remember that I must make no noise.

I remember at last I found myself down on the floor, kneeling at her side rubbing her hands, and frantically saying over and over again, "It's a lie! It's all a lie!" I was doing this when she opened her eyes again, and lay looking at me with the same fixed stare of horror which she had given me before she fainted. For the time I could think of nothing more useful than to repeat my assurance that I was merely a liar, and at last I seemed to persuade her that such was actually the case.

Then the colour rushed to her face, and refusing any help, she rose and went slowly back to her chair, where she sat and looked at me apparently with mixed wonder and disgust.

For my part, I sat quiet and waited, feeling very mean, but telling myself that at any rate I had learnt what I wanted to know, and that nothing else mattered much.

I was sure now that Maxwell's safety concerned her more than that of all the rest of us put together.

"What do you mean?" she asked me at last. "Aren't you ashamed, Dr. Armiston? How could you be so cruel!"

I *was* ashamed, though I still kept reminding myself that, at any rate, I knew what I had needed to know.

"Yes, it's all a lie," I said, "but I had to know. I'll tell you all about it presently. My tea's quite cold, and the rest will be too strong. If you used those bags, now——" and I rambled on, really anxious to give her time to pull herself together.

"Tea!" she said. "You nearly kill a woman, and you talk about tea! Oh, you men!"

"If you like to ring——" she said, with more dignity, and then stopped, looking about her to see, apparently, whether everything was in order. She had no more wish than I had for other people to find any suspicious confusion.

"Never mind about the tea," I said. "Only understand that I have lied absolutely. There's not a word of truth in what I said. There has been no meeting, no cards dealt; Captain Maxwell is in no danger, and I don't think he will be now. I declare to you solemnly that it was for your own sake I lied to you."

"I don't understand," she said haughtily.

It was quite a good thing for her to be angry. Not only it suited her style of beauty admirably, but it kept her pulse going.

"Having confessed, I hope to be forgiven," I said. "You have frightened me as much as I frightened you. I promise there shall be no more lying—to you at any rate."

And then, as she still sat and watched me, flushed and angry, without any reply, I spoke again.

"Do you believe me?" I said. "I need your help badly. I don't know how I can manage without it, if I am to see this trouble through."

"How can I help you? What do you want of me?" she asked doubtfully, and I pulled myself together for more trouble.

"Before I tell you that," I said, "I want you to promise to be patient and to hear me right out."

She nodded. "Very well, I promise. Be quick!"

"Another thing," I said slowly, "I want you carefully to keep in your mind two plain facts."

"What are they?"

I leant forward and emphasised my points with a forefinger. I was terribly nervous, but determined not to show it.

"One thing is," I said slowly, "that I am a middle-aged, or elderly, man—which you like. At any rate I am quite old enough to be your father. Please remember that if I seem meddlesome. The second indisputable fact is—now please listen quietly—that, taking the Open Minds, living and dead, in a lump, you are more concerned for the safety of Captain Maxwell than for all the rest of us individually or collectively."

My accusing forefinger insisted on her attention until I had finished. After which I leant back in my chair, heaved a sigh of relief, and thanked heaven that, whatever Miss O'Hagan might say or do next, I had at any rate got the worst of it over, though I had not finished altogether.

"You have no right whatever to say that," she declared quietly enough and scorning evasion. "You're disappointing me again, Dr. Armiston. Surely you didn't ask for an appointment in order to tell me such things. I refuse to discuss my private affairs with a stranger. If anything else you meant to say refers to this—why, I must ask you to go without saying it."

"Even if it affects Maxwell's safety?" I asked. Again she was too proud to lie, and sat silent, looking at me and tugging at her rings.

"I would risk a great deal to ensure anyone's safety with that horrible Mummy," she said at last.

"I don't know that I would," I said, "but I'm prepared to risk a good deal for Maxwell's safety, if you acknowledge that it concerns you, and if you will help a little."

"How can I help?"

"I'm an obstinate, ill-mannered, elderly bachelor," I said, "but in spite of the lie I began with, do you believe in my honest intention?"

She looked at me in silence for a moment, and then spoke firmly.

"Yes, I do!" she said, "or I wouldn't have listened so long." And to back up what she said, she held out a slim white hand and I took it.

"Thank you," I said, "I'll try to deserve that. Now, my dear young lady, always bearing in mind what we already understand about my venerable age compared with yours, I want you to grant me something more." Honestly, I felt very awkward; she was now listening so patiently.

"If for the next few days," I said, "I seem to hang about you more than necessary, I hope you won't snub me in public."

"I don't often find it necessary to snub people," she said. "Why should I?"

"Well, perhaps I'm going to be more conspicuous than most," I suggested, "though I won't do more than I think necessary. Still, it would spoil my plans altogether if you showed me any marked coolness."

"Why should I?" she asked again, puzzled. "What are your plans?"

"Well," I said hardily, "the main point is to make people believe that I am in love with you (which isn't very difficult), and next in importance, to let them believe that you haven't altogether discouraged me. That's all."

"That's all!" she echoed, after a pause during which I wished I could leave dramatically at that point. "That's all! Really, Dr. Armiston, I think it's quite enough!"

"More than enough too, I expect," I admitted. "But I can't help it. I believe my plan will work, and I'm not bright enough to think of any other that will."

"Work—how? What will it do?" she asked.

"Now that's reasonable of you," I said. "I tell you what I think it will do. At the next deal of cards—and they all seem to think themselves bound in honour to go on—I believe it will bring the Ace of Spades—and the Mummy—to me."

"How?"

"I don't think I'll tell you yet," I said. "It isn't necessary, and I may be wrong. If I'm right we shall very soon know."

"But if you're right you'll be in awful danger," she pointed out. "What will you do?"

"Oh, leave that to me!" I said airily, having only the vaguest ideas on that point. "Forewarned is forearmed."

She looked at me curiously, and showed that she was very much of a woman after all.

"What are you doing it for?" she asked.

"There's a large fee depending on it," I said confidentially, "and I don't mind telling you I'm a poor man."

"If the Mummy kills you, you won't get your fee."

"I shan't want it, shall I?" I said flippantly. "I shall be as well off as any other dead man. But I mean to live to spend it. And now let me go before I talk any more nonsense. I've said all that's necessary."

"I'm sure you aren't going to tell anyone how you frightened me," she said, as we shook hands.

"No, I'm not going to tell that to anyone," I promised, "but I'm going to let Maxwell know that if you and I seem to have an understanding between us, we're not so absurd as we want to appear."

She flushed again. "I don't know that Captain Maxwell need be troubled with any explanations," she said.

"I shall say little," I promised, "and it will be altogether on my own responsibility. I won't say a word you could object to. On the other hand, I shall explain nothing to anyone else, and I must beg you not to. We must endure ridicule for a few days or weeks as well as we can." She frowned a little. "In fact," said I, "I'm going at once to hint pretty strongly at my hopes in a certain quarter. Please remember that you *have* allowed me to hope."

"Where are you going?" she asked, curious again.

"I think," said I, "I will go to Maundeville. As a man somewhere near my own age he may understand and sympathise."

To this she said nothing, and I never looked at her to see how she took my remark. But it took all the bravado I could muster to give me what I suppose to be the proper air of mild swagger on returning to Maundeville's house.

CHAPTER XXXII

A SUITOR ON PROBATION

It was then fully six o'clock, and I had left him about half-past three; but when I entered the little museum, twisting my moustache, I found him at the table as before. The double doors prevented my coming from being audible, until I stood near him where he lay back in his chair, his hands thrust deep in his pockets, staring at his papers.

"Ah, ah!" he said, looking up. "The bold wooer!" and then surveyed me in silence, while I stood and returned his regard with, I hoped, a contented air.

It might have been my imagination, for I knew myself to be a little excited; but I fancied that his first look of mere attention changed to one in which some amazement showed, only to disappear from his face like a cat's-paw from the surface of a deep still pool.

"Let me congratulate you," he said quietly. "I see that I can."

"I am, as it were, on probation," I explained; "I am allowed to say so much, but no more."

"And you feel that, given a fair chance, you can do the rest," he suggested. "Well, 'Faint heart never won fair lady.'"

"Also, 'Better late than never,'" I added, smiling, no doubt fatuously.

"I wonder!" he said softly.

Silence fell on us, and I found myself looking at that niche between two bureaux where the Mummy stood amongst the shadows against the wall opposite. It suddenly struck me that here was a woman of three thousand years ago, affecting actively or passively the fate of a woman of to-day. I turned impatiently from these fantastic notions to say good-bye, and I found that

Maundeville, too, was contemplating this, his uncanny importation.

"I think," I said, by a sudden impulse, "that at our next meeting connected with that thing I may ask to withdraw from the affair altogether."

Again Maundeville considered me with interest.

"Why?" he asked.

"Well, I shall have other matters to occupy me," I said, "and I can't so well afford to take risks now——"

"Faint heart surely hasn't won fair lady after all?" he asked. "You can't really suppose that thing"—he nodded at the Mummy —"is responsible for what has happened lately!"

"I said 'risks,'" I answered, "not certainties. Its visits have at any rate been followed by trouble."

"Well," he said indifferently, after a moment's consideration, "we've all discussed it, haven't we? And thought ourselves bound. But you may find a way out."

After that I wished him good-night and left him. It was then after seven o'clock, but I determined to look Maxwell up, and say what I wanted to before any reports about me reached him from elsewhere.

His man took my card, and after looking at it, told me that he already had orders to admit me whenever I came. He at once put me into a sitting-room and went away to let Maxwell know. The room was not only comfortably furnished, but had plenty of books, sporting trophies, and other signs of his usual occupations. I moved about, picking up a book here and there, a queer medley of works on fortification and explosives, on sport of several kinds, and a couple of books which I fancied to be Persian verse.

On the wall I saw a good tahr head, and another of a fine sable antelope. Before the fire-place was a large tiger-skin, and because of its peculiar smoky brindling I was pretty sure it was one which I had admired in Park Lane. I was looking at it when Maxwell came in.

"Have you seen that before?" he asked me.

"Yes, at Perceval's," I said, peering down at two bullet-holes— one a little forward from the shoulder, the other at the base of the skull. "You shot it and gave him the skin, I understand."

"It was like poor Percy to tell you that," Maxwell said moodily. "I hit it first, and so, as a matter of sporting etiquette, I could claim the skin. That's my shot," and he touched the hole in front of the shoulder with the toe of his shoe. "Here's his shot," he added, touching the larger hole at the skull-base. "That's the exit hole. I was lying under the beast when he fired into its open mouth."

"He said nothing of that to me," I replied, remembering Perceval's casual way of treating the thing as, if anything, a rather embarrassing gift.

"It's the last thing he'd do," Maxwell declared. "He disliked hearing me speak of it at all; I had some trouble in making him put the skin where it could be seen."

He stood looking down at it, and evidently forgot altogether that I had anything to tell him.

"I wish," he said, "I could fix his death on someone more easily reached than a mummy."

I looked at him with some suspicion of his meaning, but I could put no further sense into his words.

"Do you suspect anyone of having a hand now?" I asked him point blank.

"How can I?" he answered impatiently. "Who could possibly profit by such horrible brutality? Who would, even if he could?"

"I asked you," I persisted, "whether you suspect anyone—no matter how unjustly or ridiculously. You haven't answered me."

"I feel ready to suspect anybody—everybody," he said contradictorily. "I could suspect you if you had been in it at the beginning."

"Well, as I wasn't, and as you brought me into 'It,'" I retorted, "you might speak out."

"I will directly I have the least justification for doing so," he promised, "but I can't insult decent folk by blurting out notions that have no evidence to back them. Besides, I've proved myself wrong once already lately."

"What do you mean?"

"I gave you a note to look at as soon as we should know the result of the Mummy's next visit."

So he did. I had thought of it more than once before Perceval's death, but that had put it out of my mind.

"I haven't looked at it," I said. "It's locked up in my desk. What had you written?"

"The name of the man to whom I thought the Ace would go next."

"Who was it?"

"Maundeville. I could have sworn he was going to get it. How can I trust my opinion about anything connected with the Mummy after that? I hadn't the remotest notion of poor Percy's danger. Even after he got the Spade I believed he was safe."

"Why?"

"Oh, what does it matter? I was wrong, and there's an end of it. Yet——"

"Well?"

"Well, it sounds absurd, but I don't think I was altogether mistaken."

"That certainly sounds absurd," I said. "I quite agree with you in saying so. You thought Maundeville was sure to get the Ace of Spades. Well, Maundeville didn't."

I was quite annoyed with him for saying such silly things, and I wanted to rouse him up. It seemed as though Perceval's death had unmanned him. He took my sarcasm very meekly, and I was much disappointed.

"What you say is just enough," he agreed. "There's nothing gained by talking about it. What did you come to tell me? I'm bound to keep a dinner-engagement with some men to-night, though I don't feel much like it."

"I come here straight from seeing Miss O'Hagan and Maundeville."

"Well?"

"What do you say to my telling you that someone has proposed to her?"

"That often happens," he said, watching me.

"What do you say if I tell you that he has not been definitely refused?" I asked.

"Not Maundeville?" he said. "Surely not Maundeville!"

"It happens not to be. But what do you say to myself?"

"You!" He looked at me with open and uncomplimentary amazement, and then, thrusting his hands into the pockets of his dinner-jacket, walked to the window.

"I'll say the correct things presently," he said over his shoulder. "She must do as she chooses."

"And you let her go?"

His attitude of *laisser-faire* annoyed me, and I was deliberately trying to rouse him. Well, I succeeded. He turned on his heel and came back to me.

"Look here!" he said softly. "I don't know what you're driving at, but you've gone far enough. I can't stand another word. If that's what you came here to tell me, go!"

"I'm here to talk to you about what you and Perceval asked me to attempt," I said. "If my methods are brutal, they're the best I can advise. I see I've waked you up, at any rate. I ask you again, do you let Miss O'Hagan go?"

"I never held her," he said gloomily, "so I can't let her go. What has this to do with the Mummy?"

"It has everything to do with how I act in the matter," I said. "Honestly, and without meaning to be offensive, it seems to me, a much older man, that you're a pretty cold-blooded sort of a lover. I ask you, for your own sake, as well as for hers and mine, supposing she is ready to consider a proposal from me, what do you say to it? What do you think of it?"

"I say she must do as she chooses—and I think what I please."

"My temper is no better than yours," I warned him, "and my patience is nearly exhausted. If we can't understand one another better in a minute or so I shall go—as you tell me to—leaving you, as you say, to think what you please."

Maxwell's manner changed, as if he thought after all that I meant well too.

"Look here, Armiston," he said, "I don't see your game, but I'm going to be frank with you. Anything rather than failure with the Mummy, though I don't want to rant or to preach.

"A fortnight or so ago I told you plainly that I was in love with Miss O'Hagan. I'm trying to look at the situation reasonably. I don't know that what I told you makes it treachery for you to cut me out. I confess I hadn't thought of that as possible; but it couldn't bar you from falling in love with her at any rate. I wonder everybody doesn't. I believe most men do. But I somehow thought at your age——"

"D—n my age!" I broke in, and he stopped to look at me.

"It's partly true, then, at any rate," he said. "Well, don't speak loudly. We might be overheard. But to be plain with you, though I love her—shall love her in my grave, I believe—somebody else comes first—*shall* come first."

"Who's that?" I asked, though I guessed pretty well.

"Poor Percy," he answered. "I swore by his coffin that before I said a word about love to Miss O'Hagan I'd find out whether any man or woman had a hand in his death. What's more, I swore that if any living soul proved responsible I'd send that soul to judgment first too."

"You're not to blame for his death," I said.

"You don't know," he returned, "I had meant to spend that night with him. I had a chance of meeting Miss O'Hagan, and I did that instead. That's why I was so easily put off from going in that night. If I had stuck to my line poor Percy might be here now. If you're in the running for her, go ahead! I'm out of it. But I warn you! If I ever get free to speak, I'll do so, though you're at the church door!" He looked at his watch. "That's all, I suppose," he muttered. "I'm late already. I must go."

Nevertheless, instead of turning out with me, he dropped into an arm-chair and sat gloomily frowning at his patent-leather shoes. I watched, wondering what was on his mind now, when he suddenly looked up.

"If you're in love with her," he said, "why, other men of your age might be too!"

"Solomon!" I said jeeringly. "There's nothing, I assure you, to prevent a man of my age being in love. You had better remember that!" I added warningly; "it's important. But remember, too, that I've never said I'm in love with Miss O'Hagan."

He stared incredulously. "You must be," he said.

"Well, we won't discuss it. Miss O'Hagan and I understand one another perfectly. It's agreed between us that I've proposed to her, and that she hasn't refused me finally. I'm on probation."

"It's agreed between you?"

"That's for public information, and you're not to throw any doubt upon it. Miss O'Hagan knew that I was coming to tell you before you heard it outside. We've already formally announced it to another man."

"To whom?"

"To Maundeville," I said, and then left him to keep his dinner engagement. He must have been very late, for he had not stirred when I left him.

CHAPTER XXXIII

THE MALAY COMES

At about that time I was quietly doing a great many things which led me out of my ordinary humdrum routine. I consulted queer books, met some queer folk, and acquired some quaint and apparently quite useless information.

If, with a great deal that was futile, I chanced across some things of importance, I think it can't be counted altogether a mere coincidence. I searched in so many directions, and kept my slow wits so constantly stirred to wakefulness, that I deserved some return.

One evening, leaving Mudge, I fancy, under the impression that I should dine at my club, I strolled away eastward, and entered the restaurant where the gilt banyan was conspicuous in the setting sun. It seemed to me that if I dropped in occasionally, I might, without showing any extraordinary curiosity, hear something of Perceval's and Maundeville's last dinner there.

Having dined I sat over my port, and looked about me. Here Maxwell had brought me first; and in one of those little rooms at the back he had scribbled his false prophecy of who next would entertain the Mummy.

Here Maundeville and Perceval had dined. At which table, and which of those soft-footed foreigners had waited on them? I sat sipping my port and speculating, until I remembered that I had an evening engagement. I went to pay at the desk, and stayed a moment to praise my dinner, which had been excellent.

"Captain Maxwell brought me first," I reminded my host, "and I mean to come back."

"So you did, sir," said he, "and I remember you came again later one evening with Captain Maxwell and the Professor."

I agreed, and reminded him that Maundeville had dined there earlier that same evening.

He showed at once that he understood the reference.

"You'll be Dr. Armiston," he decided. "Of course I saw the report. Glad The Banyan wasn't dragged in. It couldn't have done any good, and might have taken away some of our best customers." His eye strayed to a far corner. "Yes, they sat over there."

After that, finding it inconvenient just then to accept invitations and bind myself for fixed hours, I chanced in at The Banyan some four evenings out of the next ten.

It seemed to me that this summer the prolongation of life became what I am inclined to call more shriekingly fashionable than ever. To turn one's face to the wall and die decently seemed the last thing possible.

Advertisements of vitalising agents, under suitably suggestive names, filled the columns of the daily papers, which on one page warned their readers against quackery, and on the next gave indecent details of wonderful and impossible cures.

We marvelled at the Bulgarian, who had apparently been a *médecin malgré lui* from time immemorial. We suddenly discovered that it was possible to live on rice and water—and then remembered that the mild Hindoos had done it before. We agreed that everybody (except ourselves) ate and drank too much, and we supplemented our dietary by concentrated foods and nervetonics. We all sighed for the Simple Life and to go Back to the Land. Duchesses did so, for week-ends, with the result that rents rose in the country, and the roses, particularly on Sundays, smelt of petrol and were covered with dust.

The height of simplicity was reached by the man who discovered food to be a superfluity, and found that health was to be restored and retained by complete starvation, supplemented by evacuants.

A cartload of blue pills would soon represent an army's commissariat, and one would hand a beggar an aperient instead of a penny. Meanwhile everybody said that living became more expensive.

As for me, I took small daily doses of such poisons as meat, wine, tea and coffee, and tobacco, and continued to live.

The megaphonic advertisement of all these things, and the ignorance of elementary physiology, shown in many of the advertisements and comments, prejudiced one unreasonably against them at times.

Life and Death seemed vulgarised and degraded in columns which touched on nothing that they did not disfigure. It was the most modern, and probably the most remunerative, form of literature. Life was made a sort of spotted fever, and Death a shivering whimper.

One wondered at times whether Humanity was worth keeping alive. One had to remind oneself that there were still quiet, inconspicuous folk who did not advertise.

Also even penny-a-liners, themselves probably hard-pressed and trying to provide their families with bread-and-butter, could not altogether destroy the fascination of these problems.

To combine the wisdom (say of fifty!!) with the dash and enthusiasm of twenty-five, might be a real advantage. I admitted as much to Maundeville, who confessed to me that he was still investigating these problems, and sometimes thought he saw glimpses of light on the possible way to success.

When I looked in upon him in his museum one afternoon, he told me that he had begun a graduated series of hypodermic injections upon himself, and he hinted at the lines of experiment.

"The thing really should not be left in the hands of charlatans," he said, "though Cagliostros will always flourish. Let me only get definite results—even if slight—to put before you, and then you and I might follow the matter further together. My knowledge is hardly up to date—and, besides, I need an honest man to verify results.

"Ah! what a pity there are so many allurements in this sinful world. With a narrow view and a single purpose one might go so far!"

But I merely acknowledged that I had never found I could go far in any direction. My limitations, I confessed, were very definite, and soon reached. I said, however, that when he had any experiments in which my help could be useful, I should be quite ready to listen.

"I have a wonderful physique," Maundeville said, with the matter-of-fact air of merely stating the obvious. "I don't want to change that with any man. I only want to make sure that I keep what I've got—and why shouldn't I? Wear and tear can be minimised, and repair very much accelerated. But we must stick at it!"

He turned to his papers and test-tubes with frank dismissal. "Good-bye, my dear fellow," he said. "Ask for tea up in the library if you want to look at anything there."

But I said I wasn't going upstairs, and I went straight away. I found that I could now read more comfortably at home than in Maundeville's library—though I still sometimes went there. I had begun to refuse the very excellent tea. The fact is that I have quite out-of-date notions about hospitality, and the conditions under which one accepts it.

I was now welcomed, or endured, at The Banyan, so far that I could nod to the proprietor, and feel aggrieved if my corner was occupied. The second time I dined there alone I was shown to the little corner table where Perceval and Maundeville had sat, and I made it my usual resort; though the attendant at that table, a fast, solemn person, who told me he was from Bengal, had some little difficulty in understanding anything of my English, beyond the names of the dishes.

Chatting for a moment one evening at the desk as I paid my bill, I asked the proprietor where this dusky dozen or so of hire-lings lived. Did he board and lodge them?

He shook his head, and smiled at my ignorance.

"Half wouldn't live with the other half," he explained. "They get rice, butter, some other odds and ends, and the use of two rooms at the back. They do a little cooking there, and they smoke a bit. When I've done with them at night, they go out." He made a large vague gesture, which suggested a general scattering and disappearance in outer darkness.

"How do you get them?" I asked.

"Oh, they come, doctor—generally from ships. One brings another, if there's a place to be filled. Most of 'em are old hands;

but if one means to go, the rest always know of it before I do. Then one introduces a pal, and I put him through his facings, or tell old Abdullah to do it. Abdullah bosses them a bit for me, and makes a good thing of it, no doubt. But when I want to, I can talk to them in a way they understand."

"Rice, butter, odds and ends," I repeated. I was thinking of the popular discussions on foods. "That's plain living. They seem to thrive on it."

"They're better fed than they were at home, I'll be bound, and they save a bit. They do very well if they keep off arrack and bhang and opium."

"Can they get these things easily in London?" I asked him.

"Easily! Why, there's countrymen of theirs make a good living out of it. They have to be careful, of course, and they get nailed at times. But you see, the trade's almost altogether among themselves. So I think there isn't so much fuss made. Anyway, they get it. I sacked the man who waited at your table only a fortnight or so ago. He took bhang and turned nasty. I banged him." He smiled grimly at the recollection—or at his small joke—and was going to say more. But another client came to the desk, and he turned and I went off.

One evening when I was there, and was sitting idly over my coffee, which I had ordered to be brought to my corner, I saw an unusual sort of visitor come in and stare about him.

It was a swarthy fellow in dungarees. I could see the glint of ear-rings as he turned his head from side to side.

He presently looked straight at my corner and at me, and then he began to come up the room.

I thought he was coming to me, and sat watching, rather surprised. But Samuels at his desk had been watching too. He stepped out quietly and met the man half-way, smiling good-temperedly. They spoke together for a moment, the other man in a quarrelsome loud way, Samuels nodding and apparently agreeing with everything. It seemed to me that the man's face, clean-shaven, thin, unpleasant, sinister, was not absolutely unfamiliar. Samuels went on talking quietly, till the other appeared pacified; then put his hand in his pocket, half-turned to his desk, and nodded towards a door near my corner, leading to the back premises, in which direction, after salaaming, the fellow went, passing close by my table as he did so.

Presently Samuels came after him, jingling some coins as he went.

I leant forward and stopped him.

"Who's that man?" I asked. "I seem to know him."

"Of course you do, sir," Samuels said—then corrected himself. "No, you don't, though. He was before your time. Unless the Professor asked you to take him on for a job, as he did me. He used to wait at this table."

He moved to pass on.

"Stay a minute!" I said, quite certain now. "I do know the man. What is he here for?"

"He's here for what he can get, sir," he answered, "and I'm going to give it him—as soon as I can—and fire him out by another door. He's been on the spree and got left. I can't have my gentlemen put off their feed by anyone. Your coffee's getting cold."

"Never mind my coffee," I said. "I'll have more presently with a couple of your cheroots. I ask you a favour, Samuels. Let me come with you and speak to that man."

Samuels allowed himself a grin.

"D'you know Malay, doctor? Unless you do——"

"I know the true Volapük," I said, putting my hand in my pocket, "and I can rely on you to know all other languages."

I rose, assuming it settled, and Samuels, with a sort of a grunt, gave way. The man whom we found in the back premises and who was certainly the Malay I had seen in a rough-and-tumble with Maundeville and afterwards in hospital, seemed almost starving. The fighting spirit he had shown upstairs was fast oozing away. He wept, and Samuels explained that now he merely asked for food and a warm corner to eat it in. These he was finally promised for the night, and he grovelled at Samuels's feet, talking vehemently, and shivering even in that Turkish-bath atmosphere.

Samuels said he was protesting that if he could only see "the Professor," Maundeville would help him, and he wouldn't need to trouble anyone any more.

"I don't know that I care to turn him on to a customer,"

Samuels concluded, surveying him with open contempt, "even though that customer brought the man here. He can wait table too, and he can cook more than a bit."

"Give him shelter to-night," I said, "and send him to me to-morrow afternoon. I'll perhaps do something for him. If I decide to let him have Professor Maundeville's address that will be my affair."

And so it was settled.

CHAPTER XXXIV

THE MALAY GOES

When I was at breakfast the next morning, I asked Mudge whether he had ever been in the Malay Archipelago.

"Was I ever, sir?" Mudge was amused. "One of the prettiest little maids ever I met was a Malay, sir. A headman's daughter, too. That's the way to learn anybody's lingo. Pick up with a girl o' the country, and you soon pick up her speech—leastways what's useful."

"Am I to understand, then, that you can talk Malay?"

"Like a nigger, sir," Mudge declared hardily. "I won't brag— but that little girl used to say she never 'eard any man talk it like me before."

"I can quite believe that," I assured him. "Well, I've a Malay coming to see me this afternoon. He can't speak English—at any rate, hardly any—and you can translate."

Mudge looked a trifle worried.

"It's a long time ago of course," he said, "and there's several dialecks. Some words, I suppose, though, is much the same all over," and he gave me various sounds which he said meant "love" and "drink," "money," "kiss," "knife," and so forth. "Other words'd come in conversation—like," he decided. "What is the nigger, sir?"

"He's a sailorman, a lascar."

"'E'll know all our swear-words, same as you or me," Mudge said, "and that's always a 'elp if you want to get on terms with 'em. Besides, these lascars picks up a word 'ere and a word there, just like a marine," and he seemed serenely certain of his ability to equal the occasion.

I acknowledged that he did so when the fellow came—up to a certain point.

At his own suggestion he started by giving the lascar a meal in his kitchen, and I heard him catechising the man about his voyages, and so forth. I had decided to give Mudge no idea of what I wanted to ask about.

He talked to the man in the sort of broken English with which soldiers, sailors, and a good many more are apt to address the foreigner—mixing this with words and sentences which I imagine were sometimes Malay and sometimes other Eastern languages. The man was now clean and bright-looking. His meal had apparently pleased him, and he stood to attention, looking a good-tempered, inscrutable sort of ruffian.

I told Mudge to explain that I had remembered seeing him in hospital, and that I was a doctor, interested in the habits, customs, and particularly the drugs, of foreign countries. You will notice that I did not say where I had seen him first.

Mudge piled it on in broken English, with a few foreign sentences thrown in, and the man seemed impressed. At any rate, he salaamed profoundly, and, according to Mudge, called himself a "hignorant devil."

I had lit an after-lunch cigar, and I smoked and considered, not sure of my ground, and feeling my way as best I could.

I told Mudge to explain that I collected foreign drugs. For good specimens of pure drugs I was ready to pay, I said, if not too expensive—also for information about their uses. To make this point plain in case Mudge's powers were not equal to it, I fished out some silver from my trousers pocket and separated a couple of half-crowns, putting them on the table, and jingling the rest in my hand.

Imagine us. The Malay standing to attention, but with his eyes lowered to the coins on the table, a little smile just showing his teeth. Mudge fatly impassive, but sniffing a little discouragingly, and I, puffing away quietly at my cigar, determined not to hurry matters.

"Tell him," I said to Mudge, "that I understand he is a sailor. I don't expect him to tell me anything worth knowing to-day. But probably he comes and goes between London and his own country. He might remember me and bring me some of his people's medicines. I will pay him when he does."

Mudge translated or paraphrased, and the man answered quickly. He, too, was talking a sort of pidgin-English, and I had an idea of his intention before Mudge explained.

"Ses there's lots o' fine medicines in 'is place, sir, but bloomin' dear. He must take money back to buy 'em. Says they're sort o' cash chemists over there. No pence, no pills." At the same time Mudge protested strongly against any advance being made— saying it was "too bloomin' thin," and I inclined to agree with him.

"In the words o' the song, 'D'you think that 'e'll come back?' sir. The odds is against it," Mudge pointed out.

"What do they do when they're ill over here, or anywhere away from home? Do they always go to hospital?" I asked. "Don't they carry any of their medicines with them?"

"Ship's doctor, or ship's cap'n," Mudge suggested. "Number one, Indigestion. Number two, Information. Number three, Rouser, and so on."

"Ask him!"

Mudge asked, and the man first answered carelessly enough, then suddenly bestirred himself and began talking vehemently. His eyes brightened, his face changed, his voice rose, he almost chanted a long reply, while Mudge stared in silence.

"Well, what is it?" I asked Mudge, when he stopped.

"I can't quite make out, sir." Mudge scratched his head. " 'Is feelin's 'ave run away with 'is tongue, sir, I couldn't follow 'im. There's something 'e says is medicine an' meat an' drink, with a smoke chucked in."

The fellow was feeling inside his shirt, but drew out a little bag, empty, and showing it to me shook his head.

"Stony," Mudge suggested sympathetically, "and run out of 'is stock."

"He had money last night," I said. "He can't get the stuff here, perhaps. What is it?"

No! It seemed that he could get the drug here, though not so good. He gave a name I didn't know, and I rose from my chair, and going slowly to the book-case (I didn't want to seem too much interested) I took down two or three books: *Taylor's Medical Jurisprudence*, a *Pharmacopœia*, and a *Botany*.

I knew precisely what I was looking for, though not under the name the Malay gave it, and that name I could not find.

I said so, standing at the book-case with my back to them.

"Is it opium?" I asked Mudge. "Tell him I can get good opium."

But no. The Malay knew opium, and preferred his own drug.

"Perhaps it would be of no use to a doctor," I said indifferently; but the man seemed to understand at once, and protested:

"Much good."

"Well, I don't find it," I said. "Has he any other name for it?" The man gave another, but it was no doubt Malay, and it wasn't given in my index.

"Oh, it doesn't matter!" I said, yawning. "If he thinks it worth his while to bring me a good specimen, I don't care where he gets it. Tell him so."

Mudge told him, and the fellow said he would do so quite soon.

"Perhaps it's only used by Malays," I added. "I suppose he doesn't know a name for it in any other language."

Mudge asked, and the fellow thought a moment and then gave me one word: "Bhang." And Mudge jumped slightly and brought a hand down upon his thigh.

"Lord! why didn't I think o' that?" he muttered. "What else got me Cells that time?" Bhang had evidently spelt Trouble once for Mudge.

As for me I made no particular comment, beyond repeating my former promise.

"If he could get good samples of this bhang, or any other drug peculiar to his people, I would pay him a fair price. Yes, if he were really hard up, and could get some of this stuff, even to-night, I would give him something for his trouble and pay cash for the drug, and of course for any other," I added carelessly.

I didn't want to seem over keen about this particular thing, for I had at last reached what I was driving at.

This man had waited on Maundeville and Perceval the night

they dined at The Banyan, having been introduced by Maundeville. The drug used in the preparation of the drink "bhang" is *Cannabis Indica*, or Indian hemp, and its action is somewhat similar to that of stramonium.

Even then my run of luck wasn't quite done.

The man said he could, and would, get some if he had the money, and he gave Mudge the name of a street in Soho—the street, in fact, where I had first seen him. Then, while talking, he drew something else from his shirt. Outside this was a little bit of oilskin, then two or three layers of muslin, and then a little ball of yellowish, soft, putty-like substance.

He looked at it and at me with a good-humoured smile that showed his beautiful teeth. "Very fine medicine," he said. "Much can do."

"What is it?" I asked. "What can do?"

But here his English and Mudge's Malay failed altogether. They both became most amazingly stupid, and, indeed, the Malay seemed unwilling to talk more about it. He rolled up the little ball in its muslin, wrapped the oilskin outside, and shoved it back under the breast of his shirt.

It was not for sale, he said, and he could get no more till he reached home again. Perhaps he could bring me some another time, but not now.

But the bhang was different. He could get some of that and send it back by Mudge, if Mudge would go with him. And another evening he would come back and talk more about his people's medicines. I handed Mudge the money and told him to go, and to pay for the stuff when he had it in his hand. I also made the man comprehend that I was open to buy other drugs, and in any case would pay him a trifle to come again and tell me what he could of what I bought.

He promised, but suddenly objected that first he must keep another engagement.

"Where?" I asked.

It was at another *Hakim's*, and he fumbled in his pockets and produced a scrap of paper. I didn't know the writing at all—indeed, it was a sort of printing hand. But I knew the address very well, for it was Maundeville's.

"Go with him to this address," I said to Mudge. "Wait about outside, but don't make yourself conspicuous, and then go on to Soho with him."

I turned to the Malay, repeated my promise about money for other drugs and another call from him, and I let them go off together.

As a matter of fact I was very glad to sit down and to think alone.

At about five o'clock I made tea for myself; but for once, tea and tobacco could not keep me quiet. I alternately cursed my past stupidity and rejoiced that my eyes were opened, even though without credit to myself.

At about six o'clock, neither Mudge nor the Malay having returned, I was too impatient to sit quiet any longer.

I remembered Mudge's liking for a yarn, and no less for a glass.

He might conceivably have turned aside for both, either alone or even with the lascar. Other more serious things might have happened. I finally left my flat to take care of itself, and went in pursuit of Mudge.

I found that I had done him injustice. There was a seat under a tree, just outside the Square gardens, and perhaps eighty yards from Maundeville's door.

There was Mudge, stolidly smoking, and keeping a dull but steady eye upon that door. Mudge never looks very wide awake, but I knew quite well that no one would go in or out without getting his immediate attention. He rose and saluted, and I then sat down, after satisfying myself that the windows of Maundeville's house did not give a view of the seat.

"I was wondering what on earth had become of you, Mudge," I said crossly. "If you had been worth worrying about, I should have worried."

"Knew you would sir," Mudge admitted. "But your orders was to wait for the nigger."

"You don't mean to tell me he's there still?"

"I mean to tell you 'e 'asn't come out," Mudge declared stolidly, "and this was the last of my 'baccy. So I'm glad you've come, sir, though I wasn't sure if you would."

"I suppose you've been asleep?" I said.

"Knew you'd say that, sir," Mudge remarked, philosophically calm.

"Has anyone else come or gone?" I asked.

"Not a soul, sir. The 'ouse has been as quiet as the grave," said Mudge, and proceeded to knock the ashes out of his pipe.

"Shall we go, sir? You're dinin' at 'ome, you'll remember, sir; and it's time I saw to things."

Bless my soul, no! What did dinner matter?

I believe I said something to that effect, and Mudge grunted, and stowed away his empty pipe, while I tried to think.

What was I to do? I couldn't go in and ask for the lascar. I couldn't even go in and prowl about on the chance of meeting him there. I didn't want him to know that I visited the house and knew Maundeville. I didn't want Maundeville to see me meet him.

"This is important, Mudge," I said at last. "I wish I had told you so, plainly, at the beginning."

"Pity not to, sir," said Mudge. "Still, better late than never. And it wouldn't have brought the nigger out any sooner," he added, I suppose, for consolation.

"Perhaps there's a back way out," I said.

"There may be," Mudge allowed, and then suggested that if I would watch the front he would go round and reconnoitre at the back; and reminding me that there was an area gate to watch, he went, and I sat on and smoked a cigar, with incongruous thoughts about the house I was looking at, and the nuisance of not knowing when I was going to get my dinner. Mixed with these, there was a feeling which I can only liken to what I have known once or twice, when doing a difficult stalk, and finding that my chance of a stag hung in the balance.

It was some time before Mudge returned from the opposite direction to that in which he had gone, and joined me with another of his characteristic grunts.

"There's a garden-door at the back," he said, and waited while I relieved tension by a few comminatory remarks. Then he added that no one had gone out that way.

"How do you know?"

Mudge hinted that in his branch of the service men learnt to use their eyes; and then he condescended to details. He said there were cobwebs on the door. He also told me that a heavy thunder-shower, which I had paid no attention to, had fallen while he and the Malay had been on the way together. It had laid the thick dust in the little lane at the back of the house, and there was no mark of a foot near this door.

"Are you sure which door it is?" I asked him.

"Numbered, sir," was his answer, and that settled it. I sat and stared at the house with a queer feeling not at all in harmony with a fine summer evening.

I handed Mudge a cigar, and told him to take that and to think.

"Is there any friend of yours who could watch this place and say nothing?" Mudge thanked me, lit up, puffed and considered, and then suggested Seymour.

"You can trust him not to talk?"

Mudge deliberated again, and then explained that Seymour had broken with the lady whom he had been taking out, and was, therefore, to be trusted.

"Find him," I said. "Get a meal, both of you, and join me here! You may have an all-night job. The garden-door must take care of itself till you come."

I had about an hour of smoking and useless watching before Mudge returned, bringing Seymour with him. I told them that this was a serious matter, and that I relied on them both to watch the house, front and back, until the morning, and to say not a word of it, except to one another. They were to come and report to me, straight from there, at eight o'clock.

I went off and dined at my club, and about eleven o'clock I went round and looked them up. Seymour, at the front, reported that Maundeville had gone out alone in his car. Mudge, at the back, had seen nothing.

At eight the next morning they turned up together. Nothing more had been seen, except that Seymour reported Maundeville to have returned in his car about 1.30 a.m.

Mudge got me breakfast, and then went off to his hammock for a nap.

For me that day chanced to be a busy one. I saw Life come, and I saw it go. It so happened that where another mortal entered this queer world it was unwelcome, and to all appearance was likely to be unhappy and unhealthy from cradle to grave; while the life ended was that of a man younger than I, and much more useful.

That night I had one of the gloomy fits to which I have always been liable, and which I fancy tend to become more frequent. It is a mercy that at such times Mudge is the only one obliged to be near me, and to bear with my sulking. I don't think him particularly sensitive to the domestic atmosphere.

I can call up a distinct image of my father, at about my present age, sitting frowning at the fire for an hour or more at a time, with his empty pipe in his hand.

I believe now that at such times he was thinking the idle melancholy thoughts that I think, with the vague, gloomy forebodings that I have.

It is a comfort to remember that he died as a man should, and that, therefore, so may I; for there are times when I call myself coward—most pitiable of mortals.

That night, however, I came to conclusions that were sensible enough when reached, but a trifle too obvious to bring any particular satisfaction.

For example, it was certain that I had set myself a certain piece of work to do, and so it must be done.

It was certain that, first, promises that I had made, and second, my own inclination, prevented me from acting as the ordinarily right-minded citizen does when he sees crime unchecked, for he appeals to the police.

If inclination made me ready to take the law into my own hand, then I must run the risk, and be ready to pay the price like a decent fellow, even though quaking inwardly.

One theory of mine, evolved that evening, although not perhaps possessed of a very substantial basis, consoled me to some extent, and helped to keep me comparatively courageous.

I believed that unless and until I got the Ace of Spades I could sleep safely.

After that, or at any rate after once getting the Mummy as a tenant, I might expect trouble at any moment—night or day.

It seemed, therefore, to some extent possible for me to decide when my trouble should begin.

Further, I even imagined that, with a little care and ingenuity, I might forecast the form in which trouble was likeliest to come.

In the end luck helped me far more than judgment. But meanwhile this fancy kept me on the alert, and more cheerful than if I had expected a blow quite in the dark.

CHAPTER XXXV

WHAT THE LASCAR LEFT

Five days passed without any developments, and I began to get angry. To sit still and wait didn't suit my nerves at all, and I fancy Mudge had a deuce of a time.

Fortunately he bore with my temper, if not meekly, at any rate in silence.

On the sixth afternoon my patience was exhausted, and having had lunch and meditated over a cigar, I called Mudge in.

"If anyone wants me this afternoon," I said, "you can remember that I am at Professor Maundeville's house. I expect to be in at five, when I shall want tea."

Mudge stood and looked at me, or least in my direction, in silence. It is impossible to say, when Mudge looks like that, whether he is thinking or whether he is asleep.

"Yes, sir," he said at last, "and what if you aren't in at five?"

"I intend to be," I said.

Mudge rubbed his chin, a trick he has when not standing rigidly to attention.

"I'm always ready to obey orders——"

"Are you?" I asked, with interest.

"And I don't pretend to know the game," Mudge went on calmly. "But you'll remember, sir, that there nigger——"

"Went out at the garden door," I suggested.

"Maybe," said Mudge; and then added, "Very well, sir, I'll get a taxi."

"Gracious, man! What d'you take me for? A millionaire? What do I want a taxi for on a fine day like this, and for that distance?"

"I'll get a taxi, sir," Mudge repeated quite impassively, "and you'll keep it waitin', and remember the tickin's goin' on all the time. If you aren't here by half-past five, me and Seymour will be coming to look for you—and we shan't wait outside."

"Now what on earth do you mean?" I demanded.

"I don't know, sir," was Mudge's somewhat unsatisfactory reply; and without giving me time to discuss the matter further, he went off and got a taxi. What was more, he saw me into it, and told the driver, in my hearing, that he was engaged by the hour, and that he was to wait and bring me back again. That's the man who declares he's always ready to obey orders! Still, on consideration, I decided to let the taxi wait, and I repeated the order when I reached Maundeville's door. But I rang with a strong belief that I should find him at home, and did so.

His first invitation, making me practically free of the house, still held. I went straight to the little museum when Bates admitted me, and there was Maundeville busy with test-tubes, bunsen burners, distilling apparatus and other instruments and appliances, which I had forgotten the use of or had never known.

To protect his clothes, no doubt, he had put on a frayed old college gown, and being, as I knew, always very careful of his white and muscular hands, he was wearing rubber gloves.

The handsome, keen, clean-shaven face which he turned to me, directly I opened the door, was paler than usual, and even, I fancied, a trifle thinner.

"Ah ha! the happy man," he said, "*ben venuto!* But fancy straying in here on a June day. It's fine outside, isn't it? *Carpe diem*, Armiston. There's no more practical wisdom. 'In delay there lies no plenty.'"

"Of course it's fine outside," I said, going to one of the bookshelves and taking a book to carry away. "You were out this morning, I suppose?"

"I don't think so," he answered, holding a test-tube against a flame. "No, I think not."

"You don't know?" I asked curiously.

"I forget," he said a trifle impatiently, and stopping to compare the test-tube in his hand with a small stoppered bottle on the table, he then began to heat the tube again.

"The Philosopher's Stone?" I suggested, "or rather the Elixir Vitæ, I suppose."

"There's a variety of things here," Maundeville replied, without turning from his work; and then suddenly, "I can do no more. The rest can wait!" and he put the tube carefully to stand in a rack and dropped into a deep easy-chair, leaving various gas-jets and spirit-lamps burning.

"Oblige me by pressing that button behind you," he said to me suddenly. As I turned from doing so, I found that Bates was already in the doorway, and Maundeville seeming to take that for granted, spoke without changing his position in the chair or raising his eyes.

"Have a good fire at once in the dining-room, and heat up the pipes too. What meal is there for me?"

"Dinner, sir."

"Order it to be served. Are my clothes laid out?"

"Yes, sir."

"When you've told them in the kitchen, come to shave me upstairs. Oh, tell them to lay for two. Dr. Armiston dines with me."

"Too early for me, thank you," I said.

"Ah, yes! I've missed a few meals, I expect. But wait a little if you've time. I want to talk to you. You'll have tea, perhaps?"

"No, thank you, but I'll wait a little while if you want me to," I said.

It would have been interesting to test the sort of dinner Maundeville could have waiting his pleasure and ready to be served in a quarter of an hour. Even at four o'clock I daresay I could have found it tempting. But apart from any other consideration, I have the old-fashioned idea that eating or drinking in a man's house implies certain obligations on both sides.

"Wait here," Maundeville suggested. "It will be more comfortable while the servants lay the table, unless you care to go upstairs?"

I said I would wait where I was, and Maundeville, rising from his chair, glanced about him.

"Put out those spirit-lamps and burners on the table," he said to Bates. "Leave everything else." And he passed out through the door which Bates held open for him.

I remembered that it was the first time I had seen him tired. I should have liked to hear from Bates what his master's hours and meals had been during the last few days. But I said nothing, nor did he, and after obeying Maundeville's orders he followed him without a sound. I never heard a door creak or a handle rattle in that house. I never saw or heard any servant but Bates and the chauffeur; and Bates moved as though he were on rubber tyres.

I dropped into the chair Maundeville had left, and glanced about without any expectation of seeing anything particularly instructive.

Chemistry was the interest of the moment obviously, and odds and ends relating to other sciences and hobbies were shoved away on to side tables and shelves.

Bates came back in a moment, noiseless as ever. Maundeville had noticed my taxi, and told him to ask if I wouldn't have the man paid and sent off.

I said no, that he was to take me elsewhere later, and Bates slipped away again.

I had not gone there with any intention of spying about, but merely of giving Maundeville an opening—to draw him.

If he had not been pretty well tired out, I am sure that I should have missed what happened now.

On the edge of the long deal table in the centre of the room—the one he had been working at—I had laid my gloves and the book which I had taken from a shelf while we talked. It was a book on archæology. I really wanted it to look up a reference to vitrified forts which I had seen in the West Highlands. I thought I would do so now, to avoid carrying it away, and I went to the table for it.

I fancy that Bates, in putting out a burner, must have slightly disturbed loose papers, sheets of memoranda, calculations and so forth, lying scattered about the table.

At any rate, as I picked up the book I saw something else that I had not noticed before.

It was only an inch or two of oilskin, sticking out from under some other things. But in such a place it was noticeable, and I pushed the papers aside.

There, half opened, lay the packet which I had last seen in the hands of the Malay sailor—the outside oilskin wrapper, the inner covering of muslin, and the yellow putty-like substance enclosed.

I have no intention of apologising for, or explaining my theft. I pulled a bit off the little ball, rolled the latter hurriedly into shape again, wrapped the bit in a corner of my handkerchief, pushed back the papers and went to my seat as quickly as possible.

Maundeville's shave and change of clothing was a very speedy operation. Certainly in a quarter of an hour from the time he left me he came in again—in dinner dress now, though it was only about half-past four. He found me sitting in the chair which he had vacated, taking a note or two from the book I had borrowed. I told him I had found all I needed, and I returned the book to its place.

He looked much fresher, and announcing that his appetite was enormous, led the way to the dining-room, taking some vermouth from the sideboard before he sat down—at the same time laughingly declaring that it was altogether superfluous.

During soup and fish, while Bates waited on him, he told me more about those West Coast vitrified forts than I had learnt from all the books I had consulted.

Then Bates put before him a cold fowl, with tongue, salad, etc., and a pint of Irroy.

Maundeville asked me to let Bates open a bottle for me, and when I refused he told him to leave the cheese on the sideboard, and come when he heard the bell.

He then drank half a glass of champagne, attacked the fowl with gusto, and began to talk again. He seemed to have the appetite of a boy of sixteen. I watched him with a certain reluctant admiration. I began to consider him more as a force than a mere man like myself.

"Well," Maundeville said, "I have news for you. My mixed serums, or sera, if you choose, promise well."

"How have you tested them?" I asked.

"Solely on myself. But in that way I've been able to exclude fallacies. My imagination is well under control, and at the same time I know the danger-signals."

"I fancy you have a good deal of imagination," I said.

"Do me the favour of assuming that I use my mother-tongue

with accuracy!" he replied, with some impatience. "I have a powerful imagination, of course, or I shouldn't conceive things. But when it has done its work I can shut it off, and go on with the job in the daylight of common sense."

I thought this quite likely. If he had a strong imagination his will was strong too, and I fancied his critical faculty pitiless, even to himself.

"A certain amount of risk in these things is inevitable," he went on. "Risk to oneself in experimenting, and great danger of fallacies. How many clever fellows have openly worked for the elixir, or some modification of it, and openly failed? How many, more wisely, have brought good brains to the job and failed, and therefore said nothing! For the time, if you'll help me, you and I will be among the wiser ones and say nothing yet. What is it that's said about fools and bairns not seeing half-done work? If you subtract the fools and the bairns from our population, how many are left?"

"You and I, apparently," I said, with absolute gravity, and Maundeville, after looking steadily over his plate at me for a minute, laid down his knife and fork and laughed hugely.

"Forgive me if I say bluntly that now and then I find we have a good deal in common," he said. "Neither of us is a fool, Armiston, and so neither of us thinks himself omniscient or omnipotent. Still, we're a good bit above the average. If we had only met earlier!" He didn't say what would have happened in that contingency, but went on: "Now let's quit our noble selves, and talk of more important things."

"With all my heart," I said, looking at my watch. "I've been rather expecting to hear from you. But I must be elsewhere by 5.30 at the latest."

I thought for a moment that he was about to ask where I was going, but he did not. After all, he was never impertinently inquisitive, and besides, I dare say that he supposed he knew.

"Well, I mustn't make you late," he said. "It amounts to this, that I have certainly found a combination which is at any rate a strong whip to one's nervous system. For three days and nights now, having work to do, and working as I do best in long spurts with complete idleness between for three days and nights, I say, I've eaten and drunk very little, and slept still less. Here am

I enjoying my dinner uncommonly, and not now particularly tired."

"You attribute this to your treatment?" I asked.

"Oh, decide for yourself—allowing what margin you like for the imagination we spoke of. I've done a longer spell than before with less effort and less fatigue. *Ergo* these injections being the one new factor, they are responsible for the new results."

"And what do you want me to do?"

"First test the effects on myself! Decide whether the treatment is merely exhausting my store of energy at an abnormal pace, or whether vital force is being abnormally produced and stored. Then——" He stopped and looked at the clock.

"You'll be late for your engagement if we're not careful," he said. "It will take you a quarter of an hour to get there."

I was sure that he assumed, quite unconsciously, that I was going to call on Miss O'Hagan.

"After you've watched me for a day or two," he said, "decide whether you care to test the thing on yourself. You and I are much the same age, I fancy. It's an age at which, for certain possible gains, one can afford to run risks. One's stake in any case is not the stake of a young life."

"You forget," I said, "that I may value my life more highly than I did, say, a week or ten days ago."

"Do I?" he asked, looking at me fixedly. "You value the possibility of another fifty years of potential youth higher still, I fancy. I should in your shoes, at any rate."

I left him helping himself to cheese, while Bates decanted a bottle of very special port under his master's supervision.

I noticed that Mudge, who came to the door before I could use my latchkey, was looking distinctly worried. All he said was, "Thank Gord! Another five minutes *and*——" Then he got my tea, and waited on me more attentively than usual, but asked no questions, and, of course, I told him nothing.

From that time he liked to know in detail what my movements were to be when I left the house. Twice when I replied vaguely, he asked me point-blank if I was going to Maundeville's.

CHAPTER XXXVI

THE TOXICOLOGIST

I had intended to spend the evening at home with a novel. I really wanted to distract my attention from these affairs of the Mummy for a while. Otherwise I was likely to have a bad time of it when I went to bed.

I did settle down to the book for an hour after my tea. But at the end of that time I decided that the bit of stuff in my handkerchief was very inconveniently placed.

I tucked handkerchief and all away in a bureau, and having gone to my bedroom for a clean one, decided that I was restless and must go out. I wanted to talk to someone about this putty stuff. So I put the other handkerchief and its contents in a pocket again.

I am not on the telephone, but I went to the nearest call-office and found that Mortimer was. Mortimer—you may know who I mean if you're a medical jurist. I was at Guys' with him. I'm only a general practitioner and he refused the chair in Medical Jurisprudence and Toxicology at —— and never leaves Gray's Inn. When I rang him up, his answer to my question whether he was at home and disengaged was, "Who are you?"

I told him, but he didn't seem to remember me. He hummed and ha'd, making difficulties and suggesting other times, till suddenly he brightened up. "Armiston, you said? You were medical witness—Perceval—Park Lane?"

"Yes."

I heard what I could swear was a cackle of laughter at the other end.

"What did you say?" I asked. I wanted to say, "What the blazes are you cackling about?" but I had just enough sense to put it the other way.

"Oh, nothing. I said nothing. Pleased to meet you! Come along now!" and I went. I could swear he was cackling again when I hung up the receiver.

At Gray's Inn I was first shown into a fairly large wainscoted room, with handsome heavy mahogany furniture, highly polished. Then after my card had been asked for and taken away, I could hear the highly respectable female who admitted me, arguing warmly close by.

"It's not fit to bring a gentleman into," I heard her say. The reply was inaudible, but she spoke again. "At any rate let me bring you another coat." "——" "Oh, very well, sir! Of course, as you say, it's not my business," and presently she returned.

"Dr. Mortimer says, sir, if you'll excuse the dreadful state of his study, he'd rather see you there. And he thinks it best, seeing you're in a hurry, not to keep you waiting, though he didn't dress for dinner to-night."

I said something about it being all the same to me, and I followed her, while she muttered something about Doctor Mortimer always being so busy that it was hard to get him out of his study to clean it.

It was years since I had met Mortimer, but when I set eyes on him now I thought there was surprisingly little change in the man.

He sat drinking tea by a small fire, though it was June. I was at once reminded that I had left Maundeville also by a fire.

His chair was very big, and he very small and frail, except his head, which seemed too heavy for the thin neck, and the upper part altogether disproportionate to what lay below the level of the bright beady eyes.

He held out a slender, small hand to me, which felt cold to the touch. His voice was harshly chirpy, suggesting a sparrow with laryngitis; and when I had taken a chair on the opposite side of the fire to his own, he sipped his tea, always regarding me over the rim of the cup, and then putting it down continued to survey me, smiling a little dry smile, with his big black head a trifle to one side.

"I remember you now!" he said. "It's a long time since we met, Armiston. I saw your name in connection with that Park Lane case. Have you come to me to corroborate your declaration about the *datura stramonium*, or to upset it?"

"Neither," I declared. "I've come about something else."

"Glad of that!" he said. "I don't want to upset an old acquaintance's faith in himself. I didn't agree with you, you know merely judging by what I read. There's only one case on record of poisoning through stramonium cigarettes."

"I didn't say it was the cigarettes," I reminded him, "though I did say stramonium. I've changed my opinion on that too," I added.

"Ha! That's awkward for you. What are you going to do, then? Ask for a fresh inquest?"

"I'm going to do nothing," I said.

Mortimer didn't seem shocked at this, but very much amused.

"You have the courage of your opinions, I see—until they change," he cackled, "and you're as brutally frank as ever. Well! What is it now?"

"I want you to tell me what this is," I said; and I held out my bit of putty, half uncovered in the handkerchief. He took it from me, displaying the frayed sleeve-edge of what was certainly a disgraceful old jacket.

He held it to the light, sniffed at it, pinched it, and looked at me sideways, still bird-like.

"I shall need to test it in various ways," he said, "and there isn't much of it. What can you tell me about it to start with? We might eliminate certain things, or get an idea to start upon. Where did you get it?"

"It belonged to a Malay sailor," I said. "I've some reason to think it's a poison."

"Oh! very likely. Why don't you ask him?"

"I don't know where he is," I said. "He talked of going home."

"A Malay sailor." Mortimer poured out more tea for himself. He didn't offer me any, but as his big tea-pot was evidently simmering on the hob, I was resigned.

"Granting the Malay," he went on, "and assuming poison, certain things suggest themselves."

He got out of the big chair in which he was hunched up like a monkey, and put up a monkey's paw to book-shelves close above his head. There were books all over the room. Many of them tea-stained and coverless, some fresh from the publishers—I dare say for review. He took one which hardly held together, and curling up in his chair again, sipped and considered in silence. He interrupted once to rise rather hurriedly, and with sundry unscientific phrases to rush off to his adjoining bedroom and wash his hands. I could hear the water splashing about in the basin. When he came back, using uncomplimentary adjectives about himself, I asked whether he thought I had better wash my hands too. He agreed to this, but evidently wouldn't have thought of suggesting it.

When I came back from the bedroom—a very clean, big, bare room where his housekeeper evidently wielded more authority and dusters—he was plunged in his books again. He had opened two more, but soon tossed them all on the nearest table.

"Naming it may be fairly simple," he said. "Don't go presenting bits to your friends, meanwhile, indiscriminately."

"What do you think of it?"

"I like to wait until I know, Armiston. It's more scientific—and besides, it would hurt me to feel that I had said what wasn't accurate—even to a coroner's jury. He! He! Come again to-morrow night if you like."

He nodded, and apparently forgot me; and I was shown to the door by the housekeeper, who came out of what seemed a spotless kitchen, and insisted on brushing my light overcoat and my hat before she would let me go.

Between that night and the next nothing particular happened.

I was restless and unsettled, but not inclined to go out and mix with other men; though somehow they and the world generally (especially in June) seemed much more charming than usual.

I wanted to give a few instructions to my lawyer, an old friend, and I asked him to let me dine with him, and chat about these little things quietly over our wine.

He gave me a very pleasant dinner, savoured by good-natured cynical views. I believe I rather surprised him by my charity towards my fellows that evening, and still more, perhaps, by suddenly returning on impulse to wring his hand, after leaving his door.

When I left him to his surmises, I returned to Gray's Inn. For anything I could see to the contrary, Mortimer might not have moved since I had left him the night before.

He was hunched up in the same way, in the same jacket and the same chair. The same teapot was on the hob, and he was still drinking strong black tea.

The housekeeper, on the way to this den of his, was still apologetic. She had had, it seemed, no chance for tidying that particular room that day. Nor ever had, I suppose. At any rate, her apologies faltered, as though she feared they were hardly good enough to delude me.

Mortimer's greeting was characteristic. He didn't rise or even say "How d'you do?" or anything else that was hospitable— though I believe he was pleased to see me.

He merely cackled one of the several names by which a certain poison is known, and then lay back and grinned at me.

Now I say plainly, and at once, that neither here nor anywhere else do I mean to give you the name of that poison. It's not readily obtainable, but it can be got; and the hypodermic syringe now seems to have become almost an article of the toilette-table.

At the same time anyone who has been obliged to study toxicology and physiology will quite readily recognise the thing, if he thinks it worth while to read on to the end.

While I was considering Mortimer's information, which I was certain would be accurate, he startled me by another remark.

"You know," he said, "I think you're considerably indebted to me for the trouble I've taken."

"I should be sorry to deny that," I said. "Indeed, I may owe you more than you suppose. If it's a question of your fee, name it!"

But Mortimer shook his head.

"Payment in kind will suit me best," he answered, still grinning impishly.

"I can't oblige you with more of this vile stuff," I said.

"I didn't mean that," he declared, "though I'd certainly like some. But I've answered a question of yours, and you seem to think my information may be useful. Now pay me by telling me something."

No doubt it seemed most churlish, but I at once began to hedge and to debate, and while I floundered through various phrases intended to convey gratitude and refusal at the same time, he sat and watched me maliciously.

"That's your gratitude!" he said at last. "Don't stray from the path of truth, my dear Armiston, for any more flowers of speech, or you'll get hopelessly bogged. Say you won't oblige me, and be done with it!"

"Hang it, then, probably I won't!" I said frankly. "Name a good fee, and let me write you a cheque. You're so confoundedly sharp that one question might include more than one thing, and more folk than myself."

"Ha! Professional secrecy? Remember, you can't plead privilege in a criminal action," Mortimer chuckled. "But I'm going to ask you my question, and you'll answer as you choose. You got this from a Malay sailor?"

"It belonged to a Malay sailor," I agreed, and Mortimer leant forward out of his chair and pointed a monkey-like finger at me.

"It would very much interest me to know," he said, "whether this Malay, to whom our identified poison belonged, was in the very least degree in touch with your Park Lane case."

"Why?" I asked.

"Then Haschish, Armiston. Haschish that time, not *datura stramonium*. That's where you went wrong, as I think you know. No fee, thanks! You see, you've practically answered my question after all—and given me considerable entertainment. Oh, I shan't say anything to anybody. It's not my business."

I rose to go, and as I did so I asked another question. "If I happened to get a dose of this stuff, what antidote should I try?"

"I don't know what quantity taken by the mouth might injure a man. It would have to be very large, and it would most likely do him no harm. But if I was unfortunate enough to have a subcutaneous injection I should certainly try a hypodermic of strychnine hydrochlorate—if I had time." He sat and considered the matter, repeating his suggestive proviso, "If I had time—if I had time," softly under his breath. "I am of opinion, however, my dear Armiston, that it would be one of those instances in which prevention is very much better—and easier—than cure."

I attempted to swear him to secrecy.

"I have some very interesting experiments in hand just now," Mortimer said calmly. "I'm likely to forget all about your visit, for the time, unless I happen to hear of any sudden death among your acquaintances."

"Say nothing if you hear of my own," I retorted. "It will be 'merely a general practitioner' the less, you'll remember."

I left him, grinning after me from among his cultures and concoctions, over his stewed tea.

The last thing I heard as I shut the door behind me was, "Haschish! Armiston, not stramonium! You were wrong there!" followed by a most exasperating chuckle.

CHAPTER XXXVII

FIAT EXPERIMENTUM?

I trust that I am always sufficiently well-dressed to pass unnoticed anywhere, but at that time I thought it right to make my attire strike a rather more pronounced note.

I tried to keep up the general impression of a man who has hope to live upon, and finds it on the whole a stimulating diet. I suppose my face wasn't precisely as youthful or as bright as my apparel. But then the lover on probation must have anxious moments anyway, and may be allowed to show the effects. I was sufficiently rewarded when I saw that Maundeville watched me with increasing attention.

I avoided his house for a few days, and he soon dropped in to call, complaining that he had become accustomed to see me come and go, and that he missed me.

"Besides," he added, "I've reached the point in my investigations where I can't do without your help. Can't Cadogan Square spare you to me occasionally?"

I did my best to produce a fatuous smile, and allowing myself the luxury of naked truth, reminded him that I was only there on sufferance.

"My dear fellow, don't be too modest!" Maundeville implored gaily. "Own that the lady listens more readily."

"Certainly sometimes I believe I shall win," I said, smiling, while I looked in a little mirror over the mantelpiece to see the effect of a fresh rose-bud and maidenhair fern in my button-hole. It might be merely a lively imagination that made me see a momentary spasm cross the reflection of Maundeville's face in the glass. At any rate, he congratulated me warmly and chaffed me lightly, and all in excellent taste.

"We must soon be choosing our wedding presents, I see," he said. "'Unto him that hath shall be given.'"

I recommended him, with a smile which I am afraid was wry enough, to leave the question of presents until he had Miss O'Hagan's assurance that the wedding was definitely arranged. Then, fearing lest I had not been sufficiently the coxcomb, I rang for Mudge and rowed him for having put out a dark waistcoat for me, instead of a light one, and told him to go to the florist's, and ask if the flowers I had ordered had gone to Cadogan Square.

Mudge's face was such a study, as he listened, that when he left the room I had no difficulty in laughing heartily enough, while Maundeville for a time became curiously silent.

I then asked him to excuse me, as I was due at Cadogan Square; and I said good-bye, making an appointment with him for two days later, at his house. Miss O'Hagan having kindly agreed to receive me whenever I thought fit to present myself, I saw her that afternoon, and stayed talking for some time over my tea. I never met any woman like her for making a man feel a whole-some contempt for his commonplace self.

Maundeville was, as usual now, in his museum or laboratory—call it which you will—when I called to keep my appointment. A thunderstorm had been threatening all the morning, and two or three electric lamps were lit, and the shutters closed. The lights were well shaded, and the shadows were deep all round the room, the table alone standing out clearly. When I entered he was apparently doing nothing, but sat outside the lighted space among the shadows, with his chin upon his hand, and his face turned towards the Mummy, which stood in its usual niche. I would have liked to know what his thoughts had been while he waited for me; for I had lately felt that, however interesting or amusing Maundeville's conversation might sometimes be, what he said was not so important as what he kept to himself. He at once began to discuss what he said he had been working at during the last few months, namely, the prolongation of life, and, of course, of youth and energy with it.

"Life *per se* is of no value," he said. "One postulates that. One does not aim at hibernation or a prolonged trance. One must preserve power of action, and of enjoyment—or nothing. Now where is the seat of vitality? A layman might say the heart. You and I know that the heart may have a bullet in it, be cut, stabbed, sewn up, and continue to do its work, so long as it is not too greatly damaged for mechanical action as a pump. But cut the connection between the heart and the vital centres higher up—or paralyse these centres by physical or mental shock—and behold! the impulse to live has ceased!"

He talked on, quoting Pythagoras, Herodotus, Bacon, Horace, Juvenal, Galen, Aristophanes and Paracelsus, besides half a dozen of our contemporaries. Laughing or sighing, jesting or in bitter earnest, as he said, man had always shown his instinct to prolong life and to preserve youth. You might have expected his talk would be satirical, if not ludicrous, but it was neither. There was an energy and passion about it that I confess impressed me. I felt as though he spoke for so many—and then I have seen so many grow old reluctantly, and reluctantly pass away.

Suddenly he stopped and laughed. "It's an interesting subject," he said. "It has fascinated a good many minds not otherwise alike. We won't speculate on the possible limits of success. Supposing that, for the time in strict confidence, I give you a certain formula, or recipe, which I have used personally. Then I give you certain evidence of what I believe to be the direct results of my treatment. Criticise my theories, analyse my concoctions, scrutinise my results. Test my prescription practically upon yourself—if you have pluck enough and then decide with me whether we can put our conclusions quietly, say, before the British Medical Association, as worth its consideration."

He stopped, waiting, I imagined, for some response from me, and then he spoke in a different tone.

"Good men and good work have been ignored and ridiculed by our liberal profession times enough," he said. "The outside public, ass though it is, would recognise the results of such a bit of work long before many of our brethren. But if I am right I shall have the best possible way of silencing my objectors—I shall outlive them. If one is not deceived one will enjoy the results *in propria persona*, whether they be recognised by the faculty or not. You, who are meeting the very personification of youth itself almost every day, will think it worth while—no, I won't advance the most selfish argument—you will be pleased if you can do anything to keep youth youthful and charming as it is now, if only for a time. It would be a wedding present that emperors can't equal."

He broke away again into the dryly matter of fact.

"That's enough windy eloquence! We'll have no more mere unsupported statements," he said. "Do you care to see my formula and the different constituents?"

"Of course!" I said. "That doesn't bind me to anything."

"Except silence," Maundeville added, and straightway went into detail.

The stuff he worked with was an ethereal extract of certain animal organs, combined with large quantities of hydrochlorate of strychnine. The constituent to which he attached most importance was extracted from the cerebellum and medulla oblongata of the calf—these parts being chosen because of the important nerve-centres located there.

"And why the strychnine?" I asked, and his reply was that since one couldn't isolate the precise vital centres, apart from their surroundings, the extract contained forces which must be counteracted. For example, in experimenting one night with an unusually large injection he found that his pulse gradually sank to thirty beats to the minute. After that he combined strychnine. He found that no apparent effect resulted from taking large doses by the mouth, and he now always used a hypodermic syringe.

I listened while he explained these things to me, and then putting down the glass-stoppered bottle which held the completed fluid preparation ready for use, he picked up a note-book from the table, and showed me the entries under different recent dates.

For example, on the night of June 10th he had returned from a reception at about eleven o'clock, and after changing his clothes had walked thirty miles, returning to breakfast at nine, and going through an ordinary day's occupations afterwards.

From the morning of June 12th to the evening of June 14th he had worked in the museum, with little food (he had noted the precise quantities) and no sleep.

On June 16th and 17th he had taken no food, except coffee, with his ordinary quantities of cream and sugar, and had gone about as usual without any particular discomfort.

"It so happened," he said, laughing, "that on the night of the 17th I turned in to dine at the club. As I went to my table I met a man just home on leave from Egypt. He congratulated me on my general fitness, and I told him if he sat down for a chat and a glass of wine at my table he'd see reason to congratulate me on my appetite too. Before I had finished dinner he did so. He said he hadn't seen anyone enjoy a meal so much, since he shot a giraffe for a native tribe that hadn't a waist-cloth or an ounce of fat between them. Similarly with sleep. I could go comfortably now for a couple of nights without any—or I could go to sleep here in this chair while you watched."

"You were always strong," I reminded him, watching. "You must have an easy conscience."

"Why should one construct a bogey for one's own mortification?" Maundeville laughed. "But you're right. I was always strong, though I'm sure I could never endure fatigue before as I have lately. There is only one way to check my results properly. Experiment upon yourself, and see how far we differ, and how far results coincide."

"Done!" I said, after a moment's deliberation and the weighing of probabilities. "Give me an injection now!"

For a few seconds Maundeville sat silent too. Whether I had taken him by surprise, or whether he too was deliberating over his actions, I can't say. But presently he rose.

"My dose is thirty minims," he said. "At starting, and to guard against any personal idiosyncrasy, I'll dose you with fifteen, and gradually increase it."

I said nothing more. I rolled up the sleeve from my left fore-arm, and watched him take fifteen minims from the little glass-stoppered bottle, which he proceeded to inject under my skin.

I confess that I should then have preferred to get away at once, but Maundeville insisted upon the necessity of sitting quiet for at least ten minutes, and I wished to be docile.

Whether it was because the approaching thunderstorm charged the hot air with electricity, or because of the injection I did not know. It might even have been mere imagination. But I seemed to creep and tingle all over, and all my senses were exalted. I even noticed Maundeville's newspaper crackle on the table as he passed it, and I told him that the sound seemed almost to hurt me.

"Ah, yes!" he said, seating himself again, and pulling the newspaper to him. "That reminds me of something. It will serve to keep your mind from magnifying symptoms while you sit quiet. When you came I had just been reading the account of the D—— murder. The man's nerve failed him, and he took so many precautions after the event that he roused suspicion. A little more patience beforehand, and a little more pluck after, and I think he'd have got clear. Although as far as that goes, some criminals and the police are so far parallels in stupidity, that like other parallels they never meet."

He laughed softly, and stopped to consider this.

"That's not so very bad!" he said appreciatively. "I know a police commissioner. Next time I dine with him I must introduce that apothegm and see how he likes it! But that's not what I was going to say."

He stopped and listened to the far-off crackling of thunder.

"The storm's coming at last!" he said. "We shall be able to breathe better then. I like a good thunderstorm, don't you? Let's open the window."

He pushed back the shutters, opened the windows, and switched off all except one light.

"Referring for a moment to poor Perceval's unfortunate death," he said, "I sometimes fear that we got on the wrong scent. Do you remember a little rough-and-tumble I once had with a lascar?"

"Yes," I said, wondering.

"Well, I happened across the fellow again. He seemed to think that because I had knocked him off work for a time he had a claim on me."

"He couldn't enforce it," I suggested.

"Oh, no! But I hate bother, and it sometimes makes me do things that seem good-natured. I found he could cook a bit and wait table, and I got him a job *pro tem.* at The Banyan. Now when I remember how mad I was myself that night (you'll recollect even better) and that he waited at our table, I sometimes wonder whether he doesn't know more about that evening than we do. I was a good-natured fool to suppose that a Malay ever forgets. Do you read Kipling? If so, you may remember *The Limitations of Pambé Serang?*"

"Yes," I remembered, and said so.

"Where's the Malay now, do you suppose?" I asked him.

"Shipped for another voyage, I expect," Maundeville said carelessly. "I know Samuels sacked him. We must do what we can to trace him again, but I was reminded of him while I read the paper."

"Why?"

"Oh, they say 'murder will out.' It's one of a good many fallacies which give the bourgeoisie a little ease, and perhaps sometimes frighten a neurotic criminal into betraying himself. The police know better, but of course they don't say so. Apart from a good many known murders unexplained, there must be many never recognised as murders at all. We can hardly prove this without getting hold of the Malay. Such a fellow is hard to trace. I don't believe he will ever come back, and if he did he wouldn't betray himself. Mark my words, I don't believe we shall see him again. There's the storm at last!"

So it was. It broke a mile or two away, and rolled over the West End, the rain falling as if in the tropics, the lightning dazzling us where we sat, and the thunder shaking us in our chairs.

Maundeville rose as it drew near, and standing at the window watched it with tremendous enjoyment, until the storm rolled muttering away eastward.

"It must have done damage somewhere, one would think," he said, as I rose to go, "and some of those discharges were as close as could be! I fancy if one of us had been struck, there at the window, one's superabundant vitality would have been a poor show, in spite of our elixir. If you have an accidental policy, Armiston, I advise you to stick to it."

I went away, feeling that after the storm, and outside that house, I could breathe more freely.

CHAPTER XXXVIII

I GET THE ACE OF SPADES

Now I knew quite well that I was playing with more than one kind of fire, and to tell you the honest truth, I don't think I shall ever quite get over the scorching. There was one element of danger, however, that I had not prepared for. Those subcutaneous doses of Maundeville's had a power which I did not anticipate, and will not attempt to explain with any precision now. Of course, the strong doses of strychnine must not be forgotten, but I never knew strychnine alone to have such results. There is this further suggestion. Maundeville found that with certain staining reagents (which he promised to tell me about later) he could map out and isolate certain brain tracts. Using these special brain tracts (parts of the brain) alone, seemed to make a much more powerful extract, especially in combination with those tracts in the spinal cord which reacted to the same agent. I make no dogmatic assertion, my data being insufficient, but I repeat that the parts of the brain most utilised contained almost entirely what physiologists are accustomed to call collectively, for convenience sake, the "lower centres."

Whatever the cause might be, at the end of that June I felt remarkably well and much more reckless. I took daily doses from Maundeville, and was ready to push them further and faster than he would allow. I kept a record of various subjective and objective tests for comparison with his—but I also noted various facts of which I told him nothing.

For example, my point of view was beginning to alter—I make no attempt to explain how or why. I began to develop a certain sympathy with Maundeville (of which there are traces still), together, however, with growing determination to put my wits against his and utterly to crush him.

I sympathised with him so much that I felt as though I could read his thoughts and feel his feelings: so much that I constantly wondered he didn't see through me.

Maundeville once outwitted and crushed, and what then? Ah! that was becoming an open question, depending partly, no doubt, on others, or another, but mostly, I sometimes dreamt, upon myself. In his museum I once, during these days, heard Maundeville humming in his strong musical baritone the "Song of Thor":

> "Force rules the world still
> Has ruled it, shall rule it.
> Meekness is weakness."

"By . . . you're right!" I rapped out suddenly, and I remember I was conscious immediately afterwards, without absolutely seeing him, that Maundeville watched me curiously, as though he had found something to consider.

I got up to leave him early that day, and, indeed, he seemed rather inclined to be alone, and gave me no encouragement to stay.

One queer thing he said, just as I left, which rather startled me. He turned from the table and put a strong hand on my shoulder.

"Tell me," he said, "if it's not indiscreet, have you gone quite out of your depth at Cadogan Square?"

"Over head and ears," I declared boldly.

"And the lady, Armiston? Honestly, I am not asking out of impertinent curiosity."

"About the lady it is not for me to say," I protested. But I know I spoke with a certain air, and his hand fell from my shoulder.

"You and I would have done great things together," he said moodily. "You're a bigger man than I thought. It seems a pity."

"Why 'would have done'?" I asked. "We will go on."

"A man can't serve two masters—or mistresses," he said, as he turned back to the table. "But—yes, we will certainly go on," and he never again asked me about Cadogan Square.

I started to go there straight from his house that day, the "Song of Thor" booming in my ears. But I found myself nearly three-quarters of an hour earlier than Miss O'Hagan would expect me, and I turned into my club. Everybody there was complaining of the heat, and I was surprised I hadn't noticed anything oppressive about it. Men talked with greedy longing for August and the moors or the sea.

One fellow, turning to me, asked, "Where have you been for your holidays?" and when I told him that I hadn't left London, and was too busy to go, he stared.

"Then you don't need to go!" he said enviously. "Never saw you look so fit in my life."

Indeed, I saw quite plainly, as I went down the wide club staircase with two others towards a big mirror, that their faces were haggard and sallow compared with mine, and I knew I was the eldest of the three.

I went on to Cadogan Square feeling a certain savage exhilaration. Once I quoted Maundeville's words aloud: "You're a bigger man than I thought," and I laughed outright. He hadn't quite taken my measure yet. I was a different man, too, at Cadogan Square that afternoon. I had never before felt so alert and so masterful. It made me less awkward, and I could see that I spoke with greater ease and more ability, and with a certain recklessness that, unless her eyes and her whole bearing were false witness, had a sort of uncanny fascination for Miss O'Hagan—for an hour.

Yes, that was my hour, and my high-water mark. However low it may be, a man must reach his highest some time, and I reached it then; though I thought I saw greater heights of selfishness and success before me.

I left, having begged an appointment for the next afternoon, and having got it.

"Here," you will say, "is an elderly braggart gasconading in poor taste!"

Well, I agree, but I do so of set purpose, for this is how I felt, and how I was ready to act, for one short afternoon. I saw, too, how I could make sure of having, at any rate, no one in my way— but my lunacy passed, and left me with nothing but a day-dream on my conscience.

It was Mudge the commonplace, Mudge the not-too-sensitive,

Mudge the occasional appropriator of unconsidered trifles, who smoked my best cigars, who suddenly turned on me and held up an uncomplimentary mirror.

Lately with Mudge I had been more exacting, more dictatorial, and sometimes pretty harsh. That night, dining at home and in a mood to be amused, I let him wait upon me and wax garrulous, while I ridiculed his "fond adventures."

There was one about himself, a certain bluejacket who had been his great pal, and, of course, a girl who, Mudge gently hinted, might have smiled on himself under a little pressure.

"Why didn't you take the girl?" I asked carelessly, cracking a couple of brazil-nuts one against the other, and admiring my own strength of grip.

Mudge smiled at my joke. "Not my way with pals, sir," he said.

"You tell that to the marines, Mudge! I don't believe you. You're too old a hand not to know better. That way one gets left."

"Not my way, sir," Mudge insisted obstinately. He was just about to pour out a glass of port for me, but he stiffened and stood with the decanter as though he were about to present arms —a ridiculous figure. I looked up at him more attentively, and was astonished to find that Mudge was really insulted. His hand trembled with the decanter, and his face was a trifle paler than usual.

"Girls is uncertain in their fancies. But I'd rot before I played that dirty game with a pal. I draw the line there," he said deliberately.

"You're a d——d fool, Mudge," I said, "and I apologise. Here's a glass of port, and here's to the man who knows where to draw the line!"

Mudge saluted, drank his wine, saluted again, faced about, and retired in good order with all the honours. But I sat for an hour or so just where I was, with meditations which I need not inflict upon you. Then, though it was pretty late, I went out, telling Mudge not to wait up for me.

I walked to Maxwell's quarters, and finding that he was out for the evening, I waited for him, lighting a cigar and turning over some of his books. When he came in a little after midnight,

I remember I was reading *The Making of a Frontier,* by Colonel Durand.

I recommend it as likely to have a salutary effect on any man inclined to overrate himself. I was being reduced to my proper dimensions when Maxwell found me.

I did not stay long. Maxwell, I thought, greeted me with some coolness, but I showed no sign of noticing that.

I told him that I had made an engagement to call on Miss O'Hagan the following afternoon, but found I couldn't go.

"Can you manage to call instead?" I asked him. "She hasn't gone out, practically, to any extent since the Park Lane trouble, and I think the young lady is moping."

"And can't you divert her?" Maxwell asked me, bluntly.

"Oh, I!" I answered carelessly. "I'm useful *faute de mieux.* She knows I have every desire to be. But the fact is that an old friend nearer her own age could do more. Frankly, I think you've been neglecting the young woman lately, and I've a notion that she thinks so too."

All Maxwell said about it was that he could call if I thought he could help; but his manner changed very perceptibly. When I rose he pressed me to stay and chat, telling me that he meant to have a whisky-and-soda, and I must have one with him.

I agreed, ready to meet him half-way, and presently he began to speak of the Mummy.

"I've often wished I could take your view," he said. "It's the merest common sense to agree mutually that bets are off and the Mummy visits no more."

"Oh, but I've changed my opinion," I said. "I quite agree with you that the affair must be carried through—if only because of the men who've done their share already."

"You've changed more than your opinion lately, it seems to me," he said, looking at me attentively. "How is that, I wonder?"

"Youth! Youth!" I answered, chaffing. "Youth and development. And why have your views altered?"

"Oh, as for me, I'm growing older," he said chaffingly too, and then altered his tone. "I'll tell you one reason," he said. "Laugh if you like. It seems merely brutal to allow another deal, when you're sure where the danger will fall, and know that you're safe."

"You spoke like that before," I reminded him. "You were a false prophet."

"I know," he agreed, "but I repeat it. I swear Maundeville is the man most in danger."

I was on the point of expressing my satisfaction, but checked myself.

"Come! What would you call a really first-class cigar?" I asked him. "Never mind the price."

He stared. "You're certainly younger," he muttered, and then named a cigar. I'm not a tobacconist's tout, so if you like we'll call them "Almas di Cuba."

"Very well," I said. "I'm a poor man, as you know, but I'll bet you an even fifty 'Almas di Cuba' that next time there's a deal, Maundeville doesn't get the Spade—and I'll bet you another fifty that I do."

"I don't like——" he began.

"Are you afraid to lose?" I asked.

"Done! If I'm right I'll tell you my reason—whatever you may think of it."

"If I'm right I may have to tell you mine," I said. That ended our talk.

The next morning I had a few professional calls to make, and was passing through Vigo Street when I met Maundeville. On the impulse of the moment I stopped him, as he nodded and seemed to be passing on.

"I know you're interested in my progress," I said. "I was at Cadogan Square after I left you yesterday. I'm open to receive your congratulations on my success, though we're saying nothing yet except to personal friends like yourself. The fatal step is taken."

He looked at me in silence for a moment, and then smiled.

"Well," he said, "you must accept my congratulations. From a purely selfish point of view, I'm sorry. But I'm sure you'll never live to regret it. I've lost a valuable colleague."

He smiled again, and went on. Then I began to wonder at my own impulse, and I had to explain to Miss O'Hagan as clearly as I could over the telephone how matters were supposed to stand between us. When she began to expostulate angrily, as naturally enough she did, I merely said that of course I was an awkward ass, but that I had acted on impulse, and that I was doing my best according to my lights. I then added that Maxwell would be calling on her that afternoon, and I rang off without waiting for any further reply.

On the following Friday I got the usual note saying that we were to meet for "cards" and tea at Maundeville's on the Monday afternoon.

I went, and I was the one to propose that Maundeville should deal. At the third round I got the Ace of Spades, and sat looking at it with more trepidation than I had anticipated. It was a pleasant surprise to be congratulated later on my *sang-froid*.

Well, an immediate compensation was a box of a hundred "Almas di Cuba," which came that very evening while I was at dinner. I smoked three before I went to my bed, feeling some uncertainty as to how much of the box I had time to enjoy.

I now tried so to order my affairs as to be prepared, as far as possible, for whatever the Mummy might bring me.

CHAPTER XXXIX

MAUNDEVILLE VISITS THE SICK

The first thing it brought me was a row with Mudge. Indeed, the row came first, after I had casually told him at breakfast that I had a large case coming to store for a few days, and that it would be safest and most convenient to stow it away in a corner of my bedroom.

He was silent at the time, but when waiting on me at dinner that night—and a particularly nice dinner he gave me—he opened fire.

"About that there Mummy, sir," he said.

I was thinking about it, and I said, "Well?" and only remembered too late that he wasn't supposed to diagnose a Mummy before he saw it. There was nothing to be gained by fencing about it then, so I listened as patiently as I could while Mudge, becoming more presumptuous with the exuberance of his own verbosity, did the heavy father and the familiar retainer of popular melodrama to perfection. The amount of information he had obtained rather surprised me; and the point of view which he tried to make me take was unexpected. His argument was that it wasn't respectable. "Me and you's single men," he said more than once. He went into the history of priestesses in general, hinting that, broadly (very broadly) speaking, they had at all times been no better than they should be.

"I've come on 'em," he said darkly, "'ere an' there." You'd think he was indulging in memories of past incarnations. I yawned openly when he stopped for a fresh argument, or to get his wind.

"You've been talking to Seymour," I said. "Is he here now?" and Mudge acknowledged that Seymour was now in the back premises.

"Give me my coffee," I ordered him, "and bring him in when I ring." And I added that I didn't see the use of his cooking a good dinner for me if he meant to worry me into indigestion afterwards.

I took my coffee leisurely, with one of Maxwell's cigars, worried the matter over for a little, and then rang the bell.

"Bring a couple of chairs to the table," I said to Mudge, "and a couple of glasses." I filled the glasses, and I told them both to sit down, which they did a trifle stiffly.

"Now," I said, "we're talking man to man. I won't say I'm going to tell you everything, for it isn't my business only. But what I do tell you will be the plain truth, and I expect to get the plain truth from both of you. Do you agree?"

They looked at one another, and at last Mudge spoke.

"Man to man," he said, "it shall be God's truth as far as it goes." And Seymour muttered that he was agreeable.

"Well, then, you, Seymour, what do you know about this Mummy?"

Seymour mentioned the names of Scrymgeour his master, of young D'Aurelle, and of Perceval, and reminded me that the Mummy had visited them all, and that they were dead.

"Anything more?"

"I know you can expect risks, sir. It's not for me to say how I know, because it came to me privately."

"Now," I said, "I'm going to be plain with you as far as I'm at liberty to be. You both know Miss O'Hagan. You'll agree with me that if it will help and please her for me to have that Mummy, and for you to hold your tongues about it, why, it's got to be done. She's a soldier's daughter, Mudge, with no men-folk of her own to help her. You, Seymour, know, I expect, what a lot Mr. Perceval thought of her. I can't tell you more because, like you, I find out things professionally that I can't talk about. But I tell you both that, as far as I can see, Miss O'Hagan will be helped best by my keeping the Mummy here for a fortnight or so, and by your holding your tongues and doing what I tell you. Now, it's a clean job, and we're none of us going to get anything out of it, unless it's her thanks, perhaps, some day. Are you on?"

Perhaps it was admiration for Miss O'Hagan, perhaps it was the second glass of port they had more or less absent-mindedly swallowed. Anyway they said, not without some enthusiasm, that they were on—and I closed the interview at once, handing each of them an "Alma" to smoke in the kitchen.

The next morning the Mummy came to my door in its coffin-like case.

I stood and watched the thing being carried up. For the life of me I couldn't help wondering whether it or I would be carried down first.

For the next few days I was, at any rate, well looked after, for Seymour joined Mudge in attending to me.

The fact is that I found my nerves weren't what I had thought, and I had to do what I could to ensure that at certain times I could go off guard without much risk. So when Mudge had to go out, Seymour was generally in his place. Nevertheless, I own to moments, even in broad daylight, when I would turn suddenly in the street, or in my chair, expecting to find trouble at my back; and at night more than once I waked suddenly, sweating, to find that I was sitting up in my bed, waiting for I knew not what.

Once Miss O'Hagan came hurriedly up the stair late in the afternoon, asking the imperturbable Mudge if I was quite well. She had telephoned to Maxwell to meet her at my place; but when he came she could only say that she had a sudden impulse to do so, and seemed puzzled and annoyed about it.

I made them both stay to tea; and it was not until after Miss O'Hagan had gone, with Maxwell to see her to her door, that Mudge told me Maundeville had called, but had refused to join us, saying something jokingly to Mudge about leaving young folks alone.

Another time my own nerves played me a silly trick. It was evening, and I had sent the two men out together, merely telling them not to be late home. Then while I sat alone reading, a sort of panic came upon me. Of course it was disgraceful, but if I brag of some things I must be frank about others.

I became suddenly sure that I was no longer alone in the house; and instead of getting up like a sensible man and going round to investigate, if necessary with a poker, I sat and listened, suddenly chilly, and with a queer crawling sensation over me as though my skin moved under my clothes.

Though I could hear nothing, I had a very distinct impression that this Something came nearer, and I felt quite unfit to meet it. Indeed, I felt as though if I even saw the door opening I should go crazy. All at once it occurred to me that I was supposed to be alone, and that I must suggest the reverse.

Sitting there, with my reading-lamp making grey, uncertain distances of shadow, I suddenly began to talk. Imagine me chattering away rather loudly, with now and again a break, during which I listened, with my hands clutching the arms of my chair, and heard nothing. Then this unformed horror went as suddenly and as silently as it came. I rose and stretched myself, saying aloud that I was a fanciful, shivering coward, and I carried my lamp round the flat. Nevertheless, I was not sure how far fancy was responsible for the notion that I saw a light print, of a smaller foot than mine, on a rug in the hall that night.

Up to that time I had continued my investigations with Maundeville, doing a certain small amount of work in his museum. I got a daily hypodermic injection when he did too, and kept a taxi always waiting for me at the door, regardless of expense, explaining that it enabled me to keep to my engagements elsewhere.

Two or three times I told Maundeville that I found it difficult to arrange a time for meeting him. Once I failed in my appointment; and at last he suggested that it would serve our purpose if I took away three doses or so with me. I did so on two occasions, meeting him at the end of each supply to compare notes and to get more. It was on the ninth day after the Mummy had crossed my threshold, that I had a slight but curious sensation of powerlessness. I had been in a bad quarter of the West End, and having a fancy to change my clothes before lunch, found a difficulty in tying my scarf. I fumbled with it for a minute or two before I realised my condition. It was not long in passing off, and I had my lunch; but I remember that I broke my usual rule, which is not to touch alcohol until dinner-time.

That afternoon I looked in upon two or three friends, meeting Maxwell, and calling upon Mortimer the toxicologist at Gray's Inn, among other places.

I wanted to see Maundeville, but he was not at home. I asked Bates when he would be back, but Bates could not tell me, though he knew that Maundeville was making arrangements to spend a week out of town.

"I'll write," I said, and after leaving the door, turned again and wrote my letter up in the library. I was looking at the somewhat scrawling calligraphy caused by the numbness in my right hand, when Bates, always attentive, brought up a tea-tray. But I declined this, explaining that I was not quite well, and I went away home, had an early dinner, and took to my bed.

Maxwell called with an anxious face to see me, but I would not let him stay. I ordered Mudge and Seymour out, too, for the evening, forbidding them to return till midnight, and, indeed, putting them on their honour not to do so. After eight o'clock I lay quiet, listening, and wishing vaguely that I had a better life-record to look back upon. It was just nine o'clock. I had heard my clock chime in the hall, when close upon the last stroke came the sound of a lightly limping foot. I have heard men speak of the excitement felt when you have tied up a wretched bullock or donkey, and sit above it, waiting, hidden, for creeping death to show itself.

Only a few nights ago a man tried to tell some of us what he felt when he suddenly found, one dusky night, that a tiger had sprung, and was already there, on its miserable victim, without a sound.

"You've no idea how creepy it was," he said, turning to me.

"You'd find it still more so if you were the bait as well," I suggested, "instead of being up a tree," but this was considered a mere joke of rather a feeble character. Nevertheless, when I close my eyes and call up the picture of Maundeville limping cheerfully into my bedroom (as I easily can), smiling and well groomed, in speckless evening-dress, I have a very clear notion of what a "kill" may feel.

CHAPTER XL

MAUNDEVILLE EXPLAINS

"What! As bad as all that?" he asked sympathetically. "I expected to find you all right again."

"My right hand is still a trifle numb," I said, not taking his; "I thought I should be best in bed. But how did you get in? I warned you that Mudge would be out now."

"So you did! So you did!" he agreed, pulling a chair to the bed. "But sick friends mustn't be neglected for want of trifles like latch-keys. I consulted the constable now standing at the street corner, explaining the situation—a friend of yours, I fancy. Prudent man, to keep in with the force!"

"He couldn't let you in."

"No, so he said. So I assured him it didn't really matter, and that I could leave you till to-morrow. After we parted I remembered your staircase window, and I carried your defences by escalading from the mews."

He stopped again and laughed softly. "Not a soul saw me," he said, "otherwise you might have had to bail me out. Now let me hear all about it! A medical man's fist is generally pretty bad, and your letter was shaky as well."

I again told him of the numbness, which I said was passing off.

"I had better drop the injections for a few days," I said, "and then perhaps continue them in smaller doses?"

He considered this, rocking himself to and fro, and finally glanced at his watch.

"No, I think not," he said at last. "I'm due at the French Embassy to-night," and even as he spoke, leaning forward a little, I caught sight of the cross and ribbon on his breast. "But first," he went on, "as your hand is shaky I'll give you a small dose myself. I had the same experience a few days ago, but with half-doses the thing went."

I lay quiet for a moment or so, and reminded myself that I had undertaken a job that was likely to be completed now, whatever might happen to me. Also, anyway, wasn't it something to be useful, at my age?

"Do as you think best," I said. "You'll see my hypodermic and the stuff itself, there on the mantelpiece."

"Right!" Maundeville agreed, rising and crossing the room. "May I shut this window, just till I go? I find the room quite chilly. Ah! there's our friend the constable, presenting a stolid back to us!"

He pushed the window up gently, and turned to the mantelpiece. I could hear him fiddling behind me with the things; for my bedstead is never pushed back against the wall.

"A small dose," he said, "will make all the difference."

And a few seconds later, though I had thought I was ready for anything, I was startled to feel the needle driven in under the skin at the back of my neck.

"You'll be quite comfortable presently," he said, "and I have still half-an-hour to spare. Half-an-hour soon goes in your company, my dear Armiston," and he returned to his chair and sat down.

He had hardly begun to talk again, however, when I felt an increasing difficulty in breathing; and all muscular power seemed draining away as though I was being severely bled.

In spite of my determination to keep from panic, I was taken by surprise, for he had used the needle standing where I couldn't see him, and sooner, much sooner than I had intended.

By now I was choking, and half rose.

"What have you done?" I gasped. But he bore me backward as if I had been a child, and in a moment gagged me with a towel.

"A superfluous precaution, I believe," he said. "The deafening is excellent. Now, my dear blockhead! A little increase of your dose has made your limbs as wooden as your head always was.

You'll make an admirable listener, for you can neither contradict, nor get up to go away. No, you're not going to die yet."

He sat facing me, in my own easy-chair, nursing his knee with clasped hands, one leg being thrown across the other.

"I defy anyone to say," he went on smoothly, "that my methods of achieving my object are not in general most humane. Why not? I have had no more animus against those I have removed, than I have against this hassock, which is rather in my way."

He pushed the hassock gently aside with the point of his small patent leather shoe.

"But you," he went on, "are unfortunately in a different position, and I cannot pretend to forget it. The other men were old acquaintances. You are, if you will forgive me for saying so, an outsider. They were inconvenient in ignorance, and almost against their will. You pushed into what didn't concern you in the least. Oh! you want to contradict that? My dear fellow, fussy folk always have an excuse for interfering. It isn't worth while ungagging you merely to hear arguments which I'm sure I know already, and which don't in the least satisfy my logical faculty. But I'm straying a little from the point. This flat is so quiet (thanks to me), and your chair is so comfortable. You won't mind my smoking, I'm sure?" and he took out his cigar-case, but suddenly stopped to consider.

"I might be forgetful later, might I not?" he said. "It wouldn't do to leave my own cigar-end behind me, would it? I'm sure you won't mind my taking one of your cheroots."

He went away, and returned, smiling faintly, with one in his hand—and in the other he held the miniature of Miss O'Hagan.

"You will have no further use for them, you know," he said, "I never grudged you a smoke when you honoured my poor house—and I have let you keep this property of mine quite long enough. Now let us get on. It's very pleasant, though, not to be obliged to hurry. Where was I?" and having lit my cheroot and pocketed the miniature, he leant back in my chair, and sent a smoke-ring or two eddying across the room.

"There are no draughts here," he said meditatively. "That's always a comfort. I hate draughts—don't you? Oh, I forgot! Well, I'm sure you do, without troubling you to say so. Now for my explanation, why I don't treat you quite so considerately as I have treated others.

"Not only you forced yourself in upon a little circle of friends that didn't want you. Not only you gave me a fresh problem to work out, and another mind (fortunately a dull one) to pit my poor wits against. But you actually longed for the moon, and the moon sank to you!"

As he spoke he gradually worked himself into a cold passion. I had never seen him in the slightest degree angry before, and it fascinated me. He crouched in the chair, gripping its arms, and looking as though he were holding himself back from me.

"By God," he said softly, "I have had patience! I have had miraculous patience!" and he sat muttering to himself inaudibly, his eyes staring into mine, the pupils contracted to pin-points, for some seconds before he went on.

"There's your unpardonable sin," he said at last. "It's not enough merely to wipe you out like the rest, for she has lowered herself by raising you above them. The insufferable ridiculousness of it all! You have degraded her in my eyes, though ever so little, and you have made me feel a fool, a hood-winked fool."

He sat quiet again for a minute or so, and the room was so still that I could hear my own watch ticking under my pillow.

Watching him as I did all the time, stretched out under his eyes, I noticed everything. I saw that the hand he raised to his mouth shook with passion, and I saw, too, that when he moved the cheroot—my cheroot—the end was bitten to bits.

"Well, what is your punishment?" he went on presently. "You're going to die, of course, but that's a mere detail. Since you've meddled with the affair of the Mummy, you shall hear how you and the rest have been fooled." He stopped and looked at his watch. "There's plenty of time. Since you think yourself favoured by Miss O'Hagan, you shall hear what her future will be, and whom she will favour after you're gone and forgotten—like that."

He sent another vortex-ring rolling away, and watched till it broke and disappeared.

"If it's too much of a monologue to please you, my dear Armiston," he said, smiling at me again, "pray remember that when it ends I add Finis to your own story. That may make it seem less prolonged."

He thought a moment.

"We will say nothing of the lady's charms," he decided. "It would take too long to recount them all, and you've shown a certain amount of good taste, in acknowledging them yourself. We agree that they are worth the risk of death, hell, anything, everything. To be worthy, a man must have courage, brains, patience, audacity, invention, and devotion to the one end.

"I have all these and more.

"Long ago I counted the cost. There were a score of men dangling about, but most of them had no earthly chance, and I have left them alone—a case of the survival of the unfittest, my dear Armiston. There were just half-a-dozen who, for different reasons, seemed dangerous, and it was safest to eliminate them. There are only three now after you—and they will go in various ingenious ways, if I think it necessary. The study of each individual case is most fascinating and sympathetic. I fancy I owe my success mainly to fixed habits of concentration, formed upon other lines of study for years before. The main point was to avoid letting any of them think me a competitor. Thus none of them avoided me, or suspected me of any unfriendliness."

He paused again and considered.

"I was *not* unfriendly," he said, quite seriously. "I was merely logical. They were in my way—I moved them out of it as gently as I could. Perhaps Perceval suspected at the last. I can't be sure about that scrawl of his. But in any case, by that time he was barely conscious, and must have been almost indifferent.

"It was they themselves who suggested the Mummy as a stalking-horse, by their silly chaff and bravado. I had been waiting some time for an inspiration.

"Scrymgeour's case was child's-play.

"I knew his habits, and his man's ways. I went there while the valet was out, saw, I told Scrymgeour, a fresh resemblance between him and his beloved ancestor, lured the fool on to his hobby and his step-ladder, and jerked him off backward. He had bragged a little one night, or I should hardly have thought him worth while.

"D'Aurelle was known by his friends to have a marked tendency to heart trouble. I was at Dene Court, where we came and went very casually. My luggage went early to the station one morning, and I was supposed to follow on foot. I purposely met D'Aurelle, and agreed to show him an attack with the gloves which we had talked of. I struck him over the heart, and he collapsed. I was ready to be discovered, and to plead misadventure. I could have done the thing before a dozen witnesses without risk of detection. But no one saw it or knew of it, so I went quietly away, and it was never asked what train I went by.

"In Perceval's case you helped me. For that you shall go painlessly. After all, I don't want to be brutal, and I daresay you have acted according to your lights.

"Hitherto I had dealt the cards—and someone else suggested it, mind you—so of course the Ace went where I thought fit. But the night you came *she* was absent, so I made you deal, and let the Spade go where it might.

"Perceval got it, and an overdose of stramonium—according to you. You will remember a certain Malay——What?"

My face must have been expressive, for he leant forward and watched me even more closely.

"Now, shall I make you speak, and hear how much you suspected?" he muttered. "No. It's not worth while—now," and apparently he put the notion away from him, and went calmly on:

"You can easily understand that lately you've been the one most annoying to me.

"I took care to deal again, myself, at the next meeting, and this is the result. In every case I've managed to adapt my means to the individual. You, my dear Armiston, in your new role of ardent lover, wanted renewed youth, and you were fooled by the hope of it. I won't insult your understanding by naming the drug which paralyses motor-nerve endings and lays you where you are, with all your rather poor wits still about you.

"It keeps you quiet while I admonish you; and presently a stronger dose from your own hypodermic syringe will dismiss you.

"Your friends already know that you are experimenting with

some new *elixir vitæ*, and it will be obvious, to the stupidest of them, that you have pushed your experiments too far.

"I myself shall be forced to admit that I thought you were overdoing it, and that I warned you. Maxwell, no doubt, will remember hearing me do so. He goes next, by the bye. We all have our limitations. I confess to you frankly that even now I can't understand how you found favour while he was about. I know the lady's thoughts and ideals wonderfully well. I've studied her as I've studied nothing else. He was the man I feared most."

He checked himself, and amended that.

"No," he said, "I never feared him. I never feared man or devil. But he was the man who counted most in my calculations. Well, it seems I was wrong—but he certainly goes next. I have sent out cards for another meeting to be held to-morrow afternoon. Your notice will come to-morrow morning—but I fear it won't interest you. Indeed, I suppose we must adjourn the meeting out of respect for you. I needn't bore you with details of Maxwell's trapping. Besides, I'm always ready to drop the most elaborate preparations if another way seems more open. Most men are so pig-headed. If they have pluck enough to carry a bold plan through, they haven't wit enough to drop it for another. I nearly had to deal with you and Maxwell together, that night after leaving Perceval. You hesitated about going in, but we had a very pleasant little supper instead, and I was sorry Perceval couldn't be there."

He sat quiet again, hugging a knee, and to all appearance forgetting his errand. "Without the women," he said, "it would be a pleasant, friendly world. I humbly think the scheme of creation is open to severe criticism. But you may be better able than I to judge presently, and meanwhile I must take it as I find it—with its compensations.

"Each one of you removed is one distraction less for her, and one obstacle less for me."

He went on singing her praises, which he mixed with reference to his recent experiments, and assertions of his certainty of a prolonged and active life. I still believe that he had made valuable discoveries.

"The theme is inexhaustible," he said suddenly. "There's no

time for more. If you're as altruistic as you pretend to be, you'll be satisfied, my dear Armiston, that her future happiness is assured. That is the main thing. On the other hand, if your love is mere selfishness, you're suffering the tortures of the damned—and you deserve them all.

"Now, I will use your own hypodermic, and make an end. I expect to meet her at the French Embassy to-night."

He found it, complimenting me casually upon its spotless condition.

"We needn't sterilise it, I think," he added, smiling, and then went to the mantelpiece, and filled the syringe before my eyes with the undiluted solution of his preparation.

"This will be about forty times above the normal dose," he said. "Please observe that I've no wish to give you any physical pain. It will act at once."

He returned to my bedside, pulled the easy-chair closer, and sat down.

"You're a scrupulously honourable man, my good Armiston," he said, "and I've implicit faith in your word. Promise me, by closing your eyes, that you won't make any noise—which might conceivably be risky, though I don't think so—and I'll remove the gag in case there's anything you wish to say before going into the Unknown."

I closed my eyes, and without any further stipulation he removed the gag.

"Now, briefly," he said, "can I do anything for you afterwards? Give me your instructions and I'll carry them out, as far as I can without risk to my own plans."

I whispered a word or two about Miss O'Hagan and Mudge, and he nodded.

"These things can be arranged," he said. "Now, are you ready?"

He bent over the bed, picked up a fold of skin from my forearm with his left finger and thumb, and was about to introduce the needle, when it was dashed from his hand. Maxwell's dark face suddenly peered over his shoulder and Maxwell's arm was flung round his neck.

At the same moment I threw myself forward on him, and we all fell together. In spite of the amazement that convulsed

Maundeville's face, it was characteristic of the man that he never uttered a sound. Twice he flung us both off, and I got a scar then that I shall carry to my grave. Though the first injection had been, fortunately, much weaker than Maundeville had intended and supposed, it was quite strong enough to make me of little help to Maxwell. But at last we had him fairly mastered, and he lay staring up at us, without having said a word since our struggle began.

CHAPTER XLI

WHAT THE MUMMY-CASE HELD

On the following afternoon, within a few minutes of the time fixed for the meeting of the Open Minds, I drove up to Maundeville's door, which was opened by Bates.

In answer to my inquiry, he said that his master was not at home. "He told me, sir," Bates added, "that he would be back from the country by this time. He went out of town yesterday. He expected you to-day, and three other gentlemen whose names he gave me. They're here already. I expect he won't be long."

"I expect not," I agreed, "and I have brought back the mummy-case which I had from Dr. Maundeville. Where are the others waiting?"

"In the studio, sir."

"Then get my man and the driver to carry the case up to the studio with you," I said; and I stood watching while they lifted the Thing down from the roof of the taxi, and followed them up the stair when they carried it to the studio.

Maxwell at once met me, and told Mudge and Bates we should not want them any more. Just then a bell rang downstairs.

"That may be Maundeville," said Steyne, who was looking impatiently out of the window.

"He wouldn't ring at his own door," the other man pointed out. He was sitting on one chair, with a leg in splints upon another. It was obvious that he was the man who had been absent from our last two deals.

"Better wait," I said to Maxwell. A moment later Bates opened
the door widely, without knocking or announcing anyone, and
the President of the Plain Speakers came quietly in. Bates closed
the door at once again, and the President stood alone just inside,
looking from one to the other of us, as if to see who was there.
The man with the splinted leg moved to rise, but the President
said a word, and he sank back again on his chairs. The President's
eye rested on the mummy-case, ranged over us one by one, and
returned to the case again.

"I'm here uninvited, gentlemen," he said, "and for that I'm
ready to apologise to our host when he comes." He paused a
moment, and then pointed to the mummy-case. "But before I go
I must hear all about *that*," he said.

No one answered, and after watching us he asked when
Maundeville was expected. "I assume," he added, "that this is
a meeting of what one might call an inner circle of the Open
Minds, and that you're waiting for Dr. Maundeville—possibly to
arrange where that goes next. I understand that wherever it has
gone death has followed. I have come to join your circle and help
as far as I can in solving the puzzle."

There was silence again, and he stepped forward deliberately
and took a chair which Maxwell offered. We looked at him, and
at one another, and then Lethredge, the man with the broken leg,
spoke out.

"I think, Mr. President, I may say that when we began this business we did so in a fit of bravado, not knowing what we were in
for. I speak frankly for myself, at any rate. Speaking for myself
still, I say plainly that if I had known more, I would have had
nothing to do with the thing; and I advise no one else to be mixed
up with it."

The President listened and gave him an ironical little smile.

"I'm sure Major Lethredge's advice is valuable," he said—
"too valuable to be given until it is asked for. This affair has gone
much too far already. I am determined to have the mystery
exploded, either as President of the Plain Speakers, or in my
other capacity, where perhaps I can bring greater pressure to
bear." He paused a moment, and then added, "I am most anxious
to be here merely as a member of the Plain Speakers, who

happens to have learnt too much of this coterie to be kept out. Where is Maundeville?"

This time it was Steyne who answered from where he still stood, coughing, in the window.

"We don't know where he is, Mr. President," he said. "We're waiting for him. With regard to this mummy-case, those who wish can back out. For myself, I'm willing to take the Lady as my guest this evening, whether you help to solve the riddle or not."

"There's nothing left to solve," I said. "The Mummy has been very quiet, Mr. President, and I have found out all that we need to know. So you have no need to concern yourself with the matter at all."

All except Maxwell stared at me, astonished, and the President eyed me and the mummy-case alternately, with very obvious curiosity.

"If there is no further mystery," he said, "I suppose even I may hear all about it, without any breach of confidence."

"You have told us," I reminded him, "that you came to prevent further trouble with the Mummy; and I have told you there will be none. It's better that you should know nothing more about it."

"Gratuitous advice again!" he pointed out.

"Given to an uninvited disturber of a private meeting," I said, not liking his manner. "If curiosity makes you attempt to stay where you're not wanted, Mr. President, at least don't let yourself suppose you can be useful," and being annoyed I endured with equanimity the angry stare which I had brought on myself.

"This is Professor Maundeville's house, I believe," the President said, turning to the other men, after treating me to another prolonged stare. "I will save you all from any further responsibility, or temptation to—ah—express your opinion. I will wait for him as long as you think fit to do so yourselves."

"In that case, Mr. President," I said, "it is useless to waste more time in trying to save you from the results of your own interference. Listen to me, all of you!"

It was useless to tell them how I had first begun to suspect Maundeville. I merely reminded them of the three deaths—Scrymgeour's, D'Aurelle's, and Perceval's—each a host of the Mummy. I went on at once to my own turn.

"I had seen him as a conjurer," I explained, "and when I believed him to be a murderer too, I annoyed him purposely; and he dealt me the Ace of Spades, as any cardsharper might."

I then spoke of the first attempt on me, the limping foot, and the tracks on the mat.

I went on to the second attack, without details of his methods, and I told them very shortly how, thinking I had only a few minutes to live, he had boasted to me of what he had done with the other three, who had died before me.

"If he's still alive," said the President, "this is a hanging matter, three times over. We have, I suppose, with no offence to you, only your word against his?"

"He is still alive," I said, "and what he will say I neither know nor care. I have a witness," and I nodded at Maxwell, who nodded back.

"Where is he, then?" asked the President.

"If you ask me again, I shall tell you," I warned him; "but once that is done you are bound to take a share in what follows."

"I have had to take responsibility occasionally in my time," he said stiffly. "I ask you again. Where is Professor Maundeville?"

"Here," I replied, and I knelt beside the mummy-case, and beckoned to Maxwell for his help, which he gave, while the others watched. We lifted the cover off, and Maundeville, tied and gagged, lay before them.

"I suppose no one expects any apology from me," I said, "for my way of dealing with a man who has murdered three of his friends, and is ready to treat three more in the same way, if only he gets the chance?"

"Still, we must hear what he has to say, before we can do anything," the President said.

"This man is quite unscrupulous, as you all know," I said to the others, "and very quick. But we don't want to torture him, and he has been tied several hours."

"Ungag him and loose the cord," the President said at once; "Captain Maxwell and I will answer for him to you all," and I loosed the cords, helped him to step out—though to touch him troubled me—and then took the gag out of his mouth. That done, he stretched himself and yawned several times, and then stood quietly watching us with a bitter little smile. You would think, on looking at him, that he still had the best of the awful game he had played.

"Now, Professor Maundeville," said the President, "have you heard the charges made against you by Dr. Armiston?"

"I heard them," he said, yawning again.

"Do you deny them, or any of them?"

"Dear me, no!" he said, with a negligent air. "Didn't I foolishly supply him with most of the information? Let it be a warning to you all against bragging," and he looked mockingly round on us.

"You admit all that he has said," the President insisted.

"All the main facts," Maundeville agreed, looking across at me. "His delightfully moral comments are matters of opinion and taste. But the dear doctor always lacked humour."

"I must own," said the President, looking at him and then at us, "I find it almost impossible to credit such statements. The thing is monstrous, and seems absolutely impossible."

"It is a wicked world," said Maundeville mockingly. "Which means that we don't all think alike, or, if we do, some of us are afraid to say so."

"If all this is really true, madness is the only possible explanation of his crimes," the President said to us. "A criminal lunatic asylum is the only place for him."

"Madness! Crimes!" Maundeville jeered openly. "Merely words applied by fools to the unconventional," he added, "before they stamp it out."

The President looked at him as if marvelling, and then turned to Maxwell.

"You say that you were there in Dr. Armiston's room. That you heard this man own to having killed D'Aurelle, Scrymgeour, Perceval, and saw him attempt to kill Armiston?"

"Yes, sir. I agree with all that Dr. Armiston has said."

"Armiston and Maxwell agree," the President said, speaking more particularly to Major Lethredge and Steyne, "and Maundeville admits. Yet, I confess, I find the thing incredible. What possible motive could drive the man so far, so low?"

He turned to Maundeville again.

"What was your object?" he asked, and even I, who knew,

waited almost as curiously as the others to hear what he would say. He shrugged his shoulders as if such questions were beside the mark.

"They were in my way," he said, "and I had to move them," and beyond that he would tell nothing, though the President questioned him further, pointing out that a full explanation might decide what we did more favourably for himself.

"Who cares what you do?" he asked carelessly. "Certainly not I. The fact that my game has been seen prevents my winning the stake. Nothing else matters."

I can't guess how long we might have gone on without doing anything, for we were startled by an interruption which I confess I ought to have foreseen and guarded against.

"Someone is calling here," Steyne said, from the window. "A carriage is stopping." Then a moment later, with a queer breathlessness in his voice, "Miss O'Hagan is at the door!"

"The man will keep her out," suggested the President.

"He will not," said Maundeville sharply. "Miss O'Hagan has come like everybody else, but yourself, at my invitation. She will say so."

"Go out and stop her!" the President ordered Maxwell hurriedly.

"Wait!" Maundeville cried, and Maxwell waited, though he, at least as much as any of us, must have dreaded Nora's entry at such a time.

"You want to keep the meeting quiet," Maundeville said. "You fear what I shall do if she comes in. You mean to keep her out. I say she must come. If you don't bring her in quietly I have ways of letting my man know when I'm here, without opening the doors, and I'll use them. You can't keep anything private after that. Let her in for five minutes, and she shall go away quietly and willingly, without any suspicion."

"I don't bargain with criminals," the President answered coldly. "Why do you want Miss O' Hagan?"

"Only to see her once more," he answered simply; and I suppose if anyone in the room had failed to understand Maundeville's real motive up to that time, he had no more doubt about it after that one sentence. The man's voice and manner when speaking of her was altogether changed.

"Preposterous," I heard the President mutter.

While we looked at one another, hesitating, an electric bell somewhere in the room began to ring shrilly. I don't remember that one ever thrilled me so much before. I've hated the sound ever since.

"Remember," said Maundeville softly.

"I believe him," I said. "I'm going to bring her in. Be careful that no one else makes her suspicious."

CHAPTER XLII

SENTENCE AND EXECUTION

I unlocked the inner door, and finding there was just room for me to stand between the two, I shut that behind me before I opened the outer one.

Bates, with his usual inscrutably solemn face, was waiting in the gallery, with Nora close behind him. He began to apologise and explain, but I cut him short.

"It's all right," I said. "I had forgotten about Miss O'Hagan." I took her in, shutting the door behind us before opening the inner one.

Maundeville limped forward to meet Miss O'Hagan with his ordinary sprightly welcome. He was undoubtedly by far the most self-possessed man in the room.

She shook hands with him (I would have given a small fortune to prevent her from touching that hand) and she bowed to the rest of us, eyeing the President with some surprise, and bowing to him with more ceremony. Perhaps she had hurried, perhaps she was excited. Her face was flushed, her eyes were bright, her black dress and big black hat set off her delicate skin. I had never seen her look more bewitching. I involuntarily looked from her to Maundeville, and saw how his eyes lingered on her face, while his little compliments and words of welcome stopped, and there was an ominous silence all through the room. She noticed it at once, as she was sure to.

"What is it? What is happening?" she asked. "Why are you all looking so startled? Is this another deal of the cards?" Her eyes roved round angrily until they rested upon Maxwell with quite a different expression. One could see her immediate relief on knowing him to be there, and I am sure that Maundeville felt it as quickly as I did. He never took his eyes off her face; it was his high-pitched little laugh that broke the silence again; and it was he who took it upon himself to explain, without a trace of excitement in his voice or manner.

"We've been favoured, as you see, by an unexpected visit from the President," he said smoothly. "He has found out a good deal about this silly business with the Mummy, and has persuaded us to stop it."

No one contradicted or added anything to this explanation; and Miss O'Hagan, after waiting a moment, perhaps for someone else to speak, accepted it.

"I'm grateful," she said, turning to the President. "I'm very grateful, sir. I only wish you had heard about it sooner." And from the chair where Lethredge sat came a solemn "Amen," that made her turn and look at him, startled. Then a terrible comedy went on in which we all joined, Maundeville more coolly and more cleverly than any other. She saw that the mummy-case was empty, and questioned me about its contents. Was I quite safe now, and where was the Mummy?

I answered clumsily that I was in no danger, and that the Mummy was still at my rooms. "Quite undisturbed in its wrappings," I added, knowing her feeling about it.

She thanked me with a glance, and then suddenly asked why the case was here alone. I was altogether nonplussed, and it was Maundeville who smoothly explained that the Mummy was taken out to be examined with other things in the case, and we could not pack all neatly back again. "So Dr. Armiston brought over as much as the case would hold for examination," he added, "and the rest will follow."

She sighed, saying she supposed it had been best to make an examination, and then made an unexpected proposal.

"Everybody knows what I've always felt about the way she has been treated," she reminded us, "and my feeling hasn't changed. You have opened the case, and you've had the opportunity of finding out all there is important to know, I suppose. As a favour to me, let it end there! Dr. Armiston, I beg you not to touch the wrappings. Professor Maundeville, promise me now that you'll let me undertake the task of getting her back to her own old resting-place. You must think what you choose of my fancies; but I tell you plainly that I believe I shall sleep better when that is done."

I muttered a promise that, as far as I was concerned, the Mummy should not be further interfered with.

"Now," said the President, "I must ask you to retire, Miss O'Hagan. We have some business that only men can settle."

"Will you forgive me if I don't come down?" Maundeville asked her. "My limp bothers me more than usual to-day. Armiston, I'm sure you'll be glad to take Miss O'Hagan to her carriage for me," and he stood in the doorway, his eyes fixed upon her, until she passed out on to the stairs, and I closed the door behind us.

"What does it all mean?" she whispered, as we went side by side down the broad stair, watched by Bates, who stood in the hall below. "I feel horribly frightened, and I can't tell why. If I had stayed I thought I should scream. Are you quite certain there's no more danger to anyone?" and she went on to say, very kindly, how glad she had been to see me quite safely through my own ordeal.

"Our troubles are ended, I think," I said. "It's better that I shouldn't tell you more just now. Yesterday I was in danger, and Maxwell saved me. You shall hear all about it some day. Now go, and remember there won't be the slightest danger for him any more."

She then went quietly away, obviously satisfied with my assurance, though protesting that he was not the only one whose safety concerned her. I waited at the door until the carriage had moved off, being determined to make sure that Bates had no chance of learning the whereabouts of his master. I then went slowly back to the studio, very much dreading what I expected there.

"You've heard my accusations against this man," I said. "They're backed by Maxwell, and the man himself doesn't deny them. Is there the least shadow of doubt in anyone's mind?"

I made each one answer for himself in turn. Each said "No," and Maundeville himself said "No" when the others had spoken —jeeringly adding that he claimed a voice in the matter, and telling me to be done with my solemn tomfoolery.

"You're infernally proud at having trapped me, Armiston," he said; "but if we hadn't worshipped at the same shrine your poor wits would never have been sharpened. You've a lonely crabbed old age before you, Armiston!" and he jeered away, and we waited.

Sympathy wouldn't be the right word to use about our feeling, but one doesn't wrangle with a dead man.

It was at this point that I again suggested the President had better leave us, and the others backed me up. But, after considering, he refused, saying that it was too late, and he even took the lead to some extent in what followed.

"Here, then, is a criminal," I said, "with these deaths to answer for, and ready for more. What shall we do with him?"

"Call in the nearest policeman, and let him hang like any other," said Lethredge, and it was Maundeville himself who turned on him.

"You blundering fool!" he said fiercely. "Am I like any other? And is she like any other? Will you have her name tossed about through all the gutter-press of Europe? It's a pity your pony didn't break your neck as well as your leg! It's a pity I didn't deal you the Spade, though I knew she couldn't love such a fool!"

One sees the ludicrous side of this now, but at the time I think no one felt anything except his blighting contempt. Maundeville was more like a scorpion writhing in fire than a human being— though the root of it all was human enough.

"Let's hang him ourselves!" said Steyne, and took no notice of the taunts Maundeville flung at him.

"There's no hurry," Maxwell said quietly, "and no risk of failure. He can't possibly escape. One way or the other, the time has come. Can no one see——" He broke off, staring fixedly at Maundeville, who seemed oddly impressed and made no attempt to interrupt.

"We all agree that there must be no fuss," Maxwell went on in a matter-of-fact tone, "and we all agree about what is to be done,

one way or another. We can't let him live, of course."

"I have forced myself on you, gentlemen," the President said, "and I wish to be perfectly frank and to shirk no responsibility now. I absolutely agree with Captain Maxwell. This man"—and he nodded towards Maundeville—"has to die. I will ensure it, even if Miss O'Hagan's name cannot be kept out, and even if I must give evidence myself."

"Even if!" sneered Maundeville. "What self-sacrifice! What self-satisfaction!"

"Be more respectful!" Major Lethredge said angrily.

The four of us drew round Lethredge's chair, leaving Maundeville to stand alone. We were none of us afraid of the responsibility; our case was clear, and no one doubted what would happen if we appealed to the law. The President insisted upon being the one to tell him our decision, saying plainly that since he had pushed himself into the investigation, he was determined to take his full share of the responsibility.

"We have decided," he said to Maundeville, "every one of us, that you shall die. So long as that happens quickly we are not concerned as to the manner of your death. For reasons which are merely sentimental we understand your crime, and pity you just enough to let you choose. If you like to be your own executioner you shall be."

"You will not fight?" Maundeville asked.

"I will not fight you, and I will allow no one else to do so," the President said solemnly. "It has already been suggested, these gentlemen condescending so far as to be ready to meet you here and now, any one of them. But this is an execution and not a quarrel. You have forfeited your life three times over. But you may choose the means yourself."

For a moment the wild beast in Maundeville broke loose, and he cursed us all where we stood waiting round about him, even Lethredge rising to lean upon the chair's back.

"You sanctimonious ravens!" Maundeville hissed. "You vampires! I'm more alive than any of you. More of a man than any two of you! You haven't vitality enough to break your d——d laws except all together. Your law's made by cowards to protect themselves against men."

But no one answered him, and he became silent. I felt in my pocket and found my hypodermic syringe case.

"We all agree in the judgment and sentence," I said, "but no one is anxious to be executioner. To blot him out is all that we want, is it not?"

"And quickly," the President added.

"I am ready, if need be," young Steyne said. "I've done less than anyone;" but the President raised a hand to him to be quiet and nodded for me to go on. I showed them the case.

"There's death here for twenty men," I said, "and he understands the working of it. He has prostituted his knowledge to evil purposes. Let him make good use of it now."

I remember that in reply Maundeville jeered at me as a sanctimonious hypocrite and a blabber, and he spoke with such conviction that I stood wondering whether he might not be right. Perhaps there had been times when, if I thought as he did and had his courage, I might have gone some distance in the path he had chosen. But I believe his object was not to make us think, but to taunt us into a fight—and in that he failed, and recognised it, and tried another way.

"Very well," he said, suddenly calming down. "There's nothing left worth wrangling about. 'All or naught' holds to the end. Armiston, you have some comprehension of my work. Come over here for five minutes and get some instructions about it."

He limped away to the far end of the room, and after a look at the others I followed him, the President saying a word of warning to me as I passed.

"Listen, Armiston," Maundeville whispered, "and take your time to answer. Don't speak without thinking. I know you better than you know yourself. You're madly in love with Miss O'Hagan, and you'll lose her, man, you'll lose her. Think of that! Lose her! Lose her!"

As I listened there rose in my memory a lunatic I once seen tearing his own flesh.

"You say you want to speak of your work?" I reminded him. "Be quick."

"The two are inseparable," he whispered. "Your interests and mine. Listen! My experiments have succeeded and reached a point of the utmost importance. Without me nothing can be done, and the world is the loser. Our names shall go down to all time together."

"Heaven forbid!" I said hastily, but added that I would do anything reasonable for him if he gave me precise instructions.

"My work comes first," he said. "I don't deny that I loved her, but she takes a second place. Science is a jealous jade. I'm punished for dividing my allegiance, Armiston, and henceforth I will be single-hearted."

"Henceforth!"

"Yes," he nodded emphatically. "It's to your own interest to help me. I know you love her, Armiston, and I know she admires you. I will help you with her, and you will help me with my work. Together we will succeed with both."

"Think of other things!"

"Why? We should concentrate on what we want, you and I, and think of nothing else. That's the secret of power, Armiston."

I remember shivering a moment, though it was a hot June evening.

"Give me your instructions," I said, "and let us end this quickly."

"Yes, let us end this quickly!" He caught at my words and interpreted them as he chose. "We are both strong men, Armiston, and one of these four is a cripple. If we keep them off the windows no noise will be heard. Let us move back to them talking, and take them unawares. Two will be dead before they know what we're doing. Listen! I'll take Maxwell and that fool who thinks himself our better. You take Steyne and Lethredge, and then help me if I need it—but I shan't. Come, before they suspect."

"And what after?" I asked, horribly fascinated by the man's desperate cunning.

"What after?" he echoed. "Take things as they come. I recommend short views. We can make a tale later—and Bates will swear to anything."

"Finish! Finish!" the President called to us across the room.

"We have finished," I said, and, turning my back on Maundeville, went to join them. I might have guessed my risk. Looking at these men as I went, I saw a sudden movement among them, and instinctively jumped without turning round, and partly avoided a blow Maundeville had aimed at me from behind.

In an instant Maxwell had him, and the others helping, he was powerless, and at once stopped struggling. "I give it up," was all he said about it, and no one else said anything at all of what was his last effort.

I held out my pocket-case to him again, and he looked at us and saw, no doubt, that his time had come. He took the case and limped away silently towards the door leading to the bedroom.

"Is it safe?" the President asked softly.

"Let him be," Maxwell answered, and then added sharply, "I see his shroud to his lips." And again I noticed I was shivering.

When Maundeville reached the bedroom door he turned and looked back at us. A more evil, more malignant face I never saw. He stood there a moment, his lips silently writhing, and then went through, shutting the door quietly behind him. That was the last any man ever saw of Maundeville alive.

Later, when Miss O'Hagan begged me to tell her how I had managed to house the Mummy without harm to myself, I refused to say. But I honestly confessed that I owed my life probably to Maxwell's help at a critical moment.

It may amuse you to know that it was while she was thanking him, and they were both apparently engaged in singing my praises, that Maxwell found himself protesting his own love and unworthiness.

He came to tell me, with mixed pride and amazement, that the lady didn't insist on any such preliminary as a V.C. before admitting she loved him—and I think she was quite right.

They were married before she heard any of the truth about Maundeville's life, and I believe the actual facts of his death are not known to her. Even she can't get anything from Maxwell that he isn't ready to tell.

Up to the point of their engagement her stammer had been practically as bad as ever. But I now took a more hopeful view of her case and, the Mummy being off my mind, I gave it more attention.

I made her practise certain fixed exercises daily in breathing, speaking and singing, and I quietly suggested to Maxwell that his help would be useful.

The result was a cure for which I got great *kudos* in the fashionable world; and a good many such cases were brought to me. Alas! their circumstances were different, and my success was poor. I soon ceased to be consulted to any extent by the Upper Ten, which was perhaps just as well—as a little more of it, and Mudge would have insisted on my moving to Harley Street.

I got my fee from Maxwell just after his engagement to Nora O'Hagan.

He brought the cheque himself, and presented it with a certain amount of embarrassment. I may be mistaken, of course, but I fancy he was a trifle surprised when I took it without any particular comment, and gave him a properly stamped receipt—which he protested he didn't want. I banked it, together with the cheque which I had received from Perceval's lawyers and, taking a deposit receipt for both, decided that I must be developing a business faculty. Later still, the great jewellers' windows became more fascinating than anything else. I haunted them in the late summer, and, I fancy, roused vague suspicions in the minds of many goldsmiths and policemen.

At last, in despair at the shockingly costly and ugly things I had seen everywhere, and the date of Miss O'Hagan's and Maxwell's wedding being definitely fixed, I went to an artist friend of mine who had an opulent imagination, and took him into my confidence.

His enthusiasm wasn't properly roused until I had made some excuse for introducing him to Miss O'Hagan.

He then swore I had better taste than he had given me credit for, and over many pipes and sundry small dinners he devised a jewel which I thought worthy, and then went with me to a dealer in precious stones, and then to a working goldsmith.

The result was a combination of emeralds which pleased me, and which I hope to see Mrs Maxwell wear often, though so far she has pretended that they offer an overwhelming temptation to every thief in London.

Mudge and I went to the wedding, and my name is down in the church register as one of the witnesses to the marriage.

At the reception afterwards I was pretty much out of my element, and it was only at the last moment that I was glad I had gone.

I was hanging about with my hands in my pockets, mistaken by some, I heard, for a private detective, and having no particular inclination for rice or confetti, when Maxwell brought his wife to me.

"Nora says you didn't offer her a kiss in the vestry," he said, "so I've brought her to offer you one now. We hope you won't refuse."

I never felt hotter in my life, but I didn't refuse. Well, there's something in playing the part of heavy father, after all! I suspect it suits me better than that of a lover on probation, which farce you will remember had a very short run.

As for the rest, I overheard Mudge in his kitchen that night telling Seymour that "We can't hall be 'appy." I imagine he's right.

There's only one thing more I will tell you. I took the Mummy back to Egypt myself, and found its tomb and buried it there. For purely sentimental reasons I took Methuselah, the tortoise, too, and left him sunning himself in the desert sand outside the tomb.

THE END

CPSIA information can be obtained
at www.ICGtesting.com
Printed in the USA
FSHW010317051218
54179FS